LAST DAY

ON MARS

Book One of the
CHRONICLE OF THE DARK STAR

KEVIN EMERSON

WALDEN POND PRESS

An Imprint of HarperCollins Publishers

Walden Pond Press is an imprint of HarperCollins Publishers.
Walden Pond Press and the skipping stone logo are trademarks
and registered trademarks of Walden Media, LLC.

Last Day on Mars
Copyright © 2017 by Kevin Emerson
All rights reserved. Printed in the United States of America.

Library of Congress Control Number: 2016938987
ISBN 978-0-06-230672-2

Typography by Carla Weise
18 19 20   BRR   10 9 8 7 6 5 4
❖
First paperback edition, 2018

FOR WILLOW AND ELLIOTT, MY INTREPID ADVENTURERS

"Have a heart? I'll take oxygen and stable air pressure, thanks. Without those, a heart has no reason to beat."
—**SAMAYA THURSTON**, *I.S.A. Director of Phase One Colonization Protocol, 2153–2211*

"Nobody survives, if you tell the story long enough."
—**PETER BARRIE**, *Captain of the Starliner Artemis, 2146–2194**

(*Lost, presumed deceased)

PRELUDE

REGIONAL GALACTIC MANAGER'S OFFICE
8TH SECTOR—SPIRAL GALAXY 93—
GALACTIC SUPERCLUSTER 714

Many hundreds of light-years from the solar system you call home, inside a spindly crystal structure floating at the edge of a great nebula shaped like an eye, a yellow light began to blink. The light was located on a map, or something like a map. Picture a regular map spread out on a table, only now picture it bleeding up and down through the air, and also forward and backward in time. Like a map of your neighborhood, but also of Tuesday. And next week, and a hundred years ago. . . .

Let's just call it a map.

This map was in an office (not exactly an office either, but close enough), and its blinking caught the attention of a nearby being. She was known as a chronologist, and she was as similar to a human being as her map was to a human map, and her office to a human office. If you picture her having dark blue, somewhat translucent skin, and wearing black robes, that will be fine for the moment.

The chronologist tapped the blinking yellow light and read the data that appeared. It was data about a star. She stepped into the middle of the map and spun it this way and that around her, checking the data from four other lights that were blinking in her sector. These lights also indicated stars, only they were red. She pressed forward, briefly, in time, and that yellow light changed to red, too.

Red was a problem.

The chronologist reached into her pocket and gripped a tiny orange crystal, perfectly round and about the size of a human golf ball. With it, she sent a thought message to the other regional galactic managers.

In turn, she received instructions.

"Establish monitors. Add your findings to the Inquiry."

She zoomed in on the yellow light, studied its surroundings, and picked a place that seemed suitable to put an observatory.

Then she had lunch.

★

After lunch, the chronologist traveled seven hundred light-years to the location she'd chosen. There's no way to easily explain to you how she instantaneously made a journey that it would take humans nearly seven thousand years to complete, nor is there any way you could truly comprehend the chronologist's intricate relationship with the fourth dimension, and that's nothing to feel bad about.

Here's the thing: The universe that you live in is really, really big. So big that most of the intelligent beings in it have had to make peace with how much they will never see and never understand. And yet that's only the beginning.

Put it this way: If reality was a blueberry pie, this universe would be just one single blueberry. And while someone like the chronologist can see this whole blueberry, as well as all the blueberries around it, the gooey filling in between, the flaky crust, and even that this pie is in an aluminum tin, sitting on a shelf by a window in a row of other pies, you are so small and so far inside your own blueberry that you can't even tell it is a berry in the first place.

Most of the time, this lack of understanding isn't really a problem. After all, you are very busy: so much homework to do, food to eat, games to play. And often, when you do actually stumble into thinking about how big the world really is, it just gets you down.

Because what's the point of going to school, or playing outside, or anything, really, if we're just insignificant little beings in one lonely corner of a vast and uncaring universe? That kind of thinking really doesn't do you any good.

But then there are those *other* times, aren't there? Those rare moments when the stars twinkle just so, when the wind rustles the leaves just right, and you have that tingling sensation that even though the world is so very big, and you are only one infinitesimal part of it, you are also *connected*. To something greater, somewhere out there beyond the moon and the black of space, something so grand . . . a pie crust even . . .

Sure enough, though, just when you feel like you might actually be able to comprehend it, something always comes along and distracts you: a car horn, an errant Frisbee, a meddlesome younger brother, and that knowledge, that *awareness*, slips from your grasp.

For most intelligent beings, that fleeting feeling can be enough to give you peace of mind. If you could speak to the chronologist—and there's almost no way that you could—she would tell you that you're lucky. Because there are some intelligent beings who react differently to this same experience: they decide that they must know more, must try to go farther, no matter what the cost. . . .

That reaction, the chronologist would tell you, can lead to all sorts of problems.

The chronologist arrived at her destination and found herself standing on a field of cooling lava. It glimmered like a frozen sea in brilliant yellow starlight.

She checked her silver watch. She was a bit early, but like any good scientist, she wanted to get some context, given the events that were to come. She spun a dial around the watch's face and time began to pass rapidly. Days and nights raced by. Then years, decades, millennia . . .

It rained in flashes. The lava cracked and plants shot out of the gaps. In the distance, mountains grew. A jungle sprouted up around her; life-forms crawled about, developing legs, scales, feathers, and wings. The jungle became a savanna, then a desert, then a jungle again. Briefly, she was under a teal-colored sea.

The creatures around her kept changing, and eventually settled on an amazing design, full of great promise. They ruled the planet with grace and harmony for a thousand generations. One day, they even looked to the stars, just beginning to ponder their significance, to wonder what this universe around them really was. . . .

Wait, was that a blueberry?

Unfortunately, it was an asteroid.

In a flash, those great, fearsome creatures were gone.

The chronologist felt a slight pang of remorse, but only for a moment. After all, these things happened.

There wasn't much to see for a while after that. Continents crawled along, ice fought with oceans, back and forth. Then two-legged beings began to appear. They were amusing: very industrious. Called themselves humans. They named the planet Earth and their star Sun. They sped around the chronologist on wheels and rails, and through the air with propellers and jets. They built dwellings and great buildings, and even primitive spaceships. They were a bit irresponsible—not ones to pick up after themselves, so to speak—but all in all, they did okay.

Too bad for them, things were about to change.

The chronologist touched a glowing symbol on her watch. She stopped in the Centauri year 13,405,007,682. These humans called it 2175; they were kind of adorable.

She produced the orange crystal from her pocket, held it up to the sun, and started recording data.

Then it happened. The sun changed, though not in any visible way . . . yet.

The chronologist checked her readings and realized that this planet would not be suitable for her observatory after all. Her monitors would need more time, time this planet didn't have. She looked around her. These humans had no idea what was coming. Briefly, she considered revealing herself and explaining the situation, but such interference was strictly forbidden. Other chronologists had tried making contact with reasonably intelligent beings in the past and it had never gone well. They were always being mistaken for gods, or getting attacked, or, in one unfortunate case, driving an entire civilization crazy. The humans would have to figure it out on their own.

In the meantime, the chronologist traveled to the fourth planet of this solar system and found the highest spot on its red surface: a rocky spire at the top of a giant, extinct volcano, about twenty-five kilometers high. The planet had a very thin atmosphere, perfect for her sensors, and it was pleasantly desolate, except for one small human colony, but that was thousands of kilometers away. Still, after she installed her observatory using an instantaneous process of matter replacement that, again, would be nearly impossible to explain, she also sprang for a cloaking system, even though it was the end of the fiscal quarter, just in case those humans ever came snooping around.

Inside, she activated many instruments that were positioned on a shelf ringing the circular room.

Graphics fluttered to life around her. She calibrated the sensors on a long black object pointing up through the roof that resembled a telescope, and then she sped up her watch and observed the readings to make sure that everything was running smoothly. The instruments hummed and whirred. The graphics flickered and morphed. One large image showed the sun in the rusty sky. Soon, it began to grow, just like those other stars in her sector had. Before long, it would explode into a supernova, another star dying out, another yellow light blinking to red on the map back in her office. And while yes, things like supernovas happened all the time in this universe, they weren't supposed to happen to these types of stars, and they definitely weren't supposed to happen this fast. Something else was at work here. Something that was putting her entire sector, and quite possibly the entire universe, at risk.

The growing sun filled more and more of the sky, turning from yellow to orange to red. As the chronologist observed the data, something caught her eye. Her silver watch had started blinking blue around the edges.

Blue was a problem. One she'd sensed coming for a long time.

"Beautiful, isn't it?"

The voice came from behind her. The chronologist

turned to discover the blurry image of a two-legged being—

A white sting of energy shot through her. She crumpled to the ground, her vision filled with dancing bolts of electricity. As she fell, she managed to slip the orange crystal from her pocket and roll it toward the wall, where it settled in the shadow beneath a shelf.

"I'm sorry to have to do this," said the figure, his voice clipped by static. "Really I am."

The chronologist felt her body beginning to numb. She concentrated as best she could, and sent a thought message to the orange crystal.

The figure was dressed in a heavy black metallic suit threaded with glowing gold wires and wore a helmet with a lavender visor. He flickered almost like a projection, an effect the chronologist recognized as space-time warping.

"I'm just afraid you won't understand what we're after," said the figure. "It's never been your way to ponder the oldest question."

The chronologist knew of no *oldest question*. The idea seemed sort of silly. And yet, maybe not *that* silly, because here she was dying for it.

As the final moment of her long life passed, the chronologist peered at the figure.

"You want to know who I am," he said.

He raised the reflective visor of his helmet, and

when the chronologist realized who she was looking at, she felt something like relief. Maybe it was for the best that she would not live to see what would surely be the end, far too soon, of this universe she had called home.

The figure watched the chronologist until the white sparks stopped firing. Always sad to have to do this kind of thing, but necessary.

"Sir," a voice said in his earpiece, "we have a report from sector fourteen."

The figure tapped a screen on his forearm. A view of space appeared, and a fresh supernova bloomed in reds and violets. The explosion formed a shape like a hand.

"Success," said the figure. He smiled and raised his own hand, mimicking the supernova's shape. *The grand design* . . . "I am coming," he whispered.

There was a flash on one of the observatory graphics. It showed a panoramic view of the Martian landscape. The figure saw fleets of ships landing in the distance. It was still fascinating to watch time pass this quickly. In what seemed like moments, more ships arrived and a dome arced across the horizon, buildings sprouting up inside it. If only they knew . . .

"Sir, power's running low. We need to get you back."

"Fine, fine," the figure replied. "I'm ready." He dissolved out of sight, leaving the observatory atop the volcano silent and still.

Years passed. The monitoring equipment kept recording. In the skies overhead, more and more human ships arrived, and the sun kept growing.

Meanwhile, in a recess at the base of the wall, the tiny crystal sphere blinked, a small light in a darkening world.

Good evening.

As you all know, for the past four years we have been documenting extremely unusual activity in the sun. Increased radiation and solar flares have wreaked havoc on daily life. The best minds in the world have studied this data around the clock, and tonight I can report that while we still do not know the cause, our conclusion is unanimous: the sun is expanding, and we are all in grave danger.

Now, we've always known that Earth would not be humanity's home forever. Our sun was classified as a main sequence star, which meant that someday, billions of years from now, it would begin running out of energy. When that day came, the sun would expand into a red giant, swallowing Earth and the inner planets of the solar system, before dying down to a white dwarf.

We've also known that, long before then, humanity's rapid population growth would require us to begin moving outward across the galaxy. When we established our first colonies on the moon and Mars, nearly fifty years ago, we thought they were our first steps on a long, gradual journey.

Unfortunately, the need for that journey has come far sooner than we could ever have imagined. Our data shows that not only is the sun expanding now, but it will become a red supergiant, and soon after that, it will explode in a supernova. Nothing in this solar system will survive. Worse, we predict that this will happen in forty years, maybe even less. We've never seen a star behave like this before. And so I cannot be more clear: *We must leave*, and we must do so immediately, or our species faces certain extinction.

Now, though our situation is dire, it is not without hope. As I speak to you tonight, leaders from every nation around the world have pledged their help to save humanity. Together, we will build a fleet of ships to carry us to safety: the Phoenix Starliners. These giant, interstellar transports will be constructed above Mars. That will buy us precious extra years to complete the construction after Earth has become uninhabitable. Over the next few years, we will begin to ferry all of humanity from Earth to temporary Martian colonies, where we will need every citizen's help to build the starliners. Life on Mars won't be easy, but it will give us a fighting chance. And before too long, everyone will be aboard a starliner and out of harm's way, hopefully with time to spare.

But then the question becomes: Where will we go? Tonight I can also report that after surveying millions of potential planets, we've found one. Located in the Cygnus Arm of our own Milky Way galaxy, the planet designated Aaru-5 appears to have the right gravity and distance from its star to sustain human life, and it is just close enough that we should be able to make it.

We have already begun Colonization Phase One, which involves gathering advanced data about Aaru and preparing the planet for our arrival. Phase Two will be to develop a terraforming system that we can use once we arrive, to ensure an Earthlike habitat. Phase Three will, of course, be getting there. We are currently designing rockets that will allow us to travel faster than we ever have, but the journey to Aaru will still take us nearly one hundred and fifty years to complete. I know that sounds incredibly long, but our advancements in stasis technology should make the trip feel like only a few months.

Make no mistake, ladies and gentlemen: this is the most serious threat our species has ever faced. But though the challenge is great, and our future uncertain, I know that humanity will do whatever it takes to survive.

LAST DAY ON MARS

1

The great ships streaked away from the red planet like shooting stars. One, ten, hundreds they went, their fusion rockets burning, solar sails unfurling, their hulls vibrating with millions of sighs of relief.

Some of the passengers looked back at the angry ball of fire they were fleeing. Some even held up small, powerful telescopes and searched for one last glimpse of the charred ember that had once been their blue home. Others kept their backs to the traitorous sun, instead gazing hopefully into the starry dark, while still others played games and tried to enjoy themselves for the first time in far too long.

For years and years the ships hurtled away, each

fleet leaving fewer lights behind. One by one, the enormous docks orbiting Mars stopped blinking; the space elevators stopped flashing. One by one, the shimmering colony domes winked off. The endless Martian wind gathered their trash into whirling clouds and coated their windows with rust-colored dust. One by one . . .

Until there was only one ship remaining, one little colony glimmering, one last collection of humans with one last day to go, on the only planet next to the only planet they had ever called home.

Even on the last day on Mars, there was still important work to be done.

Unless you were stuck at school.

"So," said Ms. Avi, "I guess we'll take a vote. Raise your hand if you want to watch *Survey of Former Earth Continents and Nations*."

No hands.

"And . . . raise your hand for *The Starliner Orientation Guide*."

Eighteen halfhearted hand raises from the back of the room. The last Year 10 students, thirteen Earth years old—or, if you wanted to annoy your parents, you could say you were almost seven in Martian years. Not long ago, the classroom had been packed with fifty kids and there had been ten other Year 10 classes in the school, but everyone else had already moved up to the *Starliner Scorpius*, which awaited them in orbit.

"Isn't there anything else we can watch?" asked Shawn Williams.

Ms. Avi just sighed, ran her fingers through her short black hair, and continued tapping at her screen-top podium.

"Not without the VirtCom," said Liam Saunders-Chang, who was sitting beside Shawn.

"Why did they have to shut it all down?" said Shawn. "What are we supposed to do after school if we can't log into the arcades or the mall?"

"All nonessential systems have been turned off to save power for the dome," said Ms. Avi. "The *Scorpius* has its own VirtCom. I'm sure you can survive one more day."

"Maybe," said Shawn. He looked at Liam and rolled his eyes. Liam shrugged.

"Could you please just show your best effort and watch this video?" said Ms. Avi. "We have one hour of school left, and believe me, you're not the only one who doesn't want to be here."

For Liam, and surely for everyone else, the day had dragged on and on. After a seemingly endless algebra review, they'd tried to have a last-day party, but without access to their VirtCom accounts, the only music they had was what Ms. Avi kept on her personal link, mostly stuff that Liam's parents listened to. And the only snacks they could find were plain-flavored nutri-bars and synthetic lime pudding, two foods that everyone was going to be glad to leave behind forever. After that, Ms. Avi had made them clean out their desks and wash the tops, even though no one was ever going to use them again. These desks would just be sitting here, perfectly clean, until the planet melted.

Liam glanced out the round classroom windows. The black buildings of the colony glinted in copper sunlight. There was one gap where you could just see a glimpse of the colony dome and, through a haze of distance, the barren red mountains beyond. Liam had spent hours gazing that way, wishing he were out there rather than in here. Strange to think this was the last day he would think that. Soon there would be no view of buildings, no mountains. Out the starliner windows there would be no solid ground at all. The thought made him shudder.

"Okay, here we go," said Ms. Avi. "Please put on your headsets."

Liam sat up. He picked up the only thing left on his desk: a thin, clear pair of virtual glasses with silver earphones dangling from the frames. He slipped them on and pushed the phones into his ears.

His view of the classroom shimmered and was replaced by a wide image of the giant starliner floating in space. A friendly voice announced, "Welcome to the official orientation guide to the—"

The image dissolved. The classroom lights blinked out. They were left sitting in the rusty orange light coming through the windows.

An alarm began to blare.

"Aw, man," said Shawn.

"Attention, all classes," said the principal over the speaker. "The solar storm is arriving ahead of schedule. Please make your way to the shelter as quickly as possible."

"You heard her, students," said Ms. Avi, moving to the door.

Liam's stomach tightened as he put down the glasses and stood. He brushed his black shaggy hair out of his eyes and rubbed the back of his neck. His tongue felt dry, his jaw tight. As they shuffled into line, he worked on his breathing: slow . . . one breath, then the next.

They filed out into the dim hallway, their heavy grav boots clomping. The wall screens that normally showed student-made art and videos were dark. Thin beams of daylight slanted across the hall from the narrow windows in the classroom doors. Up ahead, a single green light flashed above the staircase that led down to the shelter.

"Where's Phoebe?" Shawn asked over Liam's shoulder.

Liam looked up and down the hall. "No idea." When did they ever know where Phoebe was? "She said she was going to the bathroom."

"That was like ten minutes ago," said Shawn. "Ugh, I told my dad to let me stay home today."

"At least you get to go up to the starliner tonight. I'm here until the very last elevator trip tomorrow."

"That stinks. Our parents could have at least let us come to the station today. It's pointless, being here!"

"Yeah," Liam agreed, though when he'd woken up this morning, he'd actually felt the opposite: glad for one last chance to see his school and neighborhood and classmates. But the long, boring day, and now the idea of having to sit in the cramped, dark shelter beneath their school, had soured that feeling.

Liam's parents and Shawn's dad worked out at the Phase Two research station. They were there right now, frantically trying to perfect the terraforming system that they would use on Aaru-5. The project had been on schedule to finish six months from now, but the solar storms had been getting worse, growing larger and occurring more frequently than predicted. Each one peeled away a little bit more of Mars's thin atmosphere, which meant the colony's life-support system had to work that much harder. Plus, the electromagnetic radiation from the storms was frying circuits and knocking out power more and more often.

Things were even more dire up on the *Scorpius*. Without the protection of the meager Martian atmosphere, the ship had to activate its radiation shielding during every solar storm. Using the shields meant using fuel, fuel that was supposed to be used for getting to Aaru-5. They were trying to hold out for as long as possible to finish the Phase Two trials, but the *Scorpius* didn't have much fuel left to spare for its shields, and the colony's power systems wouldn't last much longer. That's why Red Line, the time at which the colony had to be shut down and the *Scorpius* had to begin its journey, had been pushed up, and pushed up again, and now—suddenly, it seemed—it was tomorrow. Liam had set a timer on his watch, counting down. They were officially under one Martian-length day now, which was twenty-four hours and thirty-nine minutes.

There was a sizzling sound and a series of loud clangs.

"Watch your step, everyone!" Ms. Avi called.

Liam felt a subtle lightening as the artificial gravity failed. Mars's native gravity was only about one-third as strong as Earth's, so all the colony floors and streets were wired to make a magnetic field that brought the gravity up to Earth level. Everyone wore specially lined clothing and boots that reacted with the field: standard-issue black shirts and pants that had been handed down at least three times and, by this point, were made of more patches than original fabric. Most of the soft lining was gone from the insides of Liam's boots, and they were too tight and giving him blisters.

But Liam actually preferred when the gravity system failed. Earth's gravity made him feel like he was covered in heavy blankets all the time. Whenever he was out at the research station, which didn't have artificial gravity, he could jump farther and climb more easily, like a stronger, faster version of himself. His parents complained that Martian gravity gave them headaches and joint pain, but Liam and Shawn never felt that way, maybe because they'd been born here. It didn't seem to bother any of the other kids in the colony, either.

The only problem with these gravity failures was when they happened unexpectedly while you were using the bathroom or, like now, walking in line. Liam had learned to take small steps these last few months, and keep a steadying hand on the wall at all times, but this latest outage still caught him midstride and he bumped right into Nita, the girl in front of him.

"Ow! Watch it!" She elbowed him in the ribs.

"Sorry."

A new beeping joined the cacophony of alarms and voices: a high-pitched chirping tone coming from the slim link pads they each wore on their wrists. A yellow light flashed there—a radiation warning.

"Great," said Shawn. "We're gonna get fried."

"Faster, everyone!" Ms. Avi called.

They all bunched together as they waited for the younger kids to file down the stairs into the shelter.

"Hey! Guys!"

The whisper came from across the hall. Liam looked over his shoulder and spied a silhouette peering out from a doorway.

"Come on!" Phoebe hissed, motioning to the two of them.

Liam craned his neck, and when he saw that Ms. Avi's attention was on the stairs, he bolted across the hall in two bounding steps.

"Aw, man," Shawn groaned, but Liam heard him following.

Phoebe flashed a smile and slipped back through a metal door and into a stairwell.

"We're supposed to go down to the shelter," Liam said as Phoebe shut the door behind them.

"Of course we are," she said. Phoebe was taller than both of them, with bright green eyes and long hair dyed pale red. "Or . . ." She jabbed Liam in the chest. "Now would be the perfect opportunity to go get that Dust Devils jersey I know you want."

She'd poked him right on the ink stamp for the Haishang Dust Devils, Liam's favorite grav-ball team.

Since they were the last ones who had to wear the gravity-assist clothing, they'd been allowed to decorate it. Phoebe had the logo of her favorite team too, the Meridian Canyon Bombers. Shawn wasn't into grav-ball, but he had the logo for his favorite band, the Gravity Minus.

"How exactly are we going to get one of those?" asked Liam.

"We'll just go grab one at the stadium store." Phoebe paused to cough. She wore an atmo pack at all times to help with her breathing. Small tubes led from her nostrils to a slender silver backpack that converted CO_2 to oxygen. "That whole part of the colony is shut down."

"We can't just steal a shirt," said Liam.

Phoebe rolled her eyes. "It's not stealing if it's left behind. Everything around there is completely abandoned. It's a ghost town. Nobody's going to care."

"Um, Ms. Avi will care if we run off," said Shawn.

"No, she won't," said Phoebe. "She'll just be glad to be rid of us."

"What if she calls our parents?" said Liam.

"Do you really think Ms. Avi would go through the trouble of calling the research station? She knows they're busy anyway."

"But if she does—"

"If she does," said Phoebe, mimicking him, "our

parents will probably be down at the turbines running trials so they won't get the call anyway. And even if they do, it'll be fine. They know we can take care of ourselves."

Liam pursed his lips. It was pointless trying to argue with Phoebe. Ever since she and her family had moved here three years ago when the colonies were consolidating, Phoebe and Liam and Shawn had spent most of their weekends together at the research station. When Phoebe set her mind to something, there was almost no way to talk her out of it.

Liam peered back through the narrow window in the door. Their classmates were starting down the stairs. He'd wanted an official Dust Devils jersey forever, but they always cost more than he had from his allowance. His parents *said* they wanted to get him one as a leaving present, but they were always too busy with work. Then, when the stadium store had its "Going Out of Existence" sale a couple weekends ago, Liam had been stuck at the research station. And now they were sold out in the VirtCom, and there was never any time to stop by the store after school because he and his older sister, Mina, were in charge of packing up not only their own rooms but their entire apartment, as well as making dinner and cleaning up since Mom and Dad were getting home so late each night. And now, the shop would be abandoned, the few remaining jerseys just left there to burn. . . .

But still: "Why do you really want to go?" Liam asked.

"Because duh, Liam, you've been whining about how much you want one of those shirts for a month. When will you ever have another chance to get one?"

"Phoebe . . . ," said Liam.

She broke into a grin. "Okay, and I also want to watch the storm come in from up on Vista."

"You want to go to Vista for the solar storm?" said Shawn. "We'll get fried up there."

"No, we won't," said Phoebe. "We can duck inside when the storm actually arrives. And anyway, one dose of radiation isn't that big a deal. Everybody's just being cautious."

"And that's a bad thing?" said Liam.

"The storms are bigger now," added Shawn.

"Come *on*," said Phoebe. "People say the storms are beautiful, that they light up the dome with all these amazing colors, like the aurora supposedly did back on Earth. But we are always stuck in some shelter, and this is our very last chance to see one. Doesn't it sound amazing?"

"Not really," said Shawn.

Kinda, Liam thought. His heart was racing, his breaths small and quick. And he kept picturing that maroon-and-gold jersey. They were taking so little up to the *Scorpius*. You were only allowed what would fit in a single, regulation-sized container. It had been taking Liam forever to choose which of his possessions to bring and which to leave behind.

He checked the hall again. The last kids were going down the stairs, Ms. Avi right behind them. Maybe she hadn't even noticed they were gone yet. Maybe she wouldn't really care, like Phoebe said.

"Ticktock," said Phoebe. She checked her link. "We've got ten minutes till that storm arrives. Running in Mars gravity I bet we can make it to Vista in five, but we've got to go."

"We should go to the shelter," said Shawn.

"Ugh, Shawn!" Phoebe snapped. "I'm sick of you always —" She doubled over coughing and clutched her chest.

"You okay?" Liam asked. Phoebe had Martian Cough. Some doctors thought it was caused by the fine toxic dust that the colony's air filters couldn't entirely remove. Others thought it was a reaction to the artificial environment. Like with the gravity, even if you simulated Earth conditions nearly perfectly, it still wasn't Earth.

Phoebe stood, breathing deep. "I'm fine."

Liam made a slight motion to his nose. One of Phoebe's nostril plugs had come out.

"Thanks," she said quietly, replacing the plug.

Then she turned and started down the short flight of metal stairs that led to an exit door.

"Phoebe . . . ," said Liam.

"It's our last day. Let's make it count."

Liam held his breath. Shawn was right . . . but Phoebe was too. It was their last day here, ever, and he'd already spent half of it in school doing nothing. By this time tomorrow, he'd be on his way up to the starliner. No more Haishang Colony, no more Dust Devils games, even these stupid solar storms . . . He'd never see any of it again.

"I'm gonna go," he said to Shawn. "Sorry." He leaped down the staircase.

"Ugh," said Shawn, following him.

Phoebe pushed open the door and they sprinted out into the bloodred afternoon.

2

The three bounded up the wide avenue that led from their school toward the center of the colony. Everything was still, the mag-shuttle shut down, the holographic signs and screens dark. Most of the windows in the blocky, black, dust-stained buildings around them had been smashed. Everything had been closed for a couple weeks and it was just too hard to resist pausing on your way to school, picking up whatever object you could find, and taking aim.

Their strides carried them three meters at a time, each footfall making rings of fine red dust and scattering trash. Yellow safety cables had been strung along the sidewalks for these gravity outages, but instead of using them, Liam and Shawn leaped up onto the elevated shuttle track and then back down, throwing spins and somersaults, while Phoebe kicked off the sides of buildings, making a zigzagging pattern up the street.

With every step, burned brown cockroaches sprang out of their way and scuttled into the shadows. The roaches had outnumbered the colonists a hundred to one even when everyone was still here. Lately it felt like they owned the place. Antennae twitched from every corner. When the colony shut down tomorrow, the lack of oxygen and air pressure would kill them. But for one more day, they could rule the empty streets.

Ahead, the puffy top of the grav-ball stadium sagged like a half-deflated balloon. Above, the colony dome arced overhead, made of slender metal beams that crisscrossed in a geodesic pattern. Sparks crackled now and then where the beams intersected. In the triangular spaces, the dome appeared nearly transparent, except for the grainy pattern of a thin layer of metallic mesh, and the slight shimmer of the energized plasma field.

Above the dome, huge and searing in the copper sky, was the ever-growing sun. Just since he was five, Liam had watched it double in size, from about five centimeters across to nearly ten. It had darkened from a warm yellow to a fiery orange, a color like you'd only ever see in pictures of the sunsets back on Earth. The star seemed heavy and unsteady, like it might tumble down on them at any moment, but Liam knew the opposite was true: in about three years, Mars would lose its orbit and fall into the sun.

The idea of his apartment, his school, the streets and the dome and the mountains beyond all being incinerated made a lump form in Liam's throat. He'd had more than one nightmare where the planet was falling and he was still on it, splashing into the sun like it was liquid. The thought of it made him glad to be leaving Mars, but at the same time, he was happy they were out here now, on one last tour through the streets where he'd spent his whole life, with the added bonus of Martian gravity.

"Yeah!" shouted Shawn. He'd bounded up a series of balconies and was now leaping all the way across the avenue, legs wheeling beneath him. Liam somersaulted off the shuttle tracks, landing in a poof of dust.

Phoebe had reached the stadium and stopped in its shadow. She was bent over coughing. Liam joined her, breathing hard, and patted her on the back. "Nice run."

She sucked in a big wheezing breath. "Thanks. That was fun."

"Just one more day," said Liam. "Your cough should get better on the starliner, right?"

Phoebe nodded and stood up. "We won't be able to run like this, though. I'm going to miss it."

"Me too."

They gazed through the wide window of the stadium store. How many times had Liam paused right here to stare longingly at the racks of crimson shirts, their gold stripes gleaming? This time, though, his shoulders slumped.

"Guess we weren't the first ones to have this idea," said Phoebe, dropping a length of carbon bar that she'd picked up on the way.

The windows were obliterated, all the racks inside overturned.

Phoebe stepped into the shop, her boots crackling on the flex-glass shards. Liam hesitated, held back by some silly worry about trespassing . . . but also because he could tell there was no reason to go in.

"All of the official jerseys are gone," he said, surveying the mess.

"Are you sure?" Phoebe pushed the tangles of remaining shirts around with her boot.

"Yeah," said Liam. "Those are just junk."

"What's up?" Shawn called from the shuttle track.

"They're cleaned out," said Liam.

"We'll find you one somewhere else," said Phoebe,

stepping out. She rubbed his shoulder. "Sorry about that."

"It's okay," said Liam.

"No, it's not. You need one. We'll make it happen. I promise." Phoebe checked her watch. "Okay, six minutes until the storm. We need to hurry!" She took off up the street.

Liam stood there for a minute. His throat felt tight, the edges of his eyes tingly.

"You coming?" Shawn called back to him.

Liam breathed deep. "Yeah."

He ran up the next two blocks with hard, giant steps, until his legs burned. Shawn jumped down beside him and they caught up to Phoebe as she entered a wide plaza.

They arrived at the base of a great building made entirely of green panels of flex-glass that reflected the sun at a hundred angles. It twisted upward in a double-helix shape, the tallest building in the colony. Inside, on a series of levels, jungles and forests fogged the glass. The Earth Preserve. Vista was a lookout point at the top. You could tell by the pristine condition of the Preserve's exterior that this had been a place of reverence for everyone in the colony. It was one of Liam's favorite spots to hang out too, but it didn't make him quiet and weepy like it did his parents. Last time they'd visited as a family, Mom had snapped at him and Mina for joking around.

A large flag flew above the entrance. It was bright green, with a blue-and-white Earth in the middle. In the center of the planet was a human shape, green like the background. There was a white moon in the bottom left corner, and a diagram of the solar system in the top right. This was the flag of Humanity. A smaller version of it hung in every classroom. Another one flew over the research station. There was one painted on the hull of every starliner, and military vessel, and personal cruiser. Even their shirts had a small patch on the back, just below the neckline.

Ms. Avi said it hadn't been easy unifying all of Earth's cultures and histories under one common flag. There had been wars, standoffs, lines in the Earth sand. For a while, the North American Federation was going to build its own starliner, the Chinese Empire their own, and so on, but ultimately, time had been so short that everyone had to work together. Those Earth identities still mattered to some people, especially the older generations. Liam's grandmother, who had left two years ago on the *Starliner Osiris*, had listed off Liam's ethnicities and nationalities one time: Thai, Irish, Nigerian, Texan, and like ten more that he couldn't remember. To Liam, they were just words for bits of land on a planet he'd never known. He was fine being one thing.

And yet what exactly was he? Once in Year 7, they'd been celebrating Humanity Day and Liam had drawn a flag for Mars: red with an orange-brown planet in the middle, the two moons, Phobos and Deimos, one in each top corner, and a colony dome at the bottom. When his teacher asked him about it, he'd said he made it because Mars was where he lived and it needed a flag, too. She'd told him not to be silly, that he was a human, not a Martian. Then she'd taken the picture away. Liam remembered feeling mad about it, but too embarrassed to protest. Maybe it had been silly.

Grown-ups never called Mars "home." Earth was *home*, humanity's home, the ol' green and blue. Liam had sat through hours of class time learning about its oceans and cities, about the wars, its pyramids, and its first missions to its moon. . . . All of it was interesting, but only to a point. Mina had at least seen Earth from orbit, but she'd only been a toddler at the time and she said she didn't remember it. Mom hated hearing that. Even if Mina had, the Earth she'd seen had already turned dried brown, only narrow green bands remaining of its once-vast oceans.

And soon Aaru-5 was going to be their *new* home. Some people were already calling it New Earth . . . so what exactly did that make Mars? Not much more than a rest area, and yet, it was the only place Liam had ever known. Even this Earth Preserve: he liked it because it was a really neat spot *here*, on *this* world. His home.

His parents didn't want to hear that, either. Nobody did, really. It seemed like all anyone wanted to do was get out of here. Sometimes Liam felt like he was the only one who was sad to be leaving Mars, and so it must be a stupid way to feel, and yet he felt it anyway.

"Okay, should we break in?" Phoebe wasn't reverent about the Preserve either. "Or go up those?" She pointed to a column of rectangular vents that curved up the side of the building. Each one had a three-sided metal shade on it. With the gravity off, they'd make a perfect staircase.

"Why don't we just go in the front door?" said Shawn. "Look. . . ." He ran over and pulled it open, pointing at the handle. "Someone pried it open."

"Boring," said Phoebe, joining him.

Liam followed, and they stepped into the humid shadows. Everything was shut down: no automated walkways humming up the sides, no glass elevators whirring down the middle, no hiss of the watering system or babble of visitors' voices.

And yet there was still a sound: a gentle sort of nothing noise, so different from the ever-yawning winds of Mars. Maybe it was the plants respiring, or gradually wilting. Liam felt like there was a presence here, and he was surprised to find that while he liked this place when there was a crowd, it kind of unnerved him now. He imagined the leaves whispering to one another, the branches drawing him in, the trunks swallowing him up.

"Hurry!" shouted Phoebe. She dashed up one of the curving walkways that hugged the walls.

"Race ya!" Shawn started up the one on the opposite side. Liam followed him. They wound first between ferns and pines, and around an enormous redwood. The next level contained a forest of wide-leaved trees. *Coniferous. Deciduous.* They'd had to memorize those words and so many more for a field trip here.

Next, a thick, tangled world of vines and broad leaves. Behind an extra wall of glass, a forest of short, thin pines, standing in melting snow. *Rainforest. Taiga.* And so many others. The very top level was a desert, with fat, spiky cacti and spindly tumbleweed. Palm fronds hissed against the glass. Here, sun poured in through the green-tinted ceiling.

"I win!" said Phoebe, arriving at a wide spiral staircase beside the glass elevators a step before Shawn.

"The race was all the way to Vista!" said Shawn, leaping up the stairs past her. Phoebe stayed behind, coughing hard.

"It was to the steps," Phoebe said hoarsely as Liam reached her.

"You're both winners," said Liam. They climbed the stairs and pushed through a glass door onto the roof. Liam came out last, the door clicking shut behind him.

They stood on the highest spot in the colony. A grid of black buildings stretched in all directions, punctuated here and there by taller, spindly towers that ended at wide mouths with whirring fans. They spun slowly, some blowing out fresh, Earth-like air, while others sucked in used air to recondition it. A single cruiser crossed the sky at the far side of the colony, nearly twenty kilometers away. It was gray and boxy: a military ship.

There was a high-pitched hum from the south, where the six gleaming gossamer lines of the space elevators stretched up through the dome and into the caramel-colored sky. One of the giant silver pods was returning, racing like a falling water drop. A panel of the dome had momentarily deactivated to let it through. Liam had seen the elevators coming and going from a distance all his life, but the pod moved so quickly that he still felt certain it would crash. And yet once again, at what seemed like the last possible moment, plumes of steam burst from the pod's base, and it settled gently onto its platform. Dad had said it looked like an egg being put in a carton. Liam had never had eggs, but he'd seen pictures of them, and of chickens, which they might have again on Aaru.

Other than the elevator, and the buzz of the air circulators, the only other sound was the slight sizzle of the dome's plasma field, a hundred meters above them. Everything else was still and dark, the streets littered with trash and dust.

"I love it up here," said Phoebe, taking a deep wheezing breath. She checked her watch. "One more minute."

"Me too," said Shawn. "Glad I talked you guys into doing this."

Liam elbowed him and they shared a smile. He turned slowly, taking in the streets and buildings and the landscape beyond: the barren wastes and canyon folds, the endless red cliffs, the mesas and sand washes.

There were telescopes mounted on the Vista railings, two facing in each compass direction except east, where there were five. There had once been an array of ten telescopes in the center of the roof for looking at Earth, but two years ago, the burned husk of humanity's home world had fallen into the sun. Not long after, those telescopes had been taken down.

Liam, Shawn, and Phoebe leaned against the east railing and gazed into the distance.

A great maroon shadow loomed over the entire horizon: Olympus Mons, the largest, tallest volcano on Mars. The large cliff at its base was nearly fifty kilometers away, and the summit was out of sight beyond the curve of the horizon. You could see it, though, through these east-facing telescopes, which were synced with a high-powered lens on a satellite in orbit. Another thing you could see with the telescopes but not the naked eye was their parents' research station, which was located at the volcano's base.

Much closer, only a few kilometers beyond the dome, a cylindrical bolt of metal thrust up at an angle from the wide, flat plain of the Amazonis Planitia. The Pioneers Memorial was sixty meters tall, gleaming silver with humanity's flag on its side. It looked like someone had stuck a rocket half into the ground. The memorial had been built to remember the *Valiant*, one of the first ships to come to Mars after the change in the sun was detected, a crash that killed five thousand people. It hadn't been the only disaster. Collapsing space elevators, an entire colony that perished in a six-month dust storm, and of course the very first starliner, the *Artemis*, lost on its eighth year out. At least it had been the prototype, with a test crew of only ten thousand—a fraction of the hundred million that would be on board the *Scorpius*.

"You guys ever worry about the trip?" Liam said quietly.

"What," said Shawn, "you mean like crashing?"

"Or getting lost, or hit by an asteroid, flying into a black hole . . ." Liam stopped himself. Every example made his chest feel tighter.

"Twenty fleets have already left and they're doing fine," said Shawn.

"I guess," said Liam. "But the First Fleet is only three years past Delphi. They're not even a tenth of the way to Aaru. Who knows what's really out there?"

"Who knows . . . ," said Phoebe distantly.

"What's really crazy," said Shawn, "is if we had been in the First Fleet, we wouldn't care about any of that stuff, because we'd only be seven months old. They've been in stasis almost the whole time, so they're only like two weeks older than when they left."

"That's so weird," said Liam.

"I think they're lucky," said Shawn. "They get to be kids on Aaru, while we had to be stuck growing up here."

"I don't know—"

"Guys," said Phoebe. "Here it comes."

The sky ignited with curtains of molten light, first pale yellow, and then iridescent purples and greens. The wavy bands of solar energy arced and rippled and feathered through the atmosphere.

"Okay, wow," said Shawn. "I can't believe we've been missing this."

"I snuck out from the station to see one once," said Phoebe. "It wasn't nearly this big."

The folds of color curled overhead, overpowering even the great sun, and lighting their faces.

Just then, something flashed in the corner of Liam's eye. "Did you see that?" He squinted toward Olympus Mons, which was bathed in blue and green light bands.

"See what?" Phoebe asked.

"There was a flash," said Liam. He scanned the great volcanic mountainside. "Never mind, I—"

"There it is!" Phoebe pointed.

This time Liam saw it clearly. Something flashing beyond their view in the direction of the summit. It pulsed in time with the waves of solar energy, almost like it was reacting to them.

"I don't remember there being anything up there," said Shawn.

"Must be big," said Liam, "for us to be able to see it from here." He put his eye against one of the telescopes. Through the satellite lens, he could see the many calderas atop Olympus Mons, ringed by craggy peaks. There it was, an object pulsing brilliant silver-white, but just when he got it centered in his view, it disappeared.

"Do you see it?" Phoebe asked.

"I did, but it stopped." Liam looked up from the lens. There was a break in the curtains of light.

"Was it at the summit?" Phoebe asked.

"Yeah."

"Figures," said Phoebe. "How many times did we ask our parents if we could go up there and they were like *It's way too far and it's not safe*."

"Yeah," said Liam. "I've looked at the map a hundred times, and there's definitely nothing up there."

"Nothing on a map, anyway," said Phoebe.

Waves of energy were hitting the dome overhead now, making hissing, buzzing sounds.

The light flashed again beyond the horizon. Liam ducked to the telescope, and this time he found it right away. Whatever it was, it seemed to be perched halfway up a giant, fingerlike spire of rock. Each passing wave of solar energy made it shine like light reflected off a mirror. Liam squinted. "It looks like maybe a ship or something." Liam zoomed in to maximum. The object had a brilliant metallic surface. It was spherical with a black band around its waist.

The flashing ceased again, and Liam was surprised to see only the bare rock spire and the rocks around it. Where had the object gone? "I lost it," he said, scanning the nearby area. Maybe it was moving, though it hadn't looked like it was.

"Could it be military or something?" said Shawn.

"I guess," said Liam, standing up from the telescope. "Maybe it's something classified and our parents don't even know about it."

"Or they do and they're keeping it a secret," said Phoebe.

"Why would they do that?" said Liam.

"Parents are always keeping secrets," she said.

Their links started to blare a single tone. The blinking yellow light switched to a constant red, and a message flashed: *WARNING. DANGEROUS RADIATION LEVELS DETECTED.*

"We should go in," said Shawn. He turned for the door.

"Just a little longer," said Phoebe. She tilted her face skyward and put her arms out from her sides.

There was a buzzing sound and then a series of sharp, loud pops.

"Whoa!" said Liam. He looked up and saw sparks shooting from the dome support beams. The energy panels shimmered and wobbled like soap bubbles, and then winked out. The air circulators stopped humming. A space elevator frozen in place on its cable.

"Okay, that's not good," said Shawn. "Backup power must have failed. No dome means no artificial atmosphere, no radiation protection—"

"I thought there were like triple backup generators," said Liam.

"There are," said Shawn. "They've never failed before."

A hot wind from the Martian wastes strafed their faces with dust. Liam's cheeks and hands started to prickle. The dust was toxic to breathe. Add to that the direct radiation with no dome or shelter to protect them. . . . Any minute, their oxygen would be gone, and maybe worst of all, Liam had been warned many times about what would happen to a human in normal Martian air pressure. Something about all the water in your body evaporating, starting with your eyeballs.

"We have to get inside," said Shawn, running for the door.

Liam touched Phoebe's arm. She was still gazing at the storm, arms out. "Hey, let's go."

Phoebe lowered her head and sniffed. She wiped at tears. "Okay."

"What is it?" said Liam.

She shook her head and brushed past him, not meeting his eyes. "Nothing."

Liam turned to follow her—

That flash again. He spun back around. It was brighter than ever, blinking out beyond the horizon. Despite the stinging wind, the air alive with dust and electrons, Liam returned to the telescope, but with the power out, the connection to the satellite was lost.

"Liam!" Shawn called.

"I'm coming!" he shouted, but he gazed at the volcano for another second. What could it possibly be? And why had they never seen it before?

"Hey! Why did you lock the door?"

Liam spun around. "What?" Shawn was yanking on the door but it wouldn't budge. "I didn't lock it! It just closed behind me."

Shawn circled behind the entryway and reappeared on the other side. "There's no other way down! Do you see anywhere we can hide?"

Another gust of wind pelted them with dust. Phoebe doubled over, coughing hard.

The breeze grew hotter, the air hissing with energy, dust stinging the back of Liam's neck, a burning sensation on his scalp. He felt stuck in place, his legs locked, his heart pounding. He looked in all directions. There was nowhere to go, and nothing to hide under. . . .

Wait. Liam spied a rectangle of metal, just below the edge of the roof. "The vents!" he shouted. "We can jump down them!"

"Yes!" Shawn ran and vaulted the railing, landing with a bang on the metal top of the vent.

Waves of blue and green shimmered all around them now. Phoebe coughed wickedly.

"Can you make it?" Liam asked.

Phoebe nodded. "Just go already."

Liam sprinted for the edge, Phoebe right behind him. He vaulted the railing and clanged onto the vent. The metal wobbled beneath his feet and he had to windmill his arms to keep from falling off the side of the Preserve. He turned to jump down to the next vent, but before he did he gazed back toward Olympus Mons one more time.

It was still flashing up there, whatever it was, like a beacon in the storm, almost like it was trying to get his attention.

Phoebe landed right behind him. The metal groaned and sagged. "Go or I'm going to push you down!" she shouted over the wind.

"Okay!" Liam turned and followed Shawn, jumping from one vent to the next, and then taking two at a time, while above them rainbow colors cascaded and swirled. Everything and everywhere was hot, but especially the top of his head. His eyes burned, and his lungs felt like they were full of sparks.

His last jump cleared the final four vents and he hit the ground and tumbled to his knees.

"In here!" Shawn yelled. He held the door to the Preserve open.

Phoebe landed beside him. They sprinted for the door and threw themselves inside.

Shawn slammed the door behind them. There was a humming, rattling sound, all the glass vibrating in the storm. And the quiet of the plants.

Outside, the world had been erased by dust. Shawn dropped to his knees and coughed hard. When he wiped his mouth, blood came away. He looked up and locked eyes with Liam.

"Your head, too," said Liam, tapping on his forehead where Shawn had a purplish blotch.

Shawn touched it and winced.

Liam ran his fingers over his face, his head . . . searing pain on his scalp.

"This was so stupid!" Shawn shouted. "We should have gone to the shelter. My dad is going to kill me when he finds out!"

Phoebe was lying back on her elbows, her chest heaving, her breaths rattling. "I didn't know the dome would shut down." She doubled over with a long string of coughs.

"None of us did," said Liam. He looked around at the shuddering glass walls. Something was hissing, too. Liam wondered if that was the air escaping. "How long do you think this building will hold out without the dome?"

"I don't know," said Shawn. "There's probably a shelter in the basement." He stood. "I'll go look for it—"

Twin beams of light stabbed through the copper dust outside. Liam shielded his eyes and saw the boxy shape of a Cosmic Cruiser lowering through the storm. It was a medium-sized craft, old and clunky and only used these days by the International Space Agency. Each of their families had one.

Liam's gut flooded with adrenaline. Great. Ms. Avi *had* bothered to call their parents. They'd probably tracked them here by their links. They were going to be so angry. . . .

The ship rocked in the whipping wind, touching down hard and leaving its lights on. Three figures emerged from the side. The two in front hunched over and rushed toward the building. They wore standard-issue black pressure suits. One of them carried a heavy duffel bag. They burst through the doors and looked around.

"Phoebe!"

Liam felt a small wave of relief. "Hey, guys," said Phoebe as her parents, Paolo and Ariana, marched toward her. "Sorry about —"

"Sorry?" Ariana's voice was tinny through her helmet's speaker. "Sorry isn't good enough." She and Paolo were both tall like Phoebe. They were always so serious, even when their daughter wasn't risking her life in some crazy stunt. Liam never really knew what to say to them.

Paolo unzipped the duffel bag and tossed a pressure suit at Phoebe. "Get dressed." He threw two more suits to Liam and Shawn.

"Thanks, Mr. Dawson," said Liam.

The door opened again, and with a clattering sound, the third figure entered: a giant panda.

"Good afternoon, Liam, Shawn, and Phoebe," the panda said.

"Hey, JEFF," said Liam. "What are you doing here?"

JEFF was the human-sized robot assistant in Liam's family. He didn't look like an actual panda, like the one they had in stasis on the *Starliner Poseidon*, but more like a drawing Liam would have made when he was five or six, complete with a big grin. There had been a time when bots had been designed to look as human as possible, but people had ended up preferring these animal styles. Apparently the humanlike versions had been even more creepy to be around than these grinning animals. JEFF was glossy black and white, though he had many scuffs and spots where the paint was chipped down to the plastic. His eyes were bright blue lights. His mouth was a square slit hidden within a wide pink grin. His thick black legs ended at wheeled feet. The rubber treads had mostly worn away, and there were no replacement parts left in the colony. As a result, when JEFF rolled along, he made a sound like crunching crackers.

"Your parents were unable to leave their work," said JEFF, "so they sent me to guide you back to school. They also wanted me to express their profound disappointment with your choices, and to let you know that they would be speaking to you about this at a later time."

"Great," said Liam. He unclipped his link from his sleeve and started tugging on the pressure suit, his heavy clothing bunching up everywhere. He yanked up the inner zipper, then the outer one, then pulled the soft helmet over his head and zipped it closed at the neck. The clear visor immediately began to fog up. Liam slipped his link into a panel on his wrist and the suit controls appeared. He activated the heating and breathing systems, and the suit hummed to life.

"Your teacher was frantic!" Ariana said, standing with her arms crossed as Phoebe put on her suit.

"We just wanted to see the light show," said Phoebe, zipping the suit closed, her voice coming through the intercom. "It's our last day and—"

"It doesn't matter what you want," said Paolo. "And it's not a *show*. This storm is lethal. Do you realize how much we have to do out at the research station? Do you realize how vital our work is to our very survival?"

"Yes," Phoebe muttered.

"Then how could you do this?" Ariana said.

Phoebe didn't answer.

"We're sorry, Ms. Dawson," said Liam. "It was our idea too."

Ariana glanced at him for only a second. "That's polite of you."

"Let's go." Paolo whirled and marched back out into the storm.

Phoebe coughed, the sound maxing out her speaker. "Aren't we going back to school?"

"You're not," said Ariana. "Apparently we can't trust you there. We're going right back to the station, and you will not be leaving the living quarters." Ariana glanced at Liam and Shawn. "JEFF will stay here with you." She walked to the door and held it open.

Phoebe sighed. "See ya, guys."

"Bye," said Liam.

"They're brutal," said Shawn, watching them board the cruiser.

"Yeah," said Liam. "Worse than usual. They're just stressed about Red Line."

The winds died down ten minutes later. The dust began to thin; the colors stopped dancing overhead. Their radiation alerts finally stopped beeping, and soon after that, there was a rumble in the floor and the walls of the Preserve.

"Power's back on," said Shawn.

Liam wobbled on his feet. "Gravity, too."

"My readings calculate that it is now safe to walk outside without pressure suits," said JEFF. "If you'd like to remove them, I can carry them for you."

They headed out into the empty plaza. The ground and all the buildings were coated with a thick layer of maroon dust. JEFF wove along behind them, avoiding larger drifts and pieces of debris. With gravity on, there was no fun to be had, just boring, human walking through the silent streets, among the cockroaches and trash.

"Ms. Avi's going to be so happy to see us," said Shawn as they trudged along.

"Yeah," said Liam. "This should be super fun."

"I do not see why your teacher would be pleased by your actions," said JEFF, "nor why seeing her in this state would be fun."

Liam rolled his eyes. "It's a joke, JEFF. Remember I told you about sarcasm?"

"Acknowledged," said JEFF. "Sarcasm: when you are saying one thing but your tone indicates a different meaning. And this is . . . funny?"

"It's funny *now*," said Shawn. "It's not going to be very funny when we're standing in front of her."

"Was that also sarcasm?" said JEFF. "I'm afraid I am confused now as to what will and will not be humorous."

"We'll keep working on it, JEFF," said Liam. "How's it going out at the station?"

"Based on your parents' elevated stress levels, I would theorize that they are making some progress, but not as much as they had hoped."

"Will they be back tonight to help finish packing?"

"Your mother instructed me to tell you that she did not think they would be home until quite late, and that she is very sorry about that."

"What else is new," said Liam. The closer they'd gotten to Red Line, the less he'd seen his parents. He knew that wasn't how they wanted it, that they were under so much pressure, and that it would all be over tomorrow, but it was still weird not having them around. Sometimes, when he was at the apartment by himself, Liam felt like he was living on his own, the last survivor on an abandoned planet. At least Mina would be there tonight, even if she mostly acted like he was annoying.

"Sounds like we'll still be here until the bitter end, tomorrow," he said.

"Ha, ha, ha," said JEFF.

Liam raised an eyebrow at him.

"You said bitter," said JEFF. "And so I pictured

someone sipping synthetic lime extract and then making a puckering face. That is funny, isn't it?"

Liam shook his head. "That's not really what I meant."

"Are you actually consuming a bitter-flavored food to end the day tomorrow? Is that some sort of departure ritual? I have seen no records of such a thing in—"

"No, JEFF. Just forget it." Liam's thoughts drifted back to that strange object up on the volcano. "JEFF, do you know of any buildings or anything up on the summit of Olympus Mons?"

JEFF's eyes flashed, a sign that he was searching through data. "I do not have access to the most current colonial satellite imagery because the VirtCom is down. However, I have no records in my local archives of any structure on the volcano summit."

"Okay," said Liam. He'd have to ask his parents about it, if there was even time. Somebody had to know what that thing was.

"What time do you finally get up to the starliner?" Shawn asked.

"Not until three. What are you doing tonight?"

"Mainly just settling in, I think," said Shawn. "And I guess the climbing domes will be open."

"Lucky," said Liam.

Shawn shrugged. "We don't go into stasis for

three days after launch. And it's not all orientations and safety trainings. We'll still have plenty of time for fun once you're up there. I mean, we're supposed to get exercise before we go to sleep, right?"

"Yeah," said Liam.

They walked in silence for a minute. Then Shawn sighed. "I'm gonna miss this place. Maybe not school. But you know, the colony and stuff."

"Me too," said Liam. His heart was already racing at the thought of seeing Ms. Avi; now he felt his chest tightening and his eyes getting hot all over again. He turned his head so Shawn wouldn't see, pretending he was looking around at the lonely buildings and streets, as they made their way back to school.

3

"Welcome aboard!"

Liam crossed a cavernous hanger, led by a cheery young officer wearing the crisp maroon uniform of the *Scorpius* staff.

"I'm Devon, and I'll be your host for this guided tour of your new home. You've been assigned to Community Twenty-Two, in Segment Eight of Core Three of the Phoenix Starliner *Scorpius*. Right this way!"

The deck whirled with activity around him. Lights flashed and buzzers sounded. People hurried from one spacecraft to another. Transports sailed back and forth and floated up and down, full of personnel and supplies. Ships were parked in lines to either side of him, and in the many crisscrossing platforms above and below this one. There were so many different kinds, from the boxy cargo cruisers to spindly military vessels to sleeker, private craft.

On one side of the hanger, Liam spied a towering rack of one-person ships called skim drones.

"I see you're interested in the skim drones. They'll be used for a variety of interesting education and adventure outings at each waypoint," said Devon. "The guided tour through the particle reef at Delphi was a big hit with the First Fleet. Should I sign you up for that now?"

"Oh, um, I'll have to check with my parents," said Liam. He flew his parents' skim drone all the time out at the research station, but technically, you had to be fourteen to get your permit. Liam could probably fly better than most fourteen-year-olds, and Dad had assured him that the rules were going to be relaxed on the journey, but he'd still have to check.

"Sounds good," said Devon. "Just keep in mind that even though we're talking about something ten years from now, we only have five conscious days until our arrival at Delphi—three before we enter stasis and two after we wake up—and the limited spots have been filling up fast in the other fleets."

"Got it," said Liam.

"Great. Right this way!"

Tall frosted-glass doors whooshed open and Liam was greeted by brilliant sun, but not the ominous red glow he knew from Mars. This light was the safe, pale gleam from thousands of banks of lamps inside one of the *Scorpius*'s six core units. The starliner was nearly twenty-five kilometers long and had three distinct sections: an X-shaped array at the front, where the bridge and control centers were located, and where the solar sails would be unfurled; four giant, egg-shaped fusion engines at the back; and in the center, a set of six long cylinders called the cores. They were arranged beside one another, making a shape that from a distance resembled the bullet chamber of an old Earth revolver.

Devon hovered beside Liam as he gazed out across the vast space. None of the photos Liam had seen quite did this place justice. The core was so large that Liam's view of the far end was blurred by a haze of distance. And this was only one segment. There were ten segments per core, each of those nearly two kilometers long and a half kilometer tall.

"The *Scorpius* will have one hundred million passengers," said Devon, "and the cores offer everything to make the long journey feel like a breeze."

The entire inner wall of the cylindrical space was striped by long decks, with door after door into over a million staterooms. Liam saw people leaning on the railings looking out, or walking back and forth, and while some of them seemed perfectly right side up, others looked like they were standing sideways, and still others who were directly above him were upside down. It seemed impossible that they could be walking normally and not falling to their deaths.

"Takes some getting used to," said Devon. "But don't worry, the cores make their own Earth-level gravity by rotating, so no matter where you are, up and down are relative to your location, and you'll feel like you're on level ground."

Liam's eye was drawn to four particularly bright strips of the cylinder wall, collections of glossy buildings and domes that blazed with an odyssey of lights.

"Those are the social centers," said Devon. "There's one for every ten communities in this segment. Social centers feature fitness complexes, dining facilities, and entertainment that will be open before and after each stasis period. Each segment of the core also has a community park that's over five square kilometers. That's much larger than New York's Central Park back on Earth. And when you don't feel like moving those muscles, the *Scorpius* is also equipped with its own dedicated VirtCom, featuring all your favorite virtual locations and lifestyles."

Liam gazed up at the park, a long green expanse stretching from one end of the core to the other overhead. He saw a miniature Earth Preserve; five climbing structures shaped like different mountain peaks inside glass domes; a fountain that, because the park was currently above him, seemed to have water shooting down and falling up; and long, long lawns, dotted with people who were sitting or running or playing.

"I see you're eyeing the climbing domes. They're designed to replicate mountains from different local planetary bodies, including their weather conditions. I've heard the ascent of Doom Mons on Titan is a real thigh burner! Remember, muscle exercise is critical to body health in between stasis periods. Would you like me to sign you up for an experience?"

"That's okay," said Liam.

"Great." Devon smiled. "Your passenger survey also said you were interested in pets."

Liam had checked that box, though he'd never actually had a pet. There were hamsters at the research station, but his parents had never let them get an armadillo, by far the most popular pet in the colonies.

"Time with pets has been shown to help with mental health during transit," said Devon. "There are a dozen different varieties available for rental in your community, on a first-come-first-served basis. You have to be eighteen or older to rent one, so be sure to remind your parents. Now, let's head up to your stateroom and check out your accommodations. Right this way!"

They stepped into a bubble-shaped pod, clear on all sides, with two rows of seats facing each other. The pod shot out across the core on a cable system that spiderwebbed through its center. As they traveled, up and down shifted. The hanging pod rotated, always staying level, but soon their starting point was above them, and the park was to their side. Liam gripped the armrest and took a deep breath.

They transferred twice before getting off at a deck lined with doors. "Your stateroom is equipped with standard amenities, as required by the ISA's Long Travel Protocol," said Devon, "as well as—"

Someone knocked. Liam wanted to ignore it.

"—stasis enhancement packages, which include—"

Another knock.

Liam sighed. He pressed a button by his temple and everything around him froze, including Devon. Background noise remained: the hum of the cable transports, the din of voices and laughter, but now it was distant.

Liam slipped off his virtual glasses.

He was back on his bed, on Mars. He blinked, adjusting to the dim, drab light of his room.

His door popped open and Mina leaned in. "Mom says breakfast."

Liam checked the clock. Only 6:35 a.m. "I thought she said we were getting up at seven."

Mina shrugged. "They want to leave sooner. Things didn't go well at the station last night or something."

"What time are you leaving?"

Mina glanced at her link. "Arlo will be here in like an hour." Mina was the singer and guitarist in the Gravity Minus, and they'd been picked to play at one of the launch parties on the *Scorpius*. She had a dress rehearsal that afternoon, so she got to go up early. Also, she was eighteen, and could travel without a parent or guardian.

"You're lucky," said Liam.

Mina blew her bangs out of her eyes. "Yeah, well . . . Just get up before Mom starts getting on your case. They're both totally stressed out." She left his door half open. Liam could hear the commotion from out in the common room, utensils clanking, dishes being stacked.

Liam had been asleep when his parents had gotten home. Before that, he and Mina had finished their packing. They'd placed each family member's single container of clothing and personal items outside their door by ten as instructed, and then made a dinner of ice cream and the last freeze-dried pizza, the kind with the protein-plus sausages that, according to his parents, almost tasted like actual meat. They'd also cooked the last few strips of GreenVeg for their parents' plates, which they left out when they went to bed at midnight. Liam had been nervous the whole evening, except for a few moments while he and Mina had been playing a virtual game called *Roid Wraiths IV*. He'd assumed that when his parents got home, they'd have words for him about ditching school, but then he hadn't even heard them come in.

And even though he'd gone to bed kind of late, Liam's eyes had still popped open at five a.m., his stomach brewing with fluttery, nervous energy. He'd heard his parents already busying about in the common room, and wondered if they'd gotten any sleep at all, but instead of joining them, he'd watched orientation guides to pass the time. He was still worried about what they'd say about yesterday, but it was more than that now: this was it. Everything he did today was the last time, ever, even lying in his bed.

He'd been on his second tour through the *Scorpius* when Mina had come in. Before that, he'd taken the Delphi tour, and checked to see if the Danos tour had been updated before the VirtCom shut down. Danos was the second waypoint on the route to Aaru-5.

There would be fifteen stops total, but only Delphi and Danos had been officially named, and even Danos was still only theoretical, as no ships had made it that far yet. On the map, the other thirteen stops just said *Coming Soon* in the general vicinity of where they'd likely be.

A few of the stops were necessary for course corrections, but otherwise, once you burned the engines in the vacuum of space, you could maintain your speed for as long as you wanted. The rest of the stops were needed because the ship's life support and navigation systems would slowly drain the fuel supply over time. Also, there was some concern about human health if you stayed in stasis for too long. The waypoints would allow people to wake up and move around and get their brains and muscles active again, and also for the stasis pods to be serviced.

The other thing Liam had done this morning was examine maps of Olympus Mons. He'd checked the satellite images and topographic maps but found no sign of any kind of structure at the volcano's summit. Liam thought about how that sphere had only appeared when the solar energy hit it. That same energy had the effect of knocking out power. Had the sphere been losing power? Was that what made it visible? And if that was true, did that mean all the rest of the time it was . . . invisible? The only problem with that idea was that technology like that didn't actually exist. Unless it was some kind of top-secret military thing. There was also the possibility that the object had disappeared because it had been moving, except Liam was pretty sure he'd seen it in the same spot each time. Besides, no ships would have been flying during the storm, and there weren't any ships that Liam knew of that looked anything like that silver sphere. The only other explanation Liam could think of was that it hadn't actually been a structure or a ship at all. Maybe the solar energy had charged some mineral in the rocks, but he'd never heard of that happening either.

"Liam," Mom called from the other room.

Liam tapped his link. His timer was still counting down: just over eight hours until Red Line. He got out of bed, still wearing the same gravity-assist outfit from the day before, and grabbed the bottle of clean-scent sanitizing spray from his bedside table. He sprayed his armpits, his feet, and then all over. It would have to do. Water was restricted to essential use only, and apparently the starliners had some sort of ultraviolet shower. It might be a hundred and fifty years before he stood under real water again.

He went to his dresser and checked his scalp in the mirror. The burn from yesterday had scabbed over. It still ached a little when he touched it. He could probably get his hair to cover it with that new product Mina had helped him pick out. A few weeks ago, when she'd announced, as she often did, that his hair was "ridiculous," he'd realized that he agreed. They'd gone to the health and beauty section at the VirtCom, and it was a good thing she'd been there, because Liam had no idea if his hair was "grumpy" or "playful," or whether he wanted to color it fuchsia or even replace it with elasti-weave, which you could style in almost any shape. Mina had informed him that the correct product was "spazzy." The putty made his shaggy black hair stick around in cool ways that weren't too crazy. The only problem was he'd already packed it in his box to go to the *Scorpius*, so his only option was to try to mat down his bedhead as best he could.

Liam headed out into the common room and joined Mina at the tiny dining table. She was eating a bowl of Grain-O's. Dad was on the couch, a holo-screen floating in his lap. Mom was in the kitchen, in constant motion to a soundtrack of clinking dishes. Liam eyed his parents, bracing for a comment about yesterday, but they both seemed busy.

Mina glanced up through the curtain of jet-black hair that covered half her face. Liam had heard her chatting seemingly all night with Arlo, her boyfriend, which seemed dumb since they were going to see each other so soon. But they were in love or something.

Her eyes flicked to Liam's head. "I thought we talked about this."

"Shut up," Liam grunted.

"Get eating," Mom said. "I need to get the washer going."

"Mom," said Mina, "the cockroaches don't care if the dishes are dirty."

Mom nodded slowly to herself. "No, of course they don't, but it's on the checklist."

Liam poured himself a bowl of cereal. He grabbed the Total Milk container but it was empty. He was about to ask Mom for more, but he paused, afraid that getting her attention would remind her that they were upset with him.

"You forgot to get milk," Mina said.

Mom sighed. "I know. The last grocery store was closed by the time we got back. Do you want to sprinkle any protein flakes on there?" She held up a half-empty plastic jar.

"Gross," said Mina. "I don't eat anything made out of mealworms. You know that."

Mom smiled. "The label says they were farm raised." She dumped the flakes into a black metal box on the counter. Liam relaxed. Yesterday did not seem to be on his parents' minds.

"Give me some of your milk," he said to Mina.

Her bowl had only a few flakes left, floating in a sea of bluish white.

Mina scowled. "We're leaving everything else behind; why can't we leave little brother, too?"

"Mina—" said Dad.

"I'm just kidding." She held out her bowl and tipped it, using her spoon to catch the flakes.

"Thanks," said Liam.

"Just know that Arlo and I made out hot and heavy yesterday and I already packed my toothbrush, so every bite you take is basically you kissing him."

Liam shrugged and started eating.

"I can't believe you're making out with my boyfriend."

This made them both crack up.

"JEFF," said Dad, "what's the latest forecast?"

"Retrieving," said JEFF from speakers in the wall. Here in the apartment, JEFF had loaded himself into the home network. His panda body was waiting out in their Cosmic Cruiser. "The solar storm is still forecast for two o'clock. Due to the predicted storm strength, Red Line will be reached at this time. Is there anything else I can help with?"

"No, that's all," said Dad.

"Actually, JEFF, there's one more thing," said Mina. "What's the forecast for my parents actually getting their research done in time to see my big show?"

"Mina . . . ," said Mom.

"I'm afraid I do not have that information," said JEFF, "nor am I capable of offering a predictive model based on those variables—"

"Fine, JEFF. What good are you if you can't predict the future?" Mina winked at Liam.

"I can still perform many helpful functions—"

"JEFF," said Liam, "that was a joke too."

"Oh, acknowledged."

"No it wasn't," said Mina.

"Shh," said Liam. He smiled but fought a surge of nervous energy. Mom and Dad had been late for basically everything the last couple months. Today had to be different.

"We'll be there," said Mom. "But the sooner we get out to the station the better."

"Did something go wrong last night?" Liam asked.

"No, we're just . . . not quite finished yet." Mom shoved the last slices of bread into the black box and pressed a button. There was flash of light and a tingle of electrons. Mom lifted the lid and looked inside, then started unwrapping nutri-bars and dropping them in.

"What do you have left to do?" Liam asked.

"It's primarily the moisture condensers," said

Dad. "A few more cloud-seeding cycles and we should have it right."

"Why do we need condensers?" Liam asked. "I thought you already figured out how to synthesize water."

"'Cause there'd be no rain without them," said Mina, "which means no trees, or lakes, or anything."

"The condensers will allow for clouds," said Dad. "A natural water cycle. Aaru-5 isn't going to be very Earthlike if we don't have that."

"Why does it have to be like Earth?" asked Liam.

"Because duh," said Mina, "that's the whole point. You don't want to keep living like we did *here*, do you? In domes with like three things to eat?"

"It hasn't been that bad."

"No, but we're trying to make a home where the natural environment isn't constantly trying to kill us," said Dad. "Somewhere humans are *supposed* to be. And we're really close."

"Can you get it done today?" Liam asked.

"We have to," said Mom.

"But what if you don't?" Liam couldn't help asking. "Are we going to have to stay past Red Line? Would the starliner wait for us?"

"No, Liam, relax," said Mom, her voice tight. She atomized the nutri-bars. "Just . . . that's why we need to get going this morning." She swooped over to the table and took their bowls. Liam still had a few bites left, but he decided not to protest.

"You could already be out there if you'd let me go up with Shawn's dad last night," said Liam. "There was a form you could have signed."

"With all our free time," said Mom. "And besides, Wesley has enough to worry about, crunching the data we sent him. I'm sorry your parents are the ones who have to operate the terraforming turbines, but that's how it is."

"I'm afraid you're stuck with us," said Dad. He got up and ruffled Liam's hair as he passed by.

"You'll be fine," said Mina, getting up too. "Your *girlfriend* will be out there today, won't she?"

"Shut up," said Liam.

"What's that?" Mom asked.

"Nothing," Liam and Mina said at the same time.

"I need your cups," said Mom as she atomized another batch of food.

Mina slugged back her juice. "Seriously, if you're in such a hurry, why are you cleaning a place that we are about to leave forever?"

"It's important to follow Departure Protocol," said Mom.

"Maybe for people who left last month," said Mina. "But it's not like there's going to be anyone left to smell some rotted food or—"

"That's how I want to leave this place," Mom snapped. "Why do you have to argue with everything, Mina?"

"Wow." Mina stormed into her room and slammed the door. A second later, the walls began to thump with music.

Mom frowned and turned toward Mina's door.

"Let her go," said Dad. "It's her last chance for a while. The building's empty anyway."

Liam just sat there, his heart racing.

"JEFF," said Mom, "what's left?"

"Optional tasks include vacuuming and lowering the blinds," said JEFF.

"Finish packing, okay?" said Mom, taking Liam's cup.

"There's nothing left to pack," he muttered, but he returned to his room and shut the door, too.

Liam stood there in the silence, until the vacuum started in the living room. Really, vacuuming? If they needed to go, they should just go!

There was a knock on his window. Liam found Mina looking in from the balcony that their rooms shared. He opened the curved window, sliding it upward like an eyelid.

"What?"

"I've got a few minutes," she said. "Time for one last game?"

"Sure." Liam climbed onto the narrow balcony. They stepped to the far wall, just out of sight of the living room windows. Here, many of the hexagonal black solar-absorbent wall panels were missing. Each was about the size of a small plate.

They dug their fingers behind the edges of the panels that were left, popping them free with a tearing of adhesive. They collected five each, then sat down with the stacks in their laps, their legs dangling through the gaps in the railing.

"Last round," said Mina, "winner will be the all-time Demolition champion of Mars. Oldest goes first."

She held a tile vertically, eyeing the rows of circular windows across the street, and snapped her arm. The tile arced and shattered against a wall, just missing a window. The pieces rained down on a deck, the sound echoing up the desolate street.

"Close," said Liam. He threw, and his tile punched a jagged hole in a flex-glass window but failed to smash it completely. Small shards fell to the street, making a chimey sound.

"Nice," said Mina. "One point for a hit, but no bonus point for total demolition."

She threw again and this time hit a smaller bathroom window. It shattered completely. "And the bonus!" She pumped her fist.

"Good one," said Liam. "If Mom knew we were doing this, she'd want to vacuum the street, too."

Mina laughed. She reached over and rubbed between Liam's shoulder blades. "Sorry I snapped at you before."

"It's okay."

"I'm sorry too that you're stuck with *them* for the day. Mom and Dad will be more fun up on the starliner. We'll have a good time, I think."

"Yeah."

They threw their other tiles, causing more damage the more they warmed up.

"I think you win by a point," Mina said at the end, even though Liam was pretty sure she had missed her last throw on purpose. "The all-time champion of Demolition!" She grabbed his arm and held it up while making a fake crowd-cheering sound. "And now you get a prize."

Mina pulled something off her neck and handed it to him. It was a small rectangle of smooth silver metal with a green-colored circle of glass at one end, and a chain attached at the other.

"What's this?"

"It's a present for Arlo, but I want to try it out and make sure it works first."

"What's it do?"

Mina held up an identical one that was still around

her neck. "They're paired radio beacons," said Mina. "It's really retro technology, like, twenty-first-century Earth stuff. They used to power things like garage doors. They might be kinda dumb but all my friends are into them."

Liam turned the cool metal over in his fingers. "How does it work?"

"Watch." Mina pressed the green glass circle on hers. The top of Liam's lit up with a green flash.

Liam waited for it to do more. "That's it?"

Mina smiled. "The idea is, every time that lights up, you—well, you for this afternoon, but Arlo—would know that I'm thinking about you . . . him. And then you can click it back."

Liam did. Mina's blinked.

"Kinda corny," said Mina, "but also kinda great, right? No annoying link chat or emoti-messaging. You don't even have to say anything, you just . . . know I'm there. They're paired to each other only, and will supposedly work at any distance. Just try them out with me this afternoon so I know they work, okay?"

"Okay," said Liam.

"And don't lose it or I'll pummel you."

"Yeah, right." He turned the beacon over in his fingers, then gazed up at the sky, tracing the lines of the space elevators until they disappeared. Far above that, the docks and the starliner glowed like a dawn star.

"Did I ever tell you it scares me?" said Mina.

"What does?"

"Space. Being out there in all that black with no home. No solid ground."

"Huh." Liam was surprised to hear this. He never thought of Mina as being afraid of anything. "Well, we'll be asleep for most of it."

"That scares me, too," said Mina. "Stuffed into those little tubes. One thing goes wrong . . . we could be asleep forever, floating in space."

"Nah," Liam said, even though the thought of it made his belly squirm. "It'll be okay. . . . I'll be there to keep you company." He wondered if that sounded silly, but Mina laughed.

"Little brother, my big hero."

Distantly, the door buzzed. They both stood.

"That's Arlo," said Mina. "Gotta run. See you in a bit, okay?"

"Okay." Liam smiled at her, but he was barely breathing. He turned and leaned on the railing.

Mina stepped away, but then her arms wrapped around him from behind.

"What are you doing?" Liam tried to worm free.

"Shh. I'm giving you a hug."

"Why?" But her hair smelled sweet, like that Island Essence shampoo she used. Supposedly this was the smell of coconuts, not that Liam had ever smelled one. Lots of things in their lives were like that. Earth smells and flavors, the origins of which none of them could be sure of.

"I don't know so just shut up." Mina wiped her eyes, and Liam's eyes started to feel hot. She pulled back and turned him around. "Make sure Mom and Dad don't mess around out at the station. You'd better be there for my show tonight."

"Definitely," said Liam.

Mina smiled. "Good."

He stayed on the deck after she left, gazing out across the colony and the copper mountains beyond the dome. Suddenly, he found it hard to breathe. It was like Mina's hug had cracked open his insides and now they were just spilling around.

"Ready to go?" Mom appeared in the balcony doorway.

Liam just shrugged and turned away, hopefully before she'd seen his tears. "In a sec."

"It's time." Except then she joined him, leaning on the railing. "Looks like there's no more wall left to rip down," she said, glancing at the area of missing tiles and smiling. "How are you holding up?"

"Fine," said Liam, but he felt the ripples getting more turbulent inside.

"We didn't have a chance to talk about you ditching school yesterday."

"I'm sorry. It was stupid."

Mom sighed. "I'm going to miss this place, too. I know it doesn't always seem that way, since we're working so hard to leave, but we did raise you guys here."

Liam wiped at his eyes. "Yeah."

"I know it's hard leaving. Your father and I had to do it with Earth, and you've got it even worse. At least back then we got to see where we were going. We even knew what this apartment looked like. But with Aaru . . ." Liam turned and saw that Mom's eyes were wet, too. "It's all just a best guess. The planet, the star-liners, even our research . . . There are so many things we don't know, that we can't possibly account for, but that's kind of how life works. It might not seem that way yet, when you've had people telling you what to do and where to be all your life, but the reality is, when you make your own decisions, you never really know where they'll lead, or what will come next. All you can do is make choices and move forward. And actually, what ends up happening is, the more you learn, the more you realize you still have to learn. The only thing we know for sure is that we can't stay here."

"I wish we could," said Liam. "I like it here."

"I know you do," said Mom. "But this place isn't even right for us. Humans aren't meant to live in this atmosphere, this gravity, these temperatures. Even the soil, the longer days and extra-long seasons, none of it fits with us."

Doesn't seem that bad to me, Liam thought, but he knew it didn't matter; *here* wasn't going to be around for very much longer, anyway.

Mom looked up at the sky. "There's only one place humans were meant to live, but that place is gone. Now we have to find the next best thing, and hope it works out."

"But we're not even sure Aaru will be right," said Liam. "And all those years in space . . . we have no idea how we'll do. I mean, there won't be *any* days, or seasons, or gravity, it will all be fake, and nobody knows yet what that will do to us."

Mom nodded. "It's the biggest question humans have ever faced: Can we survive without this sun, outside of this solar system?"

"What if it's all so different, and it changes us, and then we're not even human anymore?"

"I don't know," said Mom. "We've done all right here. We're still mostly human, except for that weird elasti-weave some of your classmates wear."

Liam managed to laugh, but only a little.

Mom smiled, but it died away. "This has only been a small test compared to what's coming."

"Sounds hopeless," said Liam.

"It can, but in a way, sometimes I feel like it might

be the opposite. There's so much we don't know that we can only do the best we can, and that will have to be good enough. Maybe that's what being human is really all about. And sure, we may not know yet what dangers are out there, but we also don't know what good things we'll find." She put her arm around him. "We'll take it one unknown at a time. Does that help?"

Liam nodded. "Maybe?"

"My little Martian," said Mom.

That made him smile. And also caused a sort of explosion in his chest.

They gazed out at the colony. A moment later, Liam felt heat on his back. The sun had risen over the top of their building.

"We should get going," Dad said from the doorway.

Mom kissed the top of Liam's head. "Do you need another minute?"

Liam traced the building tops across the street, the distant outline of the Earth Preserve, the space elevators beyond, one last time. "I'm good," he said.

He pushed away from the railing and ducked into his room. He took a deep breath, one more look around, trying to memorize every detail: his desk, empty now; his dresser, still lined with the fossil collection he'd gathered over the years out at the research station; his Dust Devils poster; his blue bedspread. . . . He exhaled hard and headed for the front door.

"Ready?" said Dad. Liam and Mom nodded. "Okay, JEFF, let's shut it down."

"Acknowledged," said JEFF. The lights flicked off and everything powered down, a hum that cycled to silence.

They all stood there, gazing back into the darkened apartment, the red Martian light through the gaps in the blinds striping the furniture and walls. Liam heard Mom sniffing. Dad hugged her.

"Okay." He closed the door and tapped the all-clear code. A green light lit on the lock.

They walked down the empty apartment hallway. There were little bits of trash here and there. The place was so quiet.

Liam reached to his neck and pressed the top of the radio beacon.

A second later, it blinked back.

4

The Cosmic Cruiser lifted off from the empty park-
ing platform behind their apartment building. Dad
piloted, while Mom sat beside him and opened a
holoscreen. There were four seats in the cockpit, and
Liam sat behind Dad. Out the curved windshield, he
watched the empty buildings slide by below. A few
other ships crossed the sky here and there, all heading in the other direction, toward the space elevators. Liam looked for the silver droplets racing up
and down their wires. Mina would be on one soon.
Zipping off-world.

"This is Cruiser Delta Four Five," Dad said into
the transmitter, "en route to Olympus Mons research

station, requesting colony departure at the east gate."

"Copy Delta Four Five," a voice replied. "Stand by for shield deactivation."

On past Saturday mornings they might have been queued up behind a dozen ships or more waiting to leave the colony, from cruisers like theirs to sport racers to giant transports taking groups out to canyon dive, but this morning there was only a single drab military ship in front of them, probably making one of the last sweeps before Red Line.

Lights blinked from red to green around one triangular section of the dome, and then with a shimmer the energy field in that section switched off.

Dad guided the cruiser through the space and then picked up speed. They were immediately buffeted by strong winds. Below stretched a sea of trash incinerators and sewage recyclers. In the past, there would have been dense clouds of smoke and steam, but the systems were mostly shut down. Trash tumbled out of the containers, the wind scattering it into cracks and canyons.

Liam got out of his seat and left the cockpit. He ducked through a short hallway into the living area of the ship in one long Martian-gravity step. Along one wall, there was a couch and a small kitchen area with a table and stools. Everything was bolted down. Cabinets and equipment lockers lined the other wall, along with the rectangular airlock door. At the back of the craft were two small rooms with a narrow bathroom in between them, as well as a hatch in the floor that led down to the skim drone mounted beneath the ship. The cruiser was designed for six to eight travelers, with supplies for a week. It had a small ion plasma engine for space travel, and enough fuel to get as far as Saturn and back. The back rooms also had eight stasis pods, in case of an emergency in space where life support was compromised.

Liam knelt on the couch and pressed his face against one of the two curved round windows. The colony shrank behind them.

"Hey, Liam," Dad called from the cockpit. "Wanna fly?"

"What?" Liam squinted, trying to spot their apartment building.

"Fly," Dad repeated. "Want to? Last chance for a while."

"Okay." Liam returned to the cockpit. Dad slid out of his seat and Liam buckled himself in.

He'd flown the cruiser on a number of trips to the research station and back. It could operate on full autopilot, but Dad liked to have Liam practice with only the navigation assistance. Flying the cruiser was nowhere near as fun as flying the skim drone—it was heavy and slow—but the thrusters were powerful, so you could get good speed.

Liam put one hand on a touchscreen and the other on a small joystick. The windshield had a digital grid of white lines, and flashing arrows mapped future turns on their route. Readings for ground speed and altitude blinked in the corner. Liam slid his fingers on the pad, adjusting for the shifting winds, and flicked the joystick to change the angle of the small wings on either side of the ship that held the thrusters. He fired them by pressing a small button atop the joystick with his thumb.

"Good," said Dad, as Liam made a slight turn and leveled off. "Remember the thermal updrafts when we get closer to the mountain."

"Got it," said Liam.

They soared over twisting canyons, plains of copper sand, and burnt sienna cliffs. Little whorls of dust spun along the flats, and above, thin, slate-colored dust wisps streamed in the high-altitude winds.

With every kilometer they flew, Olympus Mons rose before them, until its broad slopes filled their entire view. Liam's gaze returned to the horizon, where the peak was still beyond their view.

"Guys," he said, "is there anything up at the summit?"

"What do you mean?" Mom asked, tapping charts on her holoscreen.

"I don't know, like a building? I saw something up there yesterday during the solar storm."

"I thought we weren't going to talk about your behavior during the storm," said Mom.

"I said I was sorry," said Liam. "But I thought I saw some kind of building up there. And it looked big. Kind of round and silver."

"Well, I doubt it," said Dad. "We thought about putting the Phase One observatory at the summit, but the atmosphere is so thin at that altitude, it would've put too much strain on the pressure suits during construction, never mind having to get power up that far." Dad rubbed Liam's shoulder. "I know I said we'd take the space-grade suits and hike around the peak sometime. I'm sorry we never got to that."

"That's okay," said Liam. He was more interested in what his dad had said before that. His parents rarely mentioned Phase One. He knew they'd worked on it, and that it had something to do with gathering data for Phase Two, but otherwise it was classified. Of course, Phase Two was technically a classified project as well, and yet you could barely keep Mom or Dad from going on and on about condensation or cloud seeding or whatever. In Year 9, Liam's class had done a whole unit on the Aaru colonization plan, with hours about the terraforming and starliner travel . . .

but really nothing about Phase One. Maybe it was too technical and boring even for the teachers, but Liam wasn't sure.

"And please don't take your father's comment as an invitation to go up there today," Mom added. "The only thing there will be time for is hanging out at the research station, ready to leave."

"Okay, Mom, I get it."

"Maybe it was a distortion of the light," said Dad. "Things get weird during those storms."

"I guess," said Liam. But still—

"Watch out," said Dad. He pointed out the port side just as sensors began to blink. Plumes of gray vapor wafted out of fissures in the ground: the last, deepest pockets of subsurface ice, being melted by the blistering-hot days. Temperatures in the daytime now reached one hundred and fifty degrees, while at night, they dropped to three hundred below zero. The hot days had been enough to evaporate Mars's polar ice caps years ago.

"Got it," said Liam. He adjusted course.

"Hmm," said Mom.

"What?" Dad asked.

"I'm getting some odd temperature readings from the station."

"Marco might have started the trials already."

"Yeah, but . . ." Mom pointed to a graph. "These

spikes aren't normal, are they?"

"Maybe it's the monitors," said Dad. "They could be shorting out from the solar storm."

"We'll be lucky if we can keep systems online today with all the electrical damage they've sustained," said Mom.

A crosswind buffeted the ship, pushing them sideways and off axis. Liam turned the ship into the wind, changed their forward angle, and increased speed a touch. The ride smoothed out.

"Nice work," said Dad.

"Yes, very calm under pressure," said Mom, looking up from her data.

"Thanks," said Liam. There was definitely something about flying. It was almost as if having so many things to think about actually improved his focus.

Another sensor flashed and the cruiser lurched. Liam yanked at the joystick as they skidded sideways on the air.

Dad leaned over the control panel. "Rear thruster went offline. JEFF!"

JEFF appeared in the doorway, back in his panda housing, his wheeled feet making their cracker-crunching sound. "Good afternoon, Captain."

"It's still morning, JEFF."

"Acknowledged," said JEFF.

"Check the rear thruster," said Dad. "Looks like

maybe the fuel circuits are shorting out."

"Acknowledged," said JEFF. "I will get right over it."

"On it," said Dad.

"On what, Captain?"

"It's get right *on* it, JEFF. Not *over* it."

"Acknowledged," said JEFF. "I have some faulty circuit pathways myself from the solar storms, but I have been unable to order new parts since the VírtCom shut down."

"Well, tonight on the starliner we'll check you in for a full service," said Dad.

"That would be delightful." JEFF crunched out of the cockpit.

Liam fought the sideways angle of the ship. "I'm going to try a higher altitude." He increased the other thrusters. He angled toward the top edge of a massive cliff, over five kilometers high, that encircled the base of Olympus Mons.

JEFF spoke again, over the ship's intercom. "Circuits have been replaced. I will be rebooting systems now."

For a moment, the entire ship went dark, the engines shutting down, and in the quiet they started to arc toward the cliffside—

Then the ship shuddered and everything whirred back to life.

"Reboot complete," said JEFF.

"Feels better," said Liam, pulling up sharply.

"Good," said Dad. "Take her in to the station."

Liam flew along the edge of the cliff. Far below on a flat, red plain, three dome-shaped buildings came into view. They were arranged in a triangle at the base of the cliff, right beside the mouth of an enormous canyon that led back into the rock face. Beyond them, long sheets of solar panels glittered in the sunlight. There was a smoothed landing area near the buildings; Paolo and Ariana's cruiser was parked there, along with two other ships. Liam activated the landing gear and touched down beside them.

"Looks like everyone's here," said Mom. She closed her holoscreen. "Let's get our suits on."

Liam was just getting to his feet when a shrill tone sounded in the cabin.

"Attention all colonial craft, this is Scorpius *command. Updated forecasts indicate that the approaching solar storm will be larger, and arrive sooner, than predicted. We are now expecting the storm to hit in approximately four hours and for conditions to surpass Red Line at that time. As a result,* Scorpius *departure time has been accelerated to twelve hundred hours. Please stand by for an updated space elevator schedule."*

"They can't do that," Mom groaned. "We'll never get the trials done."

"Apparently they can," said Dad.

"So we're going back early?" Liam asked.

"We'll find out when we get to the lab—"

Mom's and Dad's links buzzed simultaneously on their wrists.

"A colonial transport is coming to pick us up here instead," said Mom, reading from her link. "They'll take us straight to the starliner."

"How soon are they coming?" asked Liam.

"They'll be here an hour before Red Line," said Mom. She looked at Dad. "Three hours to finish. It's going to be tight."

Liam tapped his link and reset his Red Line countdown. He was either thrilled or terrified or both.

They headed to the back rooms to change into their pressure suits. Liam took off his gravity-assist clothing and pulled on a tight-fitting black thermal shirt and pants.

Mina's beacon flashed. Liam pressed it back. She was probably on the starliner by now. He tried to imagine what she was doing: relaxing in her stateroom? At band practice? And where was Shawn? Mountain climbing on Titan? Only four more hours . . . Now that they'd left the colony, he couldn't wait to get up there.

Liam unplugged his pressure suit from its battery charger. He stepped into the heavy boots, pulled the suit up and around his arms, and zipped the helmet closed. He transferred his link, activated the heating and breathing systems, and joined his parents by the airlock door.

"Ready?" Mom said through her suit's speaker.

"Yeah," said Liam.

Dad opened the inner door and they squeezed into the small airlock. He closed the door and pressed a button and there was a whoosh of air as the outer door slid open. They were greeted by a stiff hot wind, dust pattering against their visors. Even through the pressure suit, Liam felt a brief surge of heat before his suit compensated.

His parents jumped down to the crumbled rock surface. Like most adults, Mom and Dad wore weight belts at their waists and ankles to minimize the effects of low gravity. Liam never wore those. His parents used to get on his case about it, but eventually they'd given up. He waited until they'd walked a few paces and then leaped out of the ship, soaring three meters and landing right behind them.

The three small domed buildings were just beyond the shadow of the massive cliff. Lights blinked at the canyon entrance, where a metal walkway led into the dark. The closest building housed the power systems, water recyclers, and storage; the second was the data center; and the third was the living quarters. At least one member of the team was here every night.

The most important part of the station was actually hidden from view. The giant terraforming turbines were housed in an enormous natural magma chamber far inside the extinct volcano. You had to follow the walkway over a kilometer into the canyon and then take an elevator hundreds of meters down a lava tube to reach the underground lab. Inside the cathedral-like cavern stood the two tall, conical turbines surrounded by a jungle of plants and banks of computers. Though his parents spent nearly all their time there, they'd only brought Liam down twice, and they'd made him wear ankle weights and constantly told him not to touch anything. Liam much preferred being on his own with Phoebe and Shawn, exploring the vast network of lava tubes and caves that spread throughout the volcano.

They hurried to the data center and entered through double airlock doors. There were three people inside. Two younger scientists, Mara and Idris, stood inside a glass-encased control room, working busily on large holoscreens. Banks of computers hummed all around them. The third person was walking toward Liam and Mom and Dad, wearing a pressure suit and zipping his helmet closed.

"Gerald, Lana," said Marco, their team leader, "nice of you to join us."

"Sorry," said Dad. "We had to see Mina off."

"Of course," said Marco. He was in his early eight-ies, with thick white hair, and his eyes glittered with the bionic replacements that many seniors chose to get. "Hey there, Liam," he said with a smile.

"Hey."

"Bet you wish you were with all your friends up on the *Scorpius* right now."

Liam did his best to smile. "Pretty much."

"I hear you. It's hard work being the son of two of humanity's most important scientists. But we're almost there." He turned to Liam's parents. "You heard about the updated departure time?"

Dad nodded. "Think we can make it?"

Marco shrugged. "I think we can run two more seeding cycles and hope we get lucky."

"Two?" said Mom. "We were hoping for three."

Dad shook his head. "Twenty years of work and we're going to come up two hours short."

"The *Scorpius* can't weather another serious storm," said Marco. "We *might* be able to start one last cycle and then get the results remotely, but that will only work if the storm doesn't knock out the power again, and it's supposed to be the biggest one yet. Realistically, this is it. Two cycles and we're gone, finished or not."

"Then we'd better get down there," said Mom.

"Maybe we can be superefficient and make it three anyway. Where are Paolo and Ariana?"

"They already went in," said Marco. "They should have the turbines calibrated and ready by the time we arrive." He turned and knocked on the glass wall. "We're going down!"

Mara and Idris glanced back and nodded, then resumed typing busily. Mom and Dad followed Marco toward the door. Liam trailed after them as they hurried outside.

"Don't worry about me," he called as they headed for the mouth of the towering canyon.

Mom paused and turned. "Sorry, honey. You just wait in the living quarters like we discussed, okay? We're almost done, but every second counts."

"Will do," said Liam halfheartedly.

"I mean it, Liam. There's absolutely no time for anything unexpected today."

"I know, Mom. I feel like I should be telling you guys that."

"We'll be fine," said Dad. He checked his link. "Before you know it, we'll be eating dinner on the starliner and watching your sister perform."

"Promise?"

"We need to get going," said Mom.

"Fine," said Liam. "Good luck." He waved and

they turned and jogged toward the canyon.

Liam walked to the living quarters. He yanked open the outer door and stepped in. Once the airlock had pressurized, he pulled off his helmet and opened the inner door, entering a circular room that had a kitchen and a sitting area with couches and a virtual gaming system. Past the sitting area, a short hallway led to the bunk rooms.

Phoebe was in the kitchen, dressed in her black thermal wear. She had the station's hamsters, Wallace, Misha, and Ed, out of their habitat, and was holding a stick of OrangeVeg at her waist. The hamsters sniffed around at her feet; then Wallace noticed the stick and made a Martian-sized leap for it. Phoebe let him have it, then grabbed another from the package on the counter.

She looked up at him and smiled. "Hey, you're finally here. It's been so boring. Except for these cuties. Want to try?"

"Sure." Liam pulled off his suit. He walked to the kitchen and Phoebe tossed him a stick. He held it over the hamsters, who were scurrying around on the tan plastic floor. Misha noticed his and jumped for it. Liam raised it just out of her reach.

"Don't be mean," said Phoebe.

"Fine." Liam let her get it the next time. "Sorry

about your parents yesterday. Did you get in big trouble?"

Phoebe shrugged. "The usual. Blah-blah-Phoebe-responsibility-respect-blah-blah. They couldn't really ground me when they were already bringing me here. Yesterday was so boring. All I did was play *Roid Wraiths*. How about you?"

"By the time my parents got home, they barely remembered that it happened. Did you get to pack up your room?"

"Yeah," said Phoebe. "We went home when your parents did last night. Packed our lives into those tiny boxes and came back here bright and early."

"It was hard," said Liam.

Phoebe nodded and got another OrangeVeg. She tossed Liam one, too. "So I guess we just sit here for the next three hours."

"I guess," said Liam. "Hey, um . . ." Phoebe looked up. "Never mind."

"What?"

"I was just going to say that . . . I was thinking about when you were crying yesterday at Vista . . . and I get it. I'm going to miss it here, too."

Phoebe's gaze fixed on him. A tear trembled at the corner of her eye.

"I mean . . ." Liam twisted the OrangeVeg, cracking it in half. He hadn't meant to make her sad. Or was she angry? Her eyes were narrowing. "Just," he stumbled on, "it's sad to be leaving forever. Obviously it's better than frying, but still, this was our home and nobody really seems to get that except us."

Phoebe's mouth had gotten small. The tear slipped down her cheek. Another grew behind it.

"Or, I mean, that's what it's like for me, anyway. . . ." He'd broken the two OrangeVeg halves in half. One slipped from his fingers and Misha and Wallace scrambled for it.

"I did feel that," said Phoebe. "Leaving home sucks."

"I wish things didn't have to change," said Liam.

"Yeah."

"But so, I'm glad you talked me into going, yesterday. That's all."

Phoebe nodded. More tears falling.

"Um . . ." Liam tried to think of what to say next. *"Phoebe."*

They both looked at Phoebe's wrist, a red light blinking on her link.

"Great," said Phoebe. "It's Mom." She slapped the OrangeVeg on the counter, wiped hard at her eyes with her sleeve, took a deep breath, and tapped the pad. "What?"

"We need your help," Ariana said.

"You want us to come down there?"

"No. We need you to manually open the surface air valves. The controls have short-circuited and we need them open before we can run our next trial."

"Um, okay. Where are they?"

"They're by the north array. We know you've been out that way exploring the tunnels. We'll need you to go to the surface to open the valves."

"Can't someone else do it?" Phoebe said, but at the same time her eyes lit up and she mouthed two words to Liam.

"Everyone else is busy and we need you to do this right away. The north branch tunnel should get you there quickly."

"Okay, fine."

"And Phoebe, no delays on the way. This is extremely important."

"I said *okay*."

"Good. Get going." The screen clicked off.

Phoebe looked at Liam. "Did you get what I said to you?"

"Was it *Lunch Rocks*?" said Liam.

"Yeah, they're right near where my mom's talking about. Bonus, right? She said no delays on the way, but she didn't say anything about the way *back*."

"We probably shouldn't," said Liam.

"Come on. We definitely should."

"My parents told me to stay here. They were really strict about it."

Phoebe frowned. "They just told us to go open the valves."

"Told *you*."

Phoebe crossed the living room, stripped off her atmo pack, and unplugged her pressure suit from where it was hanging on a hook. "They obviously meant the two of us. They're always saying not to climb in the tunnels alone. And especially not today. If anything went wrong we'd miss the starliner."

"True," said Liam. It did sound way better than sitting around here. And getting to stop by Lunch Rocks would be cool. He tossed his OrangeVeg pieces to the hamsters. "Should we cage them back up?"

"You heard Commander Mom," said Phoebe. She tugged her helmet on and her voice crackled through the speaker. "*Phoebe there's no time bluh-blah.* We'll round them up when we get back."

"Okay." Liam ducked into the bunk room and grabbed their hiking backpacks off the wall. He tossed one to Phoebe and then slipped on his pressure suit.

"Ready?" said Phoebe.

Liam zipped closed his helmet and nodded, and they headed outside.

5

Liam and Phoebe bounded across the red rock toward the towering canyon. Liam's heavy breaths rattled the pressure suit's microphone. Sweat was already dripping down his forehead.

"I'll be Beah Siamese!" Phoebe called over her shoulder.

"I'll be Lance Forte!"

"Ooh, Shawn will be mad."

"That's his problem," Liam said with a smile.

Lance Forte and Beah Siamese were characters from one of their favorite shows, *Raiders of the Lost Planet*. It was about rival teams of archaeologists, fortune seekers, and pirates who made risky missions back to Earth seeking forgotten treasure and rare minerals.

"Watch out for Dorval Smugglers!" shouted Liam as he vaulted a sandy creek bed. For a moment, he hummed the *Raiders* theme song to himself.

They passed into the cool shadow of the cliff and entered the narrow canyon. Their boots clomped onto the metal walkway. It zigzagged into the dark, illuminated by small blue lights along the sides. Wire railings were strung through posts at regular intervals. The walkway was level, but beneath it, the canyon floor dropped steadily away to unknown depths. They had to slow their pace, so that their Martian-sized steps wouldn't send them right over the edge. On either side, the canyon walls looked just like they had for millions of years, curved and flecked with crystals. As they went, the jagged sliver of orange daylight overhead thinned to total darkness. Liam's suit hummed at full power. He shivered and checked the readings on his link. The temperature had dropped nearly one hundred degrees from the sun outside to the dark in here. It would take another minute for the suit to acclimate.

His nerves tightened, and his humming trailed off. Sure, they knew these lava tubes and passageways extremely well, but it was still dangerous. Every step led them farther and farther from safety, and even so much as a sprained ankle could mean missing the starliner. Their parents must have been really stressed to send them out this way, after telling Liam to stay put.

A kilometer into the canyon, the walkway ended at a hexagonal platform that made a ring around a giant lava shaft. Liam gazed over the edge. Elevator scaffolding marked by blue lights led down into the inky dark. The view still freaked him out. You could just see where the elevator stopped, hundreds of meters down. From there, another walkway led a short distance through a tunnel to the magma chamber, but this main shaft kept going below that. . . . Nobody really knew how far it went.

All around them, above and below, circular voids described lava tubes leading off in different directions. Long ago, the magma had drained out of Olympus Mons and left it hollowed out like the ant farm they'd had at school.

Liam, Phoebe, and Shawn had explored many, many kilometers of the tubes, which branched like arteries away from several main lava shafts. Their parents had warned them about unseen fissures and the potential for cave-ins, but they had given up on trying to keep the kids from coming out here. And Liam and Phoebe were prepared. Their boots had metal-studded treads. In their backpacks they carried spare headlamps, rappelling cables on powered winches, med kits, suit repair patches, and snacks. At the end of each exploration, they always repacked their bags to be ready for next time. Their links had basic infrared scanning, so they could scout out a new tunnel before they climbed into it. The links also had distress signals and worked as homing beacons. And really, as long as you watched where you were going and didn't step into a bottomless hole, the lava tubes were pretty safe. Mars hadn't been volcanically active in millions of years. The biggest concern was actually the rumbling and small cave-ins that occurred when the terraforming turbines were running, but even that was only an issue if you were right around the test area. Lunch Rocks and the north array were many kilometers away.

Liam and Phoebe circled halfway around the platform and stopped where a rope dangled from a lava tube ten meters above. They jumped and pulled themselves up into the entrance. Once inside, Liam opened a screen on his link. He tapped a button and pairs of small, cool blue lights lit up ahead of them. As they walked, the three sets of lights in front of them switched on, while the lights behind them turned back off.

The tube was circular, five meters in diameter. The sides were striped with layers of rough red pumice and smooth black glassy crystal.

Phoebe started to jog. They'd run this tunnel hundreds of times—it was one of their main routes—and they knew where the curves and narrow sections were, as well as the one area that hung low with toothlike stalactites.

Every now and then they passed small blinking red lights on the wall: sensors that mapped the tunnel system. Liam watched their progress on his link as they ran. The map showed tunnels above and below them, dead ends, chambers, a cliff lookout. They'd named some of their favorite places: the Spire, Impalement Rocks, Fairy Pools—they weren't actually pools but rather patches of a pure aqua-colored mineral—the High Castle, Lunch Rocks. They passed the turnoff to a cool spot called the Dream Eater—a bottomless black pit; they made wishes by throwing flecks of silica crystal into it—and Liam almost turned, almost called to Phoebe. It might be cool to make a last wish for their journey or something . . . but she was barreling ahead.

They ran upward at a steady incline, for one kilometer, then another. The passageway got smaller and they branched left, curved right, then right again, and at one point they thrust off the wall to reach another length of cable, which they used to climb up to the next tube. The maneuver left Liam gasping for breath. He heard Phoebe cough too, but overall, the lack of dust in the tunnels helped her breathing.

The last half kilometer of tube narrowed and they had to duck. They passed the entrance to Lunch Rocks, and soon after, the tunnel opened into another large vertical lava shaft that reached from darkness below up to a distant eye of copper sky. A cluster of steel pipes ran up the center of the shaft. A short metal walkway led from where they stood out to the pipes, and then a staircase spiraled upward around them.

Phoebe bent over, wheezing. "Almost there."

Liam patted her back. "You'll be breathing clean starliner air in just a few more hours."

Phoebe nodded. She stood and gripped the railing. "Up we go."

They climbed, circling the pipes ten times. As they neared daylight, a great roaring sound reached their ears.

The staircase ended at a platform. The pipes turned at a ninety-degree angle and disappeared into the rock wall. A ladder spanned the last few meters to the surface. Beside the ladder were spools of thick red cable with metal clips at the end.

"You ever been up here?" said Liam, eyeing the safety lines.

"I came up this far one time," said Phoebe, "but the sound of that wind made it seem like a bad idea to go any farther."

"Yeah." Liam pulled one of the cables and clipped it to a metal eyelet on the waist of his suit. There was a harness built into the midsection of each pressure suit, for climbing and rappelling. Phoebe clipped one on, too.

"Be careful," said Liam as they started up the ladder.

They emerged on the broad flank of the volcano, above the cliff. The edge was a few hundred meters down a gradual rock slope. Beyond it, canyons, washes, and ridges spread across the horizon. The research station was out of view below the cliff and around the bend. The wind nearly blew Liam over before he could plant his feet. He staggered, and dust strafed his suit.

The cluster of pipes reemerged a few meters away. Each had a metal wheel beside it and a blinking red light. Next to the pipes, on a pad of concrete, was what was technically called the north array: a compact pyramid of solar panels and antennae, the backup communication system for the station. It had been permanently damaged a few storms ago.

Beyond that, standing at a crooked angle, was the skeleton of a tall, cylindrical structure. Most of its external panels had been torn away, revealing corroded beams. Inside, a staircase switched back and forth, leading up to the curved top. Through gaps in the exterior, Liam saw telescopes and radio dishes pointed skyward.

He fought against a wind gust. "Do you think that's the Phase One observatory?" he asked.

"What?" Phoebe shouted back.

Liam pointed to his link and then switched over to local link communication instead of their speakers. He saw Phoebe's name blinking on the connection screen and tapped it. "You there?" he said quietly.

"Yeah," said Phoebe in his ear. She coughed again and Liam winced at the sound. "Sorry."

"It's okay. I just asked if that was the Phase One observatory."

Phoebe glanced at the dead tower. "I don't know. I never heard of a Phase One observatory."

"I hadn't either, but then my dad mentioned it this morning, when I asked him about that object we saw up on the summit yesterday."

Phoebe glanced up that way now. Liam followed her gaze, but the peak was still too far away to see. "Did he know what it was?"

"He said there's nothing up there." Liam looked back at the tower. "I've seen the north array on maps, but never this. I mean, if we knew that thing was here, we definitely would have come and checked it out before now."

"Maybe they didn't want us checking it out," said Phoebe.

"Yeah, it does look like it could collapse at any second."

Phoebe gazed at the tower. "It seems like Phase One is really secretive."

"I know. I was thinking the same thing today."

"Maybe there's something about it that the ISA doesn't want anyone to know."

"Like what?"

"I don't know," said Phoebe. "It had something to do with studying Aaru, right?"

"Yeah, but like, just getting data for the terraforming."

"As far as we know."

"What do you mean?" said Liam.

"I mean if that's all it was, why the big secret?"

"Well, maybe it's not even a secret. Maybe it's just super boring."

"Or," said Phoebe, "maybe there's something about Aaru that they don't want anyone to know."

Liam found Phoebe gazing at him. "You mean like a problem with it or something?"

Phoebe shrugged. "Ask your parents."

"Have yours ever said anything about it?"

"They never worked on Phase One," said Phoebe. "We'd better open these valves." She knelt beside one and gripped the wheel. "It's tight." She strained to turn it, gritting her teeth and coughing again. It moved slightly. Then more.

Liam tried the one beside it. His first tug barely budged it, but then it started to twist. The pipe began to vibrate with rushing air, and the light on the side blinked to green.

"There we go," said Phoebe, opening hers as well.

They struggled to open the other valves, buffeted by wind and dust, and then stood, breathing hard.

"Plenty of time to spare," said Liam, checking his link. They'd been gone a half hour.

"I'll let Mom know," Phoebe muttered, her head down as she tapped her link.

"You okay?" Liam asked.

"Just my lungs are killing me," said Phoebe. She slapped at her wrist. "I can't get a signal. I think there's too much mountain between us."

"I'll try mine." Liam tried connecting with Dad, then Mom, but got the same result, a message reading *No Signal*. "They can probably tell that the vents are open, right?" Liam tapped on his link and selected the research station lab. "I'll let Mara and Idris know, just to be sure— "

THWACK!

He turned to see Phoebe standing with her feet apart to brace against the wind. She'd hurled a rock at the Phase One tower. She picked up another fist-sized stone and whipped it. This one clanged around inside the structure. She bent to find another.

Liam's linked flashed.

"This is Mara. Hey, Liam!"

"Hey, just wanted to let you know we got the air vents open."

"Oh . . . um, okay. Didn't even know you were doing that. Was there a problem?"

"Yeah, Phoebe's mom said they were having trouble opening them. We can't reach her from here."

"Ah, okay. We didn't see that, but we're having lots of issues with the sensors. I'll let her know you checked in."

THWACK! Phoebe picked up another rock.

"Thanks. Is Red Line still the same?"

"Sure is. Three hours and nineteen minutes until margarita time."

Liam heard Idris make a "woo-hoo" sound in the background.

"Okay, we'll be back soon." Liam reconnected with Phoebe. "We should go."

She nodded, but looked angry. She hurled one last rock, grunting as she did. It ricocheted off the side of the tower. She turned and headed for the ladder.

They descended into the quiet of the tunnel and unclipped their safety lines.

Phoebe coughed hard. Her eyes were wet and red.

"Doing okay?" Liam asked.

"Fine," said Phoebe, her voice hoarse. She breathed deep. "Lunch Rocks?"

"Lunch Rocks."

They vaulted down the stairs, sliding more on the handrails than using their feet, then ducked into the lava tube and jogged a half kilometer back down the tube. They crouched and scrambled through a small tunnel, emerging in a wide, circular cavern. They had arranged proximity lights around the base of the walls, which lit up as they arrived. The walls themselves began to glow; they were covered with a shimmering carpet of microbes, whose mineral diet and translucent bodies made them react to the proximity lights, giving the walls a ghostly glow.

When Liam, Phoebe, and Shawn discovered this cavern last year, the microbes had barely raised an eyebrow among their parents or anyone else left at the colony. A couple other life-forms had been discovered on Mars over the years: mostly bacteria, and something like a mold one time, but the only reason anyone cared about them was to make sure that they didn't accidentally get on any equipment or pressure suits that were coming to Aaru.

Phoebe and Liam sat on a large boulder in the center of the cavern.

"Too bad we didn't bring actual lunch," said Phoebe.

"Just nutri-bars," said Liam, pulling one out of his backpack. "Hopefully this is our last day eating these, too."

He tore open the bar and gave Phoebe half. She broke off a piece and tapped her link. A tiny compartment at the base of her helmet slid open. She placed the piece in the compartment and tapped her link again. The compartment closed, and then slid open inside her helmet. She ducked her chin and grabbed the chunk of bar in her mouth. Liam did the same.

"Same old plastic taste," said Phoebe.

"Yeah." Liam aimed his headlamp at the glowing walls. "I suppose these guys don't have much longer to live."

"They have no idea what's coming," said Phoebe.

"Maybe they're kinda lucky. Not having to be scared every day like we've been. One day they'll just be sitting here and—" Liam snapped his fingers.

"Hopefully they'll be that lucky," said Phoebe. She finished her bar. "Are you excited to go?"

"Actually, yeah," he said, "when I get past the leaving part. I mean, I can't wait to see space, like . . . from space. I'm excited to see Jupiter, and Saturn Station, before we go into stasis. You've been out there, right?"

Phoebe nodded. "We took a trip a few years ago.

Jupiter was amazing. So was Saturn. We stopped at that casino out there too for one night. That was really weird. Lots of strange people."

"Did you see pirates? Or Plasticines?"

"It was hard to tell which ones were pirates. Definitely some Plasticines, though."

"It's crazy to me that the solar system is about to explode and some people's biggest concerns are hiding their wrinkles with fake skin."

Phoebe shook her head. "Humans," she said.

Liam smiled. "I know, right? If we ever meet any aliens out there, they're going to be like . . . what?"

Phoebe laughed to herself. She reached over and rubbed Liam's arm. "You're funny."

Liam felt a bolt of lightning charge up his arm and right to his chest. He thought he should look at Phoebe, but instead he gazed at his boots. "Do you, uh, know if our rooms are near each other on the starliner?"

"No clue," said Phoebe. "It will be weird if we don't get to see each other. . . . Who would I trick into ditching school with me?"

"You didn't trick me." Liam looked up and his eyes met Phoebe's. They both smiled, her green eyes reflecting the iridescent walls. Liam felt a dizzy flash, and why was he suddenly sweating? Maybe his suit was overheating. He sort of wanted to put his arm around her. Except was that a good idea? But here they were in their favorite spot on this last day, with no one else around. And he didn't know how much he'd see her on the starliner. Maybe he wanted to say something to her, about, like, *her* and *him*—he could just picture how Mina would be laughing at him right now—but what would he even say? And, like, what if she freaked out, except she was smiling now. . . .

But then she turned away. "Or did I?" She dug into her backpack and then her hand whipped at Liam.

Liam fell back as fabric slapped against his visor. He pulled it off and his headlamp shone on it.

"No way," he said, holding an official Dust Devils jersey out in front of him. It was crimson with gold stitching, a giant *06* on the chest, the number of his favorite player: keeper Hans Buckle. "Where did you find this?"

Phoebe beamed. "It was one of the last ones in the VirtCom. I had to challenge this Year 11 to a *Roid Wraiths* duel to win it."

"It's so awesome." Liam turned it over in his hands. "Wait. These have been sold out on the VirtCom for like two weeks. And it was shut down last night."

"I know. I got it right before they sold out."

"So . . . you already had this when you were convincing me to go get one?"

Phoebe shrugged sheepishly. "Sorta."

"Phoebe!" Liam threw the shirt back at her. "That's . . . you . . ."

"What?" said Phoebe. "You're mad?"

"Kinda. I mean, you lied."

"No, I didn't! We might have found one yesterday."

"Yeah, but you already had this one! If I'd known that, I never would have gone."

"I know—that's why I didn't tell you. I didn't technically lie. And besides, you said you were glad you went, up to Vista and all that. I knew you would be."

"Well, I was, but you—"

Phoebe tossed the jersey back to him. "Just take it. I wanted you to have it. And I wanted you there with me yesterday. Are you really mad?"

"I don't know," said Liam. He looked at the jersey. It was so excellent. But should he be mad? He definitely felt weird about being, if not directly lied to, deceived. Phoebe should have told him the truth, and yet then he definitely wouldn't have gone, so in a way she was looking out for him, and yet that didn't really feel fair. He rolled up the jersey and stuffed it in his backpack. "Thanks, I think."

"Well, you're welcome. It was the least I could do. You've been nice to me ever since I got here. Like a brother."

Liam shrugged. "No problem." He still didn't

know what to think about the shirt—and was a girl describing you as a brother even a good thing? "It's, um, it's been way more fun being stuck out here all these weekends with you. I mean, like . . ."

Phoebe cocked her head.

"I mean," said Liam, "what I'm trying to say is—"

"Wait." Phoebe held up her hand.

"Ah, okay, sorry, didn't mean to be weird. I—"

"No, Liam, listen."

Liam finally shut his mouth, and then he heard it: a low rumbling in the cavern walls and floor. The perimeter lights flickered. The ground shifted. They slid off the rock and stumbled to their feet.

"Is that from the turbines?" said Liam. Except they were so far away from the lab. . . .

Dust sifted from the ceiling. The rumbling increased, a deep quaking that Liam felt in his back and his teeth. Pebbles and dust began to rain down.

"That's not normal," said Phoebe.

The sound grew. The rock shuddered beneath their feet.

"Let's get out of here!" Liam shouted, throwing his backpack over his shoulders.

There was a grating shriek, like metal twisting somewhere through the rock. A splitting crack, now more, and more.

Their eyes met, Phoebe's wide—

And then all at once it hit them, a wave of sound and force that shook the cavern and sent them both staggering.

A deafening roar, a tearing of rock, crashing, dust everywhere. Like the entire mountain was coming apart. . . .

Collapsing around them.

A chunk of rock hit Liam in the back of the helmet. He fell to his knees.

"Phoebe!" he called, but sound overwhelmed him. His headlamp lit only swirls of dust and falling shadows. He tried to get up, was struck again, the wind knocked from him.

"Phoebe!"

But everything roared and shook and came apart. Liam didn't know what to do other than duck his head, put his hands over his neck, and hold his breath.

6

It seemed like the roaring would never cease. Smashing, thudding of rock, tearing and cracking and shattering . . .

Then one last rumble.

Then quiet.

And a shrill beeping.

Liam finally exhaled. Pain rushed in from his back, his shoulder, his knees. He breathed in, felt his ribs expand. Slowly pulled his hands from his neck and slid his right arm down to see his suit readings: oxygen, pressure, temperature, all falling. Words flashing: *WARNING: SUIT BREACH.*

He tried to lift his head—his helmet smacked rock

two centimeters above him. Moved his elbows—rock to either side. He breathed faster. Tried to twist his head to see in front of him. *Please don't be rock . . .* but there was a space. He shuffled on his elbows and knees, crawling forward. His pack scraped against the rock above, but he was able to move a little bit farther. Tried lifting his head, hit rock again. Crawled another meter . . . Finally he emerged in a wide space and sat up on his knees. The air was choked with dust, the floor littered with boulders.

His suit beeped more urgently. He could hear the leak now. He ran his headlamp over his arms and legs. There, on his knee: a tiny hissing cloud of escaping air. Beneath it, a red wound.

He slung off his backpack. His right shoulder screamed in agony but he ignored it. He unzipped his pack with trembling fingers and flipped it over. The contents spilled over the ground.

A new warning flashed: *LIFE SUPPORT CRITICAL*.

Come on! He pawed at the supplies on the dusty ground. There was one of the fibrous black patches he needed. He picked it up, dropped it, cursed the thick gloves, then got it again and tore away the thin packaging. He shook the patch violently to activate it, then pressed it over the tear. One . . . two . . . three . . .

Liam pulled his hand away. The patch rippled like

liquid, then hardened, sealing itself. A coating of anesthetic on the underside began to seep into his wound.

The beeping on his suit slowed. The warning stopped flashing, and his suit levels began to rise. He fell back on his butt, gasping for breath. Looking over his shoulder, he saw that he'd been under a huge slab of rock that had landed half on a boulder, creating a triangular pocket of space. Its top was covered with smashed rocks.

That slab had saved his life. But it could just as easily have crushed him flat. Had that boulder not been there, or had he been even a meter to the right . . .

Sometimes, these are the differences that determine the fate of a universe.

"Phoebe," he said quietly.

No answer. He tried again, then checked his link. Phoebe didn't appear as an available signal. He switched over to the external speaker.

"Phoebe!" he hissed, afraid that his voice might bring down the rest of the cavern.

He gathered up his supplies and stuffed them in his backpack, and then got to his feet. "Phoebe!" he shouted now, turning this way and that. His light found only a sea of dust.

"Over here!"

"Where?"

"Here!"

Her voice echoed off the walls. Wait . . . there. A weak white light. Liam picked his way through the rocks, only to find that he'd been seeing his own light illuminating the microbe-covered walls.

"At least you guys survived," Liam said to the wall.

"Behind you."

Phoebe was leaning against the large rock where they'd been sitting. One leg was bent but the other was out straight, her hands to either side of her knee.

"I think I might have broken my leg," she said.

Liam climbed over debris to her and saw two emergency patches on the shin area of her suit. She had also applied a splint kit. Two metallic braces ran down either side of her leg, with red straps connecting them.

"Are you okay?" she asked through gritted teeth.

"Mostly," said Liam, turning and looking for the tunnel out.

"What happened?" said Phoebe. "Do you think it was the turbines?"

Liam shrugged, but his immediate thought was *yes*. And whatever had happened was bad enough to cause damage this far away. "Our parents . . ."

He tapped his link and tried calling Mom. *No Signal*. Same for Dad. He tried the research station: *No Signal*.

"I can't reach anyone."

"Me neither." said Phoebe. "Let's worry about getting out of here first."

Liam climbed over a pile of boulders beside them, toward where he thought the entrance tunnel was located. He spotted it—and the massive pile of rocks spilling from its mouth.

"It's blocked," he reported, passing Phoebe and climbing in the other direction. He scanned the walls, trying to ignore the hopeless thought that they'd been here dozens of times, and he already knew that there was only one way in and out. He checked his suit readings: back to normal, with five hours of battery life to go. But Red Line would be far sooner than that.

"Find anything?" Phoebe called.

"No." Liam slid between rocks, now and then catching light—only to find that it was the glowing walls. He checked under large boulders. Maybe a hole had opened up to a lava tube below. But there was only rock and more rock, and the more Liam climbed and searched, the more it felt like the walls were somehow lowering, the boulders growing, this whole place closing in on him, swallowing them forever in its cold darkness—

But . . . there was something. A pale orange light. Liam scrambled toward it. The light disappeared, then appeared again. He leaned over a boulder and peered into a tall, narrow crack in the wall. He pressed farther, squeezing in, his shoulder igniting as it scraped against the rock, and then he saw it: bloodred daylight, far at the end of a jagged crevice.

"I found something!" Liam clambered back to Phoebe. "Can you stand?"

"Yeah." She pushed herself up on one leg, holding the other out, but the second that foot touched the ground she gasped and fell.

Liam caught her and pulled her arm around his shoulders. "Here. Lean against me."

"Thanks," Phoebe said tightly.

They moved slowly across the cavern, Phoebe hopping, her breathing tense, like each step hurt so much. When they reached the crevice, Liam helped her ease onto a rock nearby.

"I'll climb through and make sure it's safe. Wait here."

Phoebe nodded, wincing, her hands hovering around her injured leg like she wanted to rub it but didn't dare.

The fissure was only a meter tall, a narrow triangle that was only just wide enough at the base. Liam would have to shimmy through lying down. He dropped to his knees and squeezed in headfirst. He angled himself, one shoulder against the wall, one against the floor, with his arms stuck in front of his chest. He started to inch forward, pushing with his knees and toes, wriggling with his shoulders, clawing with his fingers. With every movement, his helmet scraped against rock; his suit rubbed and stretched. A meter along and he knew he couldn't turn around, or even move himself backward. His heart rate increased. Fast, short breaths. If his suit tore . . . if this space got any narrower and he got wedged in here . . . trapped. Pinned. Until his oxygen ran out. . . .

Something smacked his feet. "Keep going," said Phoebe.

"What are you doing?" said Liam. "I told you to wait while I checked it out!"

"I know," said Phoebe, panting.

Liam sighed. He wasn't sure he would've been able to make it back to her anyway. "How's your leg?"

"I think I know what a supernova feels like. But I can move it a little. It might just be a bad sprain or something."

"Okay, well, it's not much farther."

Liam craned his neck, blinked sweat out of his eyes, and kept his gaze on the triangle of daylight. Just had to keep moving. Inching toward it.

The rocks started to feel tighter. His breathing out of control. The walls and the mountain weighing on him, the entire planet, it seemed. What if there was another tremor? What if this space collapsed?

His shoulder burned; his feet and calves ached with fatigue. . . .

But the light! Getting closer. And the space had opened up a bit now; he could get his elbows under him and crawl for real.

"We're almost there!" he shouted. He could see the jagged lines of distant mountains. . . .

"Liam! I can't!"

Liam almost didn't stop. Daylight reflecting on his visor, so close . . . "Phoebe, yes, you can!" He could just see behind him now. Phoebe was in the dark, narrower section.

"The pain's worse. Just go and get help."

Liam looked ahead at freedom. He could get out first, go to the station and get the others, if they were okay. If there wasn't another tremor. If they didn't run out of time.

He started inching backward. "I'm not leaving you."

"But I can't move!"

Liam twisted onto his back and slid his feet toward Phoebe's helmet. "Get your arms out and grab my feet. It gets wider just up ahead and then it will be easier. I promise."

Phoebe shuffled, making a cloud of dust, and got her arms free. She grabbed Liam's boots. He dug in his elbows and arched his back and pulled.

"Ow," Phoebe moaned, but he could feel her moving too, millimeter by millimeter.

"Okay," he said, out of breath, when they reached the slightly wider space. "Now turn over and get yourself onto my legs. Then I can drag you the rest of the way."

"You mean like in your lap?"

"Not really . . . sorta?"

Phoebe twisted herself around. She grabbed the rock above her and pulled herself up onto his legs, until the back of her head rested on his chest. She exhaled hard. "That hurt."

"We're close," said Liam.

"If you ever tell Shawn about this, I'll kill you."

Liam managed to laugh. "Got it." He started dragging them ahead, and now he felt wind on his back, the space around them widening. Daylight on the walls . . .

Finally, copper sky appeared above him.

"We made it," said Liam. He slid his legs out from under Phoebe, rolled over—

And froze.

He found himself gazing straight down the sheer cliff face. The red land many kilometers below.

"Turn around really slowly," said Liam. He carefully got to his knees, then sat back and dangled his legs off the precipice. He could just barely sit up on this little ledge and had to hunch to avoid hitting his head. A gust of wind made him wobble, and he gripped the rocks beside him as tight as he could.

"Nice view," said Phoebe, lying on her stomach beside him and peering over the edge.

Liam gazed down. The height made him dizzy and his legs tingled in a strange way. He had a crazy thought, or more like a certainty, that if he jumped off this ledge, he'd be able to fly. The thought brought a metallic taste to his mouth. He would soar over the canyon lands, and then all the way up to the star-liner. . . .

"Liam." Phoebe pointed to the sky off to their right.

Liam leaned out and saw it: a thick column of black smoke curling up from beyond the curve in the cliff wall.

"There's nowhere else that could be coming from, is there?" said Phoebe.

He leaned back from the edge. "Probably not." He tapped his link. Mom, Dad—still no signal. He tried the research station. *Connecting* . . .

"Liam! Is that you?" It was Marco.

"Yeah! I'm with Phoebe." He tapped his pad and added Phoebe to the conversation. "What happened?"

"We're not exactly sure yet," said Marco. "I'd just

come back up to review the data from the first trial, and there was some kind of explosion down at the turbines. The elevator was damaged and a cave-in blocked the entrance to the lab."

"What about our parents?" said Phoebe.

"I'm afraid they're trapped down there. The wireless relays were destroyed, so we've had no contact with them. We're working on sending a hard line down right now. What's your status?"

Liam swallowed a surge of fear. "We're stuck on a cliff ledge, out by the north array."

"The north array? What are you doing out there?"

"They sent us here to open the air valves."

"Who did?" Marco asked.

"Our parents," said Phoebe.

"Oh. . . . I had no idea. Are you stable?"

"Kind of?" said Liam. "But Phoebe hurt her leg and we're sitting on a pretty small ledge—"

"Okay, good," said Marco. "There's only the three of us here and we've got to focus on establishing contact with your parents. I radioed colonial, and they're sending a rescue team with the transport as soon as they can. Should be here in an hour. So . . . just sit tight, okay? I'll keep you posted."

"But if we came back we could help," said Liam.

"Just stand by and someone will be there soon, don't worry." Marco disconnected.

Liam shook his head. "Sit tight. . . ." He slammed his heels against the cliff. "What are we even doing here?"

"Escaping from a cave collapse," said Phoebe.

"I mean on stupid Mars right before Red Line! We should be on the starliner. We should be out of the solar system."

A sound caught his attention. Something like static, getting louder, harsher. "Do you hear that?"

Phoebe rolled over and looked up the cliffside.

Tiny pebbles began to rain past their ledge.

Liam craned his neck to see above him—

An avalanche thundered over the top of the cliff. A storm of dust and red rock blotting out the sky and churning down the wall toward them.

"Get in!" Phoebe shouted.

Liam threw himself backward. Phoebe scrambled, pushing herself into the tunnel.

The roar grew—

Tons of rock plummeted by, mere centimeters from Liam's boots. Dust enveloped them, the daylight gone again, the sound as loud as before.

Crack! Liam felt space beneath his legs, a section of their ledge breaking away. He scrunched back farther. Held his breath. . . .

And then it had passed. The clouds of dust swirled and dissipated, daylight seeping back through.

A moment later, a massive explosion echoed from below as the rock hit the ground.

Liam waved at the dust. He inched forward, sat up, and found that their ledge was nearly gone. The entrance to their little crevice had widened, but only because an entire section of the cliff wall had broken off beside him. Now there were two directions in which they could fall to their deaths.

There was no longer enough space to sit up. Liam gripped the rocks above him.

Phoebe edged beside him and looked down. "It's too bad we don't have wings."

"Wait." Liam leaned away from the edge, risked letting go of the wall, and tapped on his link.

"What are you doing?" Phoebe asked.

"Wings," said Liam. His link beeped.

"Good afternoon, Liam."

"JEFF! Listen, can you . . ." He was about to ask JEFF to fly the Cosmic Cruiser over here to get them, but he realized that it would be very difficult to get it close to the cliff, and if another avalanche came, it would be way too slow to maneuver out of the way. . . .

"What is it, Liam?"

"Sorry, um, okay, can you lock on my location and send me the skim drone by remote?"

"Acknowledged," said JEFF. "That is possible,

though sensors indicate that you are with another person, so I must warn you, safety protocols state that the skim drone is only designed for single-passenger travel—"

"I don't care, JEFF! We're stuck on a cliff and Phoebe's leg is broken, our parents are in trouble, and an avalanche nearly killed us."

There was a pause.

"Would you like me to override the skim drone's safety protocols?"

"Yes, JEFF! And hurry."

"Acknowledged."

Liam grabbed the wall and tried to turn toward Phoebe. "How are you doing?"

"Everything hurts."

"Okay, it won't be much longer. We'll get in the drone and be back at the station in five minutes." He didn't want to think about what came after that. About his parents trapped far beneath the mountain, about time running out.

Three endless minutes later, an electric hum reached their ears. Liam spied a glint of light in the distance. The skim drone whirred toward them: a small oval-shaped craft with a slight point at the front. It had a tarnished white exterior, with a trapezoidal canopy of gold-tinted glass over the cockpit. Its primary thruster glowed hot beneath it. It slowed and hovered fifty meters from the cliffside.

"Liam," said JEFF over the link. "You will need to take control of the remote to fine-tune the drone to your position. I'm handing off the controls now."

A graphic blinked on Liam's link, showing a little joystick and also a thrust lever.

Liam tapped at the joystick graphic. The drone swerved closer to them, too drastically at first, and nearly slammed into the wall. Liam tapped again, lighter, the ship swaying in the air, then again, until it hovered a meter from them. He tapped a button and the canopy opened with a hiss.

"Okay, now what?" Phoebe asked.

"Um . . . ," said Liam. His chest froze with the thought, so he didn't answer.

He just held his breath and let go of the wall. Leaning forward, he planted his heels against the cliff. Only one chance to get this right . . .

He launched himself into space.

7

Liam slammed against the skim drone, half in the cockpit, his legs dangling over the side. The impact knocked the wind out of him, and the drone dipped. He started to slide backward, grabbing for something, anything to hold on to.

"Liam!" Phoebe shouted.

His waist slid over the edge of the ship, but his fingers found the metal bar that ran down the side of the seat. He gripped it, got a knee atop the drone, and tumbled into the cockpit headfirst, then scrambled to sit up.

The craft bobbed in the wind. Okay. Flying. This he could do. Liam pressed his right hand to the navigation screen, where he controlled which thrusters would fire, and with his left flicked the joystick that determined the angle of his movements. In addition to the main thruster underneath, the skim drone had tiny directional thrusters on its sides and top. He raised the ship and slid closer to the cliff wall. A gust of wind caught him and the drone scraped the cliffside.

"Careful!" said Phoebe, scrambling back into the tunnel.

"I got it." Liam fired the lateral thrusters and steadied. "You're going to have to jump to me."

Phoebe nodded, but even just shifting her weight caused a wave of pain to cross her face. "I don't . . . I can't . . ."

"Hold on." Liam tapped the thrusters, raising the skim drone a meter. He inched closer, now closer, until the edge of the craft was almost touching Phoebe's helmet. "I'll pull you in."

She locked eyes with him. "You better not drop me."

"I won't." She reached out, and Liam stretched and grabbed her hands.

Suddenly the craft lurched, another wind gust shoving it away from the cliff.

"Ah!" Phoebe was dragged from the ledge, and now she was hanging, Liam's arms burning, gripping her hands as tight as he could while the craft lurched and dipped, the ground impossibly far below.

"Hang on!" Liam pulled, gritting his teeth. The craft swayed back toward the cliff face. "Grab the handle!" he shouted, trying to guide Phoebe's hand to the metal bar on the seat. She lunged, got it. Liam slapped the joystick with his free hand and they arced away from the rock.

Phoebe grunted and pulled and finally got a knee on the side of the ship. Then she threw herself, tumbling over Liam and into the cockpit beside him.

Liam jabbed a button and the cockpit canopy closed. Air vents blasted, pressurizing the cabin. A small meter rose from red to green on the drone's display.

He tore off his helmet and breathed deep. "You okay?" he asked, trying to move over and give her space. There was only one seat. It was fairly wide, but they were crammed in hip to hip and shoulder to shoulder.

Phoebe nodded, but her eyes were closed, her mask fogged. She leaned over and rubbed at the sides of her leg. "Good job," she said weakly.

"You too," said Liam.

Phoebe shifted, squeezing against the far side of the cockpit but still leaning against him. She pulled off her helmet and wiped at her eyes. "Don't get any weird . . . *boy* feelings while we're like this," she said, eyeing him, but a slight smile crept across her face.

"Shut up," Liam said, grinning back.

He fired the thruster and the drone arced up at a steep angle, cresting the top of the cliff. As he banked out over the wide flank of the volcano, the sight of the thick black smoke from the research station made him feel like a belt was tightening around his chest. He pushed the throttle to maximum. "We'll be there in just a couple minutes," he said.

"That avalanche was massive," said Phoebe. Liam glanced out her side of the cockpit and saw a wide red swath like a scar down the side of the mountain. Phoebe craned to see behind them. "It totally took out the Phase One observatory. It stretches forever, all the way up near the summit—whoa, stop."

"Phoebe, there isn't time. We have to get back—"

"Liam, just do it."

"But we—"

"Stop!"

Liam brought the drone to a lurching halt. "Fine, what?"

Phoebe pointed up the mountainside. "There."

Liam couldn't see around her. He pivoted the drone to face uphill. "What? I don't—"

But then he did. From up here, the summit was finally visible, and far away on that distant ridgeline . . .

There it was again. Reflecting the sunlight brilliantly. Round, metal, massive.

"It's that thing," said Liam. From here it wasn't much bigger than a marble. Liam aimed the drone's front camera at it and zoomed in.

If it was a building, it was unlike any he'd ever seen on Mars. It really did appear to be a perfect sphere, made of this gleaming metal that even from here seemed so smooth and so polished, with the sun reflecting off it like water. There was that dark band around the middle, like he'd seen yesterday. The structure was perched at an angle at the top of a narrow rock spire, just above where the avalanche had begun. Part of the spire seemed to have broken away, leaving the structure perilously balanced, like it might fall and roll down the mountain at any moment.

"How could no one have seen this before?" said Liam.

"It must have been hidden somehow," said Phoebe. "Maybe the explosion and the avalanche uncovered it."

"Except we saw it yesterday."

"True. But never before that. Big solar storm. Big avalanche."

"Yeah," said Liam. He felt like a balloon was expanding in his head. "Hidden . . . but by *who*?"

"Liam." Phoebe put her hand on his. "We have to go check it out."

"I know, but . . . we can't," said Liam, even though he'd been thinking exactly the same thing. "We have to get back and find out what happened to our parents, and the colonial team is coming, and—"

"And we're leaving Mars forever. How can we leave without knowing what that is?"

"I don't know," said Liam. His heart pounded. "It might just be another old Phase One thing."

Phoebe stabbed the screen with her finger. "Does it look like an old Phase One thing?"

"No," said Liam. "Maybe it's military, or like some old solar monitoring thing from the first colonists or—"

"It doesn't even look human," said Phoebe.

"But it's got to be," said Liam, and yet . . . "What else could it— Whoa."

"Where did it go?" said Phoebe.

They gaped at the video screen. Liam looked out the cockpit to be sure.

The object had disappeared. Gone. Like it had never even been there.

Then it was back, flashing into existence with a shimmer of blue sparks, right where it had just been.

"Okay . . . ," said Phoebe.

"That's what it did yesterday," said Liam.

He looked at Phoebe. She looked back at him. "We're about to head out across space," she said, "and whoever built that might be out there. . . ."

"Out there," said Liam. "You mean like . . ."

"Aliens."

"No way." And yet his chest was tight and his head felt like fireworks were going off inside and Phoebe was right, she was so right. They were heading out across the galaxy, with asteroids and black holes to worry about, with unfinished terraforming, with only enough supplies for one shot. . . .

What if they had to worry about aliens, too? Liam stared at the sleek structure. He remembered asking his mom once, years ago, if there were aliens. She'd said: *If there are any aliens out there, they're the least of our worries right now.*

But what if it wasn't *if*? What if there were *definitely* aliens, and they'd already been here? What were they like? And what had they been doing at the top of Olympus Mons? Spying on humans? Did they know the entire human race was in stasis flying across the galaxy? Were they out there somewhere waiting?

"What if there's someone—something up there, like right now?" said Liam.

Phoebe shook her head. "We haven't seen any ships, or any other evidence. That thing might just be a probe or something. Look. . . ." She ran her finger across the screen. "It looks tilted. Maybe it's damaged. If there is someone in there, they might need our help."

Liam glanced back at the smoke coming from the research station. He tapped the image of the strange structure, then the navigation controls. "If we fly at max speed, we could be up there in about five minutes. How about we take a quick look, maybe get some good pictures, and we're back at the station in fifteen minutes, tops." He looked at Phoebe. She nodded.

"Okay." Liam breathed deep and brought up the communicator on the console. *Connecting . . .*

"Liam," said Marco. "You guys still okay?"

"We're fine. We're in the skim drone and we're on our way back. What's going on there? Have you talked to our parents yet?"

"Not yet. We're in the canyon, still working on running that hard line down to them. It's like threading a needle through all the collapsed rock, but our sensors show that the cavern is at least mostly intact, so we've got our fingers crossed."

"Can we help at all?"

"Not unless you can fly that skim drone through solid rock. The rescue team is still forty-five minutes out. Just get back here safely, okay?"

"We'll be right there." Liam ended the call and swallowed hard. "We have to be quick."

Phoebe nodded. "The quickest."

Liam fired the engines, and the skim drone lunged toward the summit.

8

They raced up the long barren slope of the volcano. The skim drone's sensors chirped about falling temperatures and thinning air. Liam remembered reading that at the summit of Olympus Mons, the air pressure was so low it was nearly like being in space. The drone's systems would have to work extra hard.

"Shawn would definitely be telling us to turn back right now," said Phoebe.

"Definitely." Liam pushed the craft to near maximum speed. The battery level was at 92 percent. Flying this fast would drain it more quickly, but they couldn't risk going any slower. They flew over slopes of gray lava and fields of red boulders. Thin whorls of white clouds curled around the peaks of the caldera rim, spinning into and out of existence in the whipping wind.

They neared the gleaming silver structure, and Liam saw that it wasn't perfectly circular but had a flat top and bottom. It sat tilted on the rust-colored spire, one end hanging out into space where rock had once supported it.

He slowed and flew alongside the structure, firing short bursts from the thrusters to stay steady in the wind. He guessed that it was thirty meters across. Blue sparks shot from the black band around its middle, which was made of square panels. They glowed with orange lines like circuitry, except also feathery and layered, almost like something living. One panel flared brightly, and for a second it and a small section of the silver wall around it disappeared, like a window had opened into the caldera behind it.

"It was invisible," said Liam. "The solar storm must have damaged it. And then the avalanche made it worse."

As Liam gazed at the structure, the very likely *alien* structure, he felt a strange tingling in his mind, at his fingertips, almost like an awareness. If there were really aliens, then there was more to everything than he'd ever imagined, not just to Mars but to the galaxy, to the future and history. They were so worried about their one star and their old planet and yet there were billions of stars, even more planets, so many. His heart pounded. Right here, right now, they were two tiny humans on Mars, but this structure meant they were part of something enormous, the whole universe, limitless possibility within their reach.

"Do you see any way in?" said Phoebe. "I mean, we're going in, right?"

Liam swallowed hard. Maybe he had it backward. Maybe they were just two tiny humans in a tiny ship and it was completely insane to even consider going inside some sort of alien structure. Whatever was in there might capture them, or kill them. They had no way of knowing. And yet . . .

"Yeah," said Liam. "We're going in." He tapped the controls with shaking fingers and circled around. "Maybe if you can make your stuff invisible, you don't need doors?" He raised the drone until they hovered above the structure. "Wait, there." He pointed to a sleek instrument sticking out of the roof, made of black polished metal. There was a hole torn in the roof beside it, as if the instrument had shifted when the structure did.

"That kind of looks like a telescope," said Phoebe.

"It does," said Liam. Maybe there was a benevolent, science-loving alien in there. Then again, the ability to build a telescope didn't mean you were peaceful, or that you didn't have meter-long claws and tentacles and a mouth with six rows of teeth like the main villains in *Roid Wraiths*.

"It looks like we could get in beside it," said Phoebe.

"I'll land on the upper side," said Liam. "We don't want to tip the whole place over." He edged the drone over the flat section of roof, fighting angry gusts of wind, and lowered the landing legs. There was just enough space. . . . The legs tapped the metal, and he gradually powered down the engine, letting more and more of the craft's weight rest on the structure. There was a low-pitched groan.

"I think it's moving," said Phoebe.

Liam held his finger over the thruster. . . . The groaning ceased.

He activated the magnetic stabilizers and the legs locked into place. They slipped their helmets back on. "Ready?" said Liam.

"Yeah. Are you?"

"I don't know." He checked his link. Eight minutes since they'd talked to Marco. Their parents— they would definitely not want them to do this.

Liam opened the cockpit canopy. Wind howled, and their suits immediately began to beep. Messages lit up their links: *WARNING: EXTREMELY LOW AIR PRESSURE*. An identical message about oxygen.

His external temperature reading plummeted to seventy-five below zero. The wind howled around them.

"Our suits won't last long up here," said Liam, shivering. He could feel the suit humming, working hard, but even at max power, the internal temperature and oxygen readings were still falling.

Phoebe leaned out and surveyed the jagged hole around the telescope-like instrument. She started digging into her backpack. "We should use our safety lines." She pulled out her portable winch, a metal spool with red cable around it and a control panel on the side.

"Good idea." Liam got out his. The spool attached to the eyelet at his waist. He activated the control panel and stood, hanging on to the open cockpit against the furious wind. "What about your leg?"

"It's feeling a little better," said Phoebe, pushing herself up. "And don't even think about saying *wait here*, because there's no way."

"Right." Liam hopped out of the drone. He landed and paused, waiting for any shifting, but the structure remained still. He rounded the skim drone, holding on to a series of gold-colored towing rings to fight the wind. Phoebe leaned on his shoulder and dropped down, landing on one foot.

Liam attached the thick metal clips at the ends of their safety lines to the closest towing ring. They inched down the incline toward the opening, their spools clicking, letting out small amounts of cable, and stopped at the edge. The telescope was shaped like a bundle of cylinders, made of a black material that looked more like volcanic glass than metal. It had three silver-colored plates arranged in a triangle at its end.

Below, lights blinked. Phoebe eased herself onto her stomach and peered into the jagged hole. "There's lots of equipment, and . . ." She looked back up with wide eyes. "There's someone down there."

"Someone?"

"Yeah. Lying on the floor." She checked again. "Not moving."

"You mean an alien?"

"Probably."

"Is it dead?"

Phoebe sat up. "I can't tell."

"What does it look like?" Liam asked. "Any claws, or tentacles—"

"I don't know, kinda person-like. It's pretty dark down there." She swung her legs over the edge and took a deep breath. "Ready?"

"We don't have to," said Liam. "We could just go back."

Phoebe shook her head. "You know we do."

Liam shivered again, his nerves ringing. A dizzy

feeling washed over his mind, like he was about to fall over, or float away like a balloon in this furious wind. Maybe it was low oxygen, or the cold, but no, it wasn't any of those things. It was the almost powerless feeling that yes, he had to. Had to know what was in this structure. He glanced at the sky. Had to know what was really out there.

Curiosity. In this universe, there are few forces more powerful.

"I'll be right behind you," said Liam.

Phoebe exhaled hard, the sound distorting her microphone. "Here we go." She pushed herself over the edge and fell for just a second before her safety line caught. She dangled, her shoulders still above the rim of the hole. She glanced at Liam, a half smile, then tapped the control panel on her spool. It hummed and she slowly lowered out of sight.

Liam glanced back down the vast volcano slope. The smoke was so far in the distance now that it looked like little more than a dust whorl. He checked his link again. Eleven minutes. He sat down, held his breath, and slipped over the edge. Falling— His line caught, and he hung there, half in and half out of the structure. Then he lowered out of the whistling wind, into the dark.

At first, the gloom and silence inside seemed complete, except for his rapid breaths. The air was still, like a tomb. His boots clanged on the angled floor. He set his safety line to slack. Phoebe stood beside him, one hand on the telescope to keep her bad leg off the ground.

As his eyes adjusted to the low light, Liam saw that they were standing in a cylindrical room. The walls, ceiling, and floor were metallic and smooth. Large graphics floated at various points around the room, their imagery moving and changing. There was something like a holoscreen that showed a wide view of the Martian landscape, including their colony far in the distance. Their headlamps swept over strange silver instruments, arranged on a thin shelf that ran around the circumference of the room at waist height. Lights flashed, gyroscopes spun, pendulums swung. Beside them, the telescope's smooth black surface was adorned with glowing blue symbols, maybe some kind of language. These symbols were in other places around the room as well. The movement of the screens, the flashing symbols . . . Liam had to fight off another wave of dizziness, this one likely from the altitude. He checked his link. His suit's battery level was already down to 60 percent.

Phoebe hopped around the telescope to the body lying on the floor. Liam stepped hesitantly beside her.

The figure was tall and thin, and lying on its back. It wore simple black clothing and . . . oh, it had four legs. Its head was narrow, with a sort of diamond-shaped face. Its skin was dark blue and translucent—you could see the faint outlines of vessels and tissues beneath—and shriveled here and there. It had two eyes in a human position, open and clouded over white, but then also two noses, one above and one below the eyes. Two flat ears, and one small, closed mouth.

There was something sort of blurry about the figure. Almost out of focus. And when Liam took another step, its features shifted. Its skin looked more withered, its cheeks more hollow and sunken, an extra layer of dust on the clothes, like it had aged when he moved. Liam stepped back to where he'd been, and the figure looked like he'd first seen it. He shook his head. Maybe the altitude again . . . but he didn't think so.

The figure wore a thick belt around its waist. Metallic with more of those blue symbols. There was a black spot right in the middle of the being's chest, the shirt around it singed.

"She looks pretty dead," said Phoebe.

"How do you know it's a she?" said Liam.

"How do you know it's a he?"

Liam shrugged. "But it's . . . I mean, it's an alien. Right?"

"Yeah," said Phoebe. "Definitely an alien."

Liam knelt and pointed at the burn mark. "It looks like maybe she got shot or something. But by who?"

"I have no idea." Phoebe hopped toward one of the floating graphics. "The question is: What was she doing here?"

Liam wondered, gazing into the shadows around the room. "How do we know that whoever killed her isn't still here?" He looked back at the body and fought to calm his thoughts. Outside, he'd had that strange, serene feeling, like some kind of understanding. Now he felt panicked and like he couldn't understand less about the universe. This was an *alien*! And it was right here! In a hidden station on Mars. When had it come here? How long had it been here? Were there others of its kind, and were they dangerous?

This one didn't look dangerous, but dead things rarely did.

"You don't think this is, like, a Martian, do you?" said Liam.

"I'm pretty sure we're the only Martians," said Phoebe. "Us and those glowy microbes. I mean, I guess she could be some kind of ancient Martian or something, but you would think we would have found *some* evidence of others after all these years. Besides, this place doesn't look very ancient."

"So then, that would mean she came here from

somewhere else." Liam noticed the alien was wearing a wide silver band around her wrist, like a watch. Also she had eight fingers, or nine, if you counted the way the largest finger branched into two separate digits at its end. Who was she? Did she have siblings, parents? Was she from another planet? Multiple planets? Were others of her kind searching for her, missing her—

A small light flashed in the corner of his eye. Liam glanced toward the wall. A set of round glass instruments on the ledge there—

The light flashed again, in the shadow beneath the table. A blink of pale orange. His headlamp glinted off a small object.

Liam stepped past the being, eyeing it as he did. Her complexion morphed again and she looked nearly alive. Liam paused, almost expecting her to move. But she didn't.

He knelt by the wall and picked up the object: a perfect sphere of orange crystal that fit in the palm of his hand, and was etched with evenly spaced grooves like latitude lines on a globe.

It blinked again. In between blinks, it had a faint glow, as if there was an ember burning at its center.

"Phoebe, check this out." Liam walked over to where Phoebe was examining one of the graphics. He held out the sphere for her to see.

She narrowed her eyes at it. "Where did you find that?"

"Over in the corner." As he glanced back that way, Liam thought you could almost trace a line from the dead alien's hand to where he'd found it. Had she been holding this when she'd been killed?

"What does it do?"

"I don't know." Liam turned it over in his hand. "It doesn't have any buttons or anything."

"Huh." Phoebe turned back to the graphic. "Take a look at this."

It depicted a star, a close-up view that showed its roiling surface and arcing solar flares. A stream of data flowing vertically beside it, written in those alien symbols. Planets circled around it, their shapes familiar.

"That's the sun?" Liam guessed.

"I think so," said Phoebe.

Liam's eye wandered to the next graphic over. It showed what looked like a three-dimensional grid with little images of stars and systems. There were things that looked like black holes, and also nebulas and binary stars. The map seemed blurry too, like there was some other aspect to it that Liam couldn't quite see. Here and there on the map, red lights blinked. There were four of them. And then one yellow light.

"Maybe she was studying the sun," said Liam. "Maybe that was her job. Surveying stars or something."

"Hey, check this out." Phoebe pointed to a small device on the shelf nearby, a sleek black box, short and fat, with a rounded depression in the top. There were grooves in the depression, curving parallel lines. "It almost looks like it would fit your space marble thing."

Liam held the crystal over the depression. It was definitely the same size, and the lines matched the grooves. He pressed it into place.

There was a click, a hum, and then light burst from the crystal, a beam shooting between them.

Liam and Phoebe spun to find a glowing floor-to-ceiling projection. It showed a map of space similar to the one that Liam had been looking at. It rotated slowly, and as they watched, one of the blinking red lights grew, the view zooming in on a violet-and-red nebula that was shaped sort of like a human hand.

There was sound with the map, too, like long whispers, but also deep tones like heavy wind chimes ringing somewhere a few doors down, and then a sort of rhythmic ticking. And yet immediately these sounds began to change. The whispers gained inflections, the deep tones shortened, and the clicking smoothed out, organizing into sounds that Liam and Phoebe could understand . . . more and more familiar, until finally they had arranged themselves into a human female voice:

"*Emergency protocol activated. To any sentient being in possession of this data: please deliver it to the regional manager's office located in the eighth sector of your current spiral galaxy, at the following coordinates: 22 hours, 29 minutes, 38.55 seconds right ascension, -20 degrees, 50 minutes, 13.6 inches declination.*"

"It's translating for us," said Phoebe. "Like it knows who we are."

The map in front of them continued to rotate. The image of the hand-shaped nebula shrank back to a red light, and then the one yellow light on the map grew until Liam and Phoebe saw a graphic of their solar system, of their sun. It was time-lapsed, and they watched as the sun grew from yellow to orange and swallowed Mercury and Venus. Alien symbols flashed around the graphic.

"*Infected star five exhibits the same abnormal growth pattern as previous infected stars. Supernova is once again imminent. Rate of growth and time to explosion are nearly identical to other cases. Please see the logs for details. Further analysis of star locations and the timing of events may help to determine the location of those responsible.*"

The voice paused, and then began to repeat the same message.

Liam gazed at the graphic. "The sun is *infected*?"

"Not just our sun," said Phoebe quietly.

"She said someone is responsible. Does that mean someone caused the sun to change? Who could possibly change a star?"

Phoebe shrugged. "This alien can translate our language instantly, and make her lab invisible. Who knows what other aliens can do?"

"Other aliens." That alone was enough to make Liam's brain feel spinny again, but another thought jolted him, making his gut tie in knots. "This means that everything that's happened, the sun growing, us having to leave—it's all somebody's *fault*."

"I know." Phoebe sniffed. Liam saw condensation on her visor. "It changes everything."

Liam put his arm around her. "It's okay."

Phoebe brushed at his hand and hopped away. "No, it's not. It's really not."

"But now that we know this, we can do something—"

"Like what?" Phoebe snapped. "Sorry, this is just . . . a lot to think about."

Liam pulled the crystal sphere from its socket. The graphic winked out. "We have to show this to colonial. Maybe someone can figure out what it means."

Phoebe nodded, still looking away, biting her lip.

"I know it doesn't change the fact that the sun is

still going to explode, that someone did that on purpose, but . . ." Liam looked at the other glowing graphics. "If this has happened four times already, what if it happens again? What if whoever did this blows up a star on the way to Aaru? Or even Aaru's star? Humanity could be flying right into another supernova without even knowing it." Liam put the crystal in the hip pocket of his suit. He picked up the black square crystal reader and stuffed it in his backpack, then stepped toward the hole in the ceiling. "Come on," he said, "we have to get back to the station."

Phoebe shook her head, like she was breaking out of a trance. She held up her arm and tapped her link. "We should make a video of this room."

"Good idea." Just then, another blinking light caught Liam's eye, this one a pale blue. It was coming from the dead alien. From her watch.

Liam knelt beside the being. He gingerly gripped her arm and twisted it so that he could better see the watch. Its silver band was intricately engraved. It had a round face but no hands. The face was divided into two semicircles, one silver, one black, each with a symbol like the alien writing around the room. The blue light was coming from a dial around the face. Liam found a clasp on the inside of the band and removed the watch from the alien's wrist. As he picked it up, the dial began to blink faster. He thought about putting it in his backpack but instead fastened it around his wrist.

"What's that?" Phoebe asked, joining him.

"More evidence," said Liam, standing to show her.

Phoebe glanced at the alien body. "I guess she won't mind. Why is it blinking?"

"No idea."

Phoebe returned to the opening in the ceiling and tapped her spool. The safety line retracted with a steady clicking sound and lifted her up. Liam moved to the same spot.

He took a last look around the room, and at the alien on the floor. "Good-bye," he whispered, "and thank you." He wondered if he'd gotten a good enough look at everything. If he would be able to remember it just as it had been. He felt like he needed to, not just for himself, but for this fallen being, whose crystal he now had in his pocket, whose watch he now wore. If she was monitoring these infected stars, did that mean she was on their side, an alien ally?

Which also might mean they had alien enemies.

Liam tapped the control panel and rose into the Martian light. He clambered over the edge of the hole, buffeted by the relentless wind. Phoebe had hopped to the skim drone and was unhooking her line. As Liam stood, he noticed that the alien watch was flashing even faster—

A crack tore through the air. There was a crunch of falling rocks.

The station began to tilt. . . .

Liam locked eyes with Phoebe. "It's falling!"

9

Liam scrambled to the skim drone and lunged for the towing handle.

"Hurry!" said Phoebe, dragging herself into the cockpit.

Liam unclipped his line and grabbed for Phoebe's hand. She yanked him up, and he hauled himself in.

Metal creaked and whined. Glass smashed inside the observatory. The sphere tilted up onto its side, the top becoming a vertical wall, and with an earsplitting scrape of metal on rock, it began to fall.

"How do I start this thing?" Phoebe called, stabbing at buttons.

"Hold on a sec!"

"We don't have a sec!"

Liam struggled to get situated as the world turned upside down. He managed to hit the canopy button. As it hummed closed, he reached over his shoulder and yanked the seat belt across his body. "Here, get this around you, too!" He thrust it toward Phoebe. She took it, and he braced his legs in the footwell, grabbed the joystick, and jabbed at the main power.

Rock crunched and splintered. They were falling fast, flipping upside down. Liam glanced up and saw the mountainside rushing at them. He fired the thruster . . . but they didn't move.

"We're still stuck to the roof!" said Phoebe.

"Got it!" Liam flicked off the magnetization and hit the thruster again. They shot free of the roof just as it crashed onto the mountainside. The world was still upside down in front of them. Liam banked hard and fired the lateral thrusters. They whipped around, right side up again, but angling hard toward the rocky slope.

"I'm gonna be sick," said Phoebe.

"Almost there." Liam pulled up and fired the main thruster at full power.

The skim drone slammed against the rocky slope, a wicked tearing sound beneath the craft. Everything shaking, skidding along, rocks and dust flying.

"Behind us," said Phoebe, pointing at the rear camera.

The giant observatory sliding toward them, nearly on top of them.

Come on. Liam kept pulling up—

And then with a lurch, they shot into the sky.

Liam exhaled hard. He hadn't even realized he'd been holding his breath. "Okay, I think we made it."

"Nice flying," said Phoebe, also out of breath.

"Thanks. It was mostly luck, I think."

The craft flew with a little sideways shimmy, like it had a limp. A red light blinked on a schematic. One of the stabilizers was out, but Liam could keep it mostly straight.

He banked and swooped down the mountainside, pushing the craft to nearly full speed. It rattled and vibrated, but Liam didn't back off.

As he flew, his eye strayed to the watch. Its blinking had slowed.

"I can't believe what we just found," said Phoebe. She played her video of the room back on her link. "Nobody's going to believe it." She rewound it and watched it again.

"Yeah," said Liam. It had been so strange, so astonishing; it almost felt like a dream. Liam glanced at the rear camera. The observatory was just a silver dot. He looked out at the horizon, at the sky. There could be aliens anywhere.

But as the column of smoke grew in front of them, fresh fear began to boil over. Forget about aliens—his parents were trapped! He didn't even know if they were alive. Guilt and worry flooded over him. How could he have flown up to that observatory? He should have been back there helping. *But Marco told me we couldn't help,* he reminded himself. And what they'd found was so important.

And yet, who even cared about exploding stars or any of it if his parents didn't make it out of there alive? He checked his link. Eighteen minutes since they'd talked to Marco. Longer than he'd said they'd be. He tried Mom and Dad again: *No Signal.*

He breathed deep and tried connecting with the station again.

"Hey, Liam," said Marco. "Are you back yet?"

"We're really close. Any progress?"

"We're still at the elevator shaft. Good news, though: we got the hard line established. Sensors show that your parents are alive and their suits are intact, but they're not responding. We believe they're unconscious, maybe from the force of the blast, or perhaps smoke overwhelmed them."

"So they could be hurt," said Liam, "or suffocating. . . ."

"Calm down, Liam. They're alive, that's what matters. Now we just have to get them out."

"Okay. What's the plan?"

They were nearing the thick black smoke column now, flying over the canyon fissure. Liam banked around the smoke and cleared the edge of the cliff, then dived at a steep angle toward the research station.

"It's a tough call," said Marco. "The turbines are leaking radiation and we can't get the elevator fixed. We thought about rappelling down and sending your parents out on the emergency canaries, but it will be slow going and we're afraid the exposure to smoke and radiation will leave us just as bad off as they are. We could all end up trapped down there. The rescue team is bringing hover pods and digging equipment, not to mention radiation-proof suits. So I think our best bet is to wait for them to arrive. They should be here in half an hour, maybe less."

"Can our parents last that long?" asked Phoebe.

"Yes, their suits should have plenty of oxygen left, and while the radiation levels are unsafe, they're not lethal."

"So what are we supposed to do?" Liam asked.

"Just wait out there where it's safe," said Marco.

"I hate waiting," Phoebe muttered.

"Okay, um . . ." Liam looked over the research

station. "We'll go to my parents' ship so JEFF can look at Phoebe's leg."

"Sounds good," said Marco.

Liam passed over the station buildings and lowered beside the Cosmic Cruiser. He edged the drone beneath the ship, and then engaged the docking magnets. The drone clunked into place, syncing with the cruiser's systems. There was a hiss of pressurizing air, and the battery began to charge. Liam opened the canopy and climbed up into the short vertical tunnel that led to the hatch.

He turned back to Phoebe. "Do you need a hand?"

"Just onto the ladder, thanks." He pulled her up and then they climbed into the cruiser.

"Welcome back, Liam." JEFF's giant smiling panda face peered out from the cockpit. "Hello, Ms. Phoebe."

"Hey, JEFF," said Liam. He pulled off his helmet and dropped to the couch. "Can you come take a look at Phoebe's leg?"

"Acknowledged," said JEFF, rolling out to them as Phoebe eased herself down beside Liam.

Liam sat there, stunned. The cave-in, the alien, his parents . . . also he was starving, and yet he didn't want to move to get himself anything. He'd mostly been ignoring his aching shoulder. It sang with pain now.

JEFF handed Phoebe an atmo pack. As she pushed the tubes into her nose and ears, JEFF pressed gently in different places on her leg. A spot below her knee made her cry out. JEFF opened a medical kit and produced a half-moon-shaped device. He moved it above her leg and it made a humming sound. X-ray images appeared on its small screen.

"You did not suffer a bone break," JEFF reported. "You appear to have a bruise on your fibula, which can be quite painful but should heal fairly quickly. I recommend ice and pain medicine."

"Thanks," said Phoebe.

JEFF rolled to the kitchen and returned with an ice pack.

"I can't believe we have to just sit here," said Liam.

Phoebe stared into space.

"You okay?"

"Just thinking about our parents." She met Liam's eyes but then glanced at his side. "Why is that thing blinking again?"

Liam looked to his wrist. The watch was blinking faster again. "I don't know," he said, holding it up and studying it. "It was doing that before."

"Does it tell, like, alien time or something?" Phoebe asked.

"Maybe." He noticed now too that the symbol in

the right semicircle of the watch face was illuminated.

"It's like it's trying to get your attention," said Phoebe.

"It was blinking fast before. It started right before we climbed out of the observatory, but then it slowed down once we were flying away."

"Do you think it's a warning? Like it blinks fast if we're in danger?"

Liam shrugged, examining it more closely. He ran his finger around the edge. "It's got this dial." There were little notches in it, like the dial might click from one to the next.

"What happens if you turn it?"

"I have no idea." The blinking had increased speed even more. "Maybe it does something if you turn it toward the symbol that's lit up?"

Liam turned the dial clockwise, clicking it one notch forward into the semicircle with the glowing symbol.

All at once, everything around him changed.

Sound sucked away. What was left was muted: a muffled warbling like the world was on the other side of a thick curtain.

The ship, Phoebe, and JEFF all began to blur, like they were . . .

Speeding up.

Everything around him started to race along, the world clipping like he was watching it on fast-forward. JEFF zipped over and gave Phoebe a pill and a glass of water. She slugged the water back in a millisecond, then bolted up and hopped to the cockpit, following JEFF. Liam was moving too, or his view was moving. It was like he was watching a movie out of his own eyes.

In a blink, he was in the cockpit. Phoebe was talking to JEFF and also to a voice that was coming over the link, their voices chirping like birds. Liam couldn't make out anything they were saying.

The only thing that didn't seem to be speeding along was Liam. Except he was. He'd moved to the cockpit, but when he looked down he also still seemed to be sitting on the couch. He could hear his own breathing, felt his chest rising and falling, all at normal speed. When he looked down at his wrist, that movement seemed to happen in real time. But in the edges of his vision everything was blurry, like his contact with the world had changed.

That was what it felt like. Like he'd stepped out of reality. Or like he was in two realities at once. Still sitting on the couch, but also moving forward . . .

Time traveling. Could that possibly be what this was?

There was a flash out the cockpit window now.

A blur and then the big boxy gray colonial transport had landed in front of them. Its wide airlock door slid open and the rescue team sprinted out—not sprinted, far faster than that. They zipped toward the canyon and disappeared into the smoky dark fissure. This seemed to be what was going to happen. What hadn't happened yet . . .

The future.

Liam looked back at the watch. Still on wrist, resting on his leg on the couch. He clicked the dial one more notch to the right.

The speed of the world around him doubled.

Phoebe and JEFF became blurs, their faces and hands no longer in focus. So much movement. Sound became a stream, a kind of high-pitched whine.

Liam felt a tugging on his insides, like down in his gut. And also a light-headed static in his head. His muscles ached and the air was stale and his stomach began to knot up like he might be sick at any moment.

Everything flashed and sped. So fast . . .

And then terrible things began to happen.

The Cosmic Cruiser began to rise. They were taking off? But why—

Warning lights on the console. Frantic shouting.

Then a flash. Blinding light out the cockpit window. A giant mushroom-shaped cloud bloomed over the canyon, a thousand meters tall in a second. Double that in two seconds—

And Phoebe was screaming, and the ship was arcing away from the research station, but then there was light, only light, and a terrible melting heat and more white light.

Then darkness.

Everything gone.

But Liam could still look down. There was the watch and his body and the couch, even in the total darkness beyond him. He had an upside-down feeling of nausea and stretching, his head splitting with pain now, as if all of his thoughts and cells had become disconnected, pulling apart from one another.

More happened around him. Light filtered through smoke. Ash falling over smoldering wreckage. A mangled wing of the Cosmic Cruiser sticking out of the sand. The sun set, and Phobos crossed paths with Deimos overhead, and the smoke dissipated and the stars became clear gems and the sun rose again. A solar storm flashed by in an instant of green.

Liam felt disconnected. Like he'd lost himself, or left himself behind. No body anymore, just thoughts. And even those unraveling, becoming distant. *Too . . . fast. . . . I'm traveling too fast.*

And yet in spite of that spreading, that sense of losing track, he felt another urge:

Keep going.

Farther.

If he clicked the watch another notch . . . if he kept traveling even faster . . . days, years, ages from now. The death of the sun, the future of humanity . . . Even farther than that, when Andromeda collided with the Milky Way, when the youngest stars began to age and die out.

His head, his whole body, fading. He felt like a dust devil, momentary, about to be scattered forever. *Keep going.* But no, where was his body? Did he even have one anymore? This wasn't right.

Liam reached for the watch dial. Where was his arm? He could barely feel his own fingers. It took all his strength, like fighting a gale-force wind. Stretching across a vast distance . . . He grasped the dial, tried to turn it back, but it wouldn't move, his fingers slipping. Why wouldn't it go?

The headache increased, tearing his brain in two, now down his spine, his whole body. He kept trying to twist, but it didn't work. Like his hand was made of dust, scattering on the cosmic breeze. *Farther. Farther.*

No.

That symbol on the watch. It was blinking now. He stabbed at it with his finger. Missed. Tried again. . . .

He pressed the symbol and the watch face lit up bright white. A message scrolled across it in alien code. It seemed like a warning, or an error message—

The world around him screeched to a halt. Liam felt like he was being crushed, his molecules slamming into one another like car crashes, his head squeezing, his body mashing back into itself.

The dial snapped back to its original twelve o'clock position, and everything around him reversed even faster than it had passed before. Liam was yanked apart again, like he was being dragged, a string of atoms barely hanging on to one another. . . .

Night returned, moons reversing course, the sun rewinding from the horizon. Smoke gathered and poured down from the sky, into a mushroom cloud, sucking back into the canyon, their ship coming out of a darkness and landing at the research station, colonial troops running backward onto their ship.

And then a rush of sound and Liam was back in his body, in his time.

Sitting on the couch.

There was Phoebe, sitting beside him, eyeing him.

JEFF in the kitchen filling a water cup.

"What's up with you?" said Phoebe.

He was exactly where he'd left. *When* he'd left. Everything normal again.

Liam collapsed to his knees and barfed all over the floor.

"Ah, gross!" Phoebe yanked up her legs.

He heaved twice, then sat there gasping for breath, his head stabbing with pain, his fingers and toes tingling.

"Just one moment and I'll clean that up," said JEFF, rolling back to the kitchen.

Liam's head pounded. He had a stinging, sour taste in his mouth, and chunks of barf in his nose.

"Here, Liam." JEFF handed him a towel and he wiped off his mouth, blew his nose. He wobbled to his feet, but his vision filled with bright dots and he collapsed back onto the couch.

He laid his head back, wincing.

"Are you okay?" Phoebe asked.

The pain receded a little in his head. Liam sat up. JEFF handed him a glass of water, then began spreading a white powder over the vomit.

Liam sipped the water. Phoebe peered at him. "What just happened to you?"

"I don't . . . what did you see?"

"What do you mean? You twisted that watch, and sort of flinched, and then you just fell over and started barfing."

"You didn't see anything in between that?"

"What do you mean, *in between*? That all happened in like two seconds."

Liam breathed deep. "When I turned the watch, I . . ." He was about to say *time traveled*, except he hadn't actually gone anywhere. When he'd pressed that blinking button, he'd ended up right back here. Like he'd never actually left, even though he felt like he had. "I think I saw the future," he said. "Or like, I was in the future, sort of. . . ." He rubbed his head.

"Are you saying your alien watch just showed you the future?"

Liam nodded. "I think so."

"Okay," said Phoebe. "Well, what did you see?"

Liam's gut flooded with adrenaline. His mouth went dry.

"I saw us die."

INTERLUDE

Just over a billion kilometers from Mars, in a golden structure parked within the ice and dust of Saturn's rings, a white light began to blink. The light was on a link, worn by a woman sitting at a card table. There were many tables in the room, all filled with people who knew nothing about alien observatories or infected stars, nor about the four-legged beings or their murderers who might be out there somewhere.

There were, however, a few people in the room who were a bit more in the know about some of the larger forces at work in this universe. If you believe in fate, and it's fine if you do, you might think it was the reason why three of these people ended up at the same card table together at this particular moment. One was the woman whose link was blinking.

The card dealer, a gold-plated bot that resembled a jaguar, made a disapproving sound. "No links at the table, ma'am."

"Sorry," said the woman. She was dressed in a sparkling silver-and-lavender jumpsuit and her hair was bright purple and twisted in a seashell spiral atop her head. She finished reading the urgent message she'd just received, leaned into the man beside her, and spoke quietly in his ear. His jumpsuit was teal and orange, and his black hair was coiffed into a sideways triangle. The man nodded but didn't smile. Neither of them had smiled all night.

"Where did you two say you were from?" Simon Onatu asked from across the table.

The man looked at Simon. "We didn't." His eyes narrowed for a moment, but then he shrugged. "Where is anyone from, these days?"

Simon laughed and sipped from his signature cocktail glass: a tall funnel that spiraled twice around his forearm. "Fair point," he said.

He rubbed his free hand through his curly, graying hair and looked around the busy, circular gaming room of the Rings of Gold casino. Half of the floor-to-ceiling windows looked out on the massive, swirling tan clouds of Saturn. The other half offered a view of seemingly infinite, glassy stars. Nearly everyone was dressed like these two across from him. Wild clothing and hairstyles were part of the fun here: the chance to shed your old inner-solar-system identity and be someone new. You could purchase these outfits in the gift shop, but as someone who considered himself very much *in the know*, Simon preferred to dress simply: black jacket and pants, an expensive but subtle blue shirt, black shoes, a titanium link.

He figured this couple was like the others, here to cut loose one last time before boarding the *Scorpius* when it arrived from Mars, a day and a half from now. Or maybe, like him, they weren't planning to take the *Scorpius* at all. As to why they never smiled, Simon didn't particularly care. He'd talk to anyone to pass the time.

"If I told you I was originally from Fort Wayne, Texas province, North American Federation," said Simon, "someone your age might not even know what that meant. Then again, can you be from somewhere that no longer exists?" He glanced back out at the stars, and he sipped his drink again. "Really, we're all just orphans now."

"That is all too true," said the man. "But still, I think it matters where you're from. I think it matters very much. We are made of our memories, after all."

"I like to think I'm all about the future," said

Simon, "but here I am waiting around to watch the supernova. I tell myself I'm staying because you don't often get a chance to witness such a thing, but I guess I'd have to admit I'm also a little bit nostalgic."

The dealer's metal hands flashed across the table, dealing each of them two cards. Simon looked at his. Two kings. "Now there's some luck," he said, knocking his fist on the table. He looked to his right. "Oh, sorry, Nico."

Between him and the unsmiling couple sat an old man whose ankle was chained to the chair. His cards added up to sixteen, the worst possible hand. Nico shook his head and mumbled to himself. When the dealer pointed to him, he slapped the table. She dealt him another six and took away his cards and his chips.

"One too many," said Simon, patting Nico on his back. "Dumb luck."

"You believe in luck?" asked the unsmiling man.

"Don't you have to, in a place like this?" said Simon.

The man sat back in his chair. "Luck is just a way of explaining an event that you cannot fully comprehend. If you play any game long enough, there is no luck. There is only time, and math."

Simon made a little toast toward the man. "Maybe, but where's the fun in that?"

The dealer dealt the cards. Simon won again. Nico lost.

"Lady luck must be at the buffet," Simon said, patting Nico again and flashing a knowing smile at the man.

Nico made another mumbling sound and pressed a button beside him. A silver bot that looked like a penguin appeared and rolled Nico's chair away.

Simon saw the man and woman watching Nico go. "Bathroom break," he explained. "Nico's a lifer."

There were one or two lifers at each table: people who'd run out of money and sold themselves to the casino. The upside was unlimited play. The downside was you were stuck here playing until the supernova, at which point your game would be over, so to speak. The Rings of Gold casino promised to be "Open Until the Lights Go Out." All the human employees had already left, as had the owners; they'd traveled with the First Fleet and were building a new resort on Delphi. This place ran solely on bots now.

"Amazing," said the woman, gazing after Nico, "that a creature could be so self-centered that it can't even see the folly of its own situation."

"Is there anything more human?" the man said.

"Pretty sure Nico just really loves cards," said Simon.

"Shuffle," said the dealer. She gathered the stack

of cards and began flipping piles atop one another.

Simon leaned back and sipped his drink. A shadow passed over the table. The doughnut-shaped casino was positioned vertically right in the middle of Saturn's rings. It rotated to create gravity, and now they were passing down through the thin layer of ice and dust. Or was it up? Direction didn't really matter in space.

As they came out the other side, the bright face of Enceladus gleamed in the distance. The moon was nearly the same distance from Saturn as the old moon had been from Earth. Seeing Enceladus always gave Simon a little pang. He pictured the bands of moonlit mist over the plains beyond his childhood home, the white glow on distant rock mountains, the chirps of bats and insects, the diamonds glinting on the once-great ocean. . . .

From here, you could just make out the metallic structures that stuck up from the surface of Enceladus, connecting a network of space stations, as if the moon had been trapped in a net. This was Saturn Station, where water was mined from the moon's massive sub-surface ocean and supplied to each starliner before it embarked for Delphi.

"So, how are you getting to Aaru, then?" the woman across the table asked. "If you're waiting to watch the supernova, then you obviously aren't taking the *Scorpius*."

Simon laughed. "You got that right. Coop myself up in one of those metal buckets with a hundred million other people? No, thank you. Also that's a darn slow way to travel. I've got myself a Moon Racer IV parked outside."

"Impressive," said the man. "But I've read that the Moon Racer, at best, is only about twenty percent faster than a starliner."

Simon looked around. Only bots and lifers nearby. He leaned over the table. "That's a little trick of mine," he said. "Nanorocket technology, top-secret stuff."

"Nanorockets?" said the man. "Do you mean like what they used on the Phase One project?"

Simon narrowed his eyes. "How'd you know about that?"

"Oh," said the man. He glanced at the woman. "We saw the test results firsthand."

"Ah, part of the analysis team?"

"More or less," said the man.

Simon slapped the table and smiled. "Finally, someone who knows what I'm talking about. I mean, I didn't work for Phase One—my company just sold them the rocket designs." He put a hand beside his mouth. "For a pretty nifty sum, I might add. Those babies worked like a charm, didn't they?"

"Like a charm," said the woman.

"Yes, very impressive," said the man.

"I know, right?" said Simon. "So the minute I made the sale, I started modifying the tech for my own ship. I'm gonna watch the solar system go pop, and still make it to Aaru right along with the First Fleet, if not slightly ahead of them."

"Wow," said the man. "Does that mean that you're Simon Onatu? Of Starfire Aeronautics?"

"In the flesh," said Simon.

"You must be so proud," said the woman, still not smiling.

"Well," said Simon. "Some people do call me one of the heroes of the new frontier, but I'm just glad I was able to do my part for the future of humanity." He slid a tall stack of chips out onto his spot. "Also, just between us, with that paycheck, I've already put a nice down payment on some property on Aaru."

"Property?" said the woman. "You think you own a piece of that planet?"

"Not think, *do*. I mean, nobody really knows exactly what the landforms look like yet, but I've got a lease on an equatorial region—fingers crossed that it will be beachfront!—though I guess that's up in the air now with the reports coming from Mars."

"Do you mean Phase Two?" the woman asked. "We heard the tests were nearly complete."

"They were," said Simon, "but I saw on my link

that there's been some kind of big accident at the research station."

"The best-laid plans," said the man, shaking his head.

"Tell me about it," said Simon. "Not sure what's going to happen if we get to Aaru without the terraforming finished. Hopefully what we already have will be good enough."

There was a squeaking of wheels, and Nico returned.

"Welcome back, buddy," Simon said, slapping Nico on the shoulder.

The dealer's hand flashed around with cards. Simon smiled. An ace and a ten. "Ha-ha," he said. "Twenty-one."

Nico moaned.

"Oh, sorry, Nico. More dumb luck."

"Well, Mr. Onatu," said the woman, "sounds like you have it all figured out."

"Please, call me Simon." He shrugged. "Back on Earth they used to say, *Go big or go home*. Well, now there's no *home*, so I guess we just go big, right?"

The man and woman didn't laugh.

"What were your names?" Simon asked.

The woman sipped her drink. The man rolled up his right sleeve and started massaging the crook of his elbow. Simon noticed a tattoo there: three small, hollow circles in a vertical row. The man was whispering something to himself.

"Hey, is that a colony tattoo?" Simon asked. "Or colonial squadron?"

The man looked up, almost as if Simon had disturbed him. "More like a colony." He started rolling down his sleeve.

"Oh, which one?"

The man gazed into the table. "Telos."

"Never heard of it."

"Nobody has," said the man. He pushed back from the table. "I'll be right back."

"I meant no offense," Simon said to the woman.

She smiled at him for the first time. "Of course you didn't."

The dealer dealt another hand.

"Sorry, Nico," said Simon again, as the dealer pulled Nico's chips away and Simon raked in his winnings.

A hand fell on his shoulder. Simon found the man standing behind him.

"Let us buy you a drink," he said.

"Oh." Simon smiled too. "That would be lovely. I've been drinking the synth lime—"

"I already got you one." The man stuck a vial onto

the back end of Simon's cocktail glass, beneath his elbow. A pink-colored liquid shot into the glass, spiraling around his arm.

"Mmm," said Simon, sipping it. "I've never tasted anything like that. What did you say this was called?"

The man leaned in. "It's our own recipe, from Telos. It's made from the root of a tree we called Wind-Ache."

Simon shook his head. "Never heard of that, either." He drank again and a warm tingle spread through his chest. His fingers felt like they were floating. "This is delicious. If you are not selling this on every starliner from here to Delphi, son, you are missing out on a golden opportunity."

"Maybe you'd like to be an investor," said the man. He was very close to Simon's ear. But Simon didn't mind. His next set of cards equaled thirteen, and when he asked for another card he got a ten and the dealer took his cards and his chips and he didn't mind that either. Out the window, Enceladus looked smudged, as if by a fog rolling across the Texas plains. . . .

"Let's take a walk," said the woman. She was beside Simon now too. "Let's talk about the future."

"That sounds delightful," said Simon. "I'm so glad we happened to meet." He sipped his drink again and motioned to the dealer. "Be right back."

Then he was at the far end of the casino floor, and then he was in a hallway. The music faded away. Outside the circular windows, the stars were dancing, twinkling like they once had on those summer nights on Earth, when the humid air was thick and buzzing with life. People hated the Texas heat, but Simon had never minded it. In fact, he missed it now, more than he usually did. Something was itching in his mind. *We are made of our memories. . . .*

The man and the woman had him by his arms, guiding him along. They passed through a door to the private hangar docks and reached the security checkpoint.

"Show them your docking pass," said the man.

"Right, of course." Simon tapped his link, his fingers fat and clumsy. It was weird, the way he felt like there was a great distance between his mind and his body, like he was sort of floating.

They walked along the series of airlocks.

Simon sipped his drink again. It made his mouth fuzzy. "I never did get your names," he said.

"No, you didn't," said the woman.

"Come on," said Simon, laughing. Things were funny all of a sudden. "If we're gonna be partners, I should at least know what to call you. Say, do you want to stick around for the supernova? I've got a couple extra stasis pods in the racer, top-of-the-line comfort with the virtual dream enhancers and everything, not to mention a few freeze-dried delicacies from Earth—"

"That sounds great," said the man, "but I'm afraid we can't."

"Oh, come on, why not?"

"We're extremely busy," said the woman.

"With what, playing cards and having crazy hair?" Simon laughed.

"Not just that." The woman smiled again. "After we deal with you, we're going to plant a bunch of explosives at Saturn Station so that when the starliner arrives, we can blow it all up."

"You guys are hilarious," said Simon, laughing harder.

"Aren't we?" said the man. He smiled now too. "But that's not even the best part. We're also going to steal the final Phase Two data, and then rendezvous with the rest of our team. And after that, we're going to start shooting every single starliner out of the sky, one by one, until there are no more humans left in this entire galaxy."

Simon stopped laughing. "There will just be the three of us." He slapped the man's back. "Genius! We won't have to buy land on Aaru-5. We can own the whole thing!"

The man wrapped his arm around Simon. "Now you're getting it. Well, here we are." He stopped and tapped a console and a thick airlock door slid open. "After you, Mr. Onatu."

Simon toppled through the doorway, lost his balance, and ended up on his backside, facing his two new friends. "Boy, that drink of yours is strong!" he said, and yet at the same time . . . had they just pushed him? But come on! Why would they do that?

The man and the woman peered down at him.

Simon felt something cool on his arm. His spiral drink glass had smashed. There was a small trickle of blood on his palm. "That's too bad," he said. He tried to stand, but that space between his mind and his body seemed like a big black void now and he fell back down. "Can I get a hand here?"

"Your link has the key codes for your Moon Racer, I take it?"

"It, um . . ."

The man was holding up a link. Simon looked at his wrist. His own link was gone. He looked back at the man. "Guys . . . what's going on?"

The man and woman were no longer smiling. The man handed Simon's link to the woman. He rolled up his sleeve again. "Do you have children, Mr. Onatu?"

Simon's heart had started pounding. "I, um, well, I mean, yeah. I have two sons. Dimwits most of the time. They're on the *Starliner Mercury*. Do, um . . . do you?"

"My children are dead," said the man. "So is my wife. Do you know what I do when I need to calm myself?"

"I don't—"

"I say their names," said the man. He tapped those three black circles inside his elbow. "Nala," he said, "Gaela, Spira . . ."

"They will be counted," said the woman. Her eyes were closed and she had rolled up her sleeve, too. There were four black circles on the inside of her elbow.

Simon tried again to get to his feet. He managed to stagger into the wall, grab the edge of the window, and pull himself up. Had the gravity turned off? Everything felt sideways. He wanted to ask what had been in that drink. He wanted to ask why his friends were acting so strange, but his heart was racing and his legs were tingling and he felt like he needed to ask something else. "Who are you?"

"My name is Barro," said the man. "This is Tarra. The people of Telos send their regards."

"I've never heard of Telos," said Simon.

"No, you haven't," said Tarra. "You had no idea it even existed."

Simon gulped air. His brain was looping in a spiral. Weird thing his new friend Barro had said a minute ago. *Until there are no more humans left . . .*

Simon turned himself around. "I think I've had enough, for the moment. Going to go to my ship now . . ." He looked at the outer airlock door and his vision swam, but he focused on the number there. Twenty-two. "I think I . . . I think I parked at twenty-one?"

"Huh, must be dumb luck," said Barro.

Simon kept staring at the door. "There is no luck."

"Now you're getting it," Barro said from behind him. "The time and the math of what you did."

"What I did . . . " Simon kept staring at the door. There was something about what Barro was saying. Something he should have understood.

"Thank you for the Moon Racer."

"The—" Simon spun around. "You're stealing my ship? That's what all this is?"

"Not even close," said Tarra. "We are stealing a very fast ship from the man who made Phase One possible. It's poetic, really."

"But I don't . . . I've done nothing wrong, I'm— I'm a hero of the human race!"

"You're more than that," said Barro. "You're the first casualty in a great war."

Simon squinted at them. "What are you talking about?"

"We already told you," said Tarra. "Now if you'll excuse us, we're extremely busy."

"Busy with *what*?" Simon said.

"We told you that as well."

The words jumbled in Simon's head. *Stealing the Phase Two data, blowing up the starliner* . . . "But you can't—you don't—the Phase Two station is damaged anyway. . . ."

"And who do you think caused that?" said Tarra.

Simon squinted at her. "You?"

She just stared at him and then nodded to Barro. He reached for the airlock controls.

"No!" Simon managed to make his legs move and he threw himself forward and grabbed Barro by the arm—

But his hand slipped, and Barro hissed words that Simon couldn't possibly understand, and hands shoved him onto his backside once more.

Warning lights flashed and there was a loud beeping. The inner airlock door began to close.

Simon looked down and saw that his hand was streaked with something tan-colored, like paint, but more viscous and rubbery. He looked up. Barro and Tarra were gazing down on him, and as the door slid closed, he glimpsed Barro's arm, and the streaks there, as if his skin had been torn away—no, painted on—no . . . There was something beneath it, the purple color of a predawn sky and dotted with black.

"What are you?" Simon whimpered.

"That's the first smart thing you've said all night," said Barro. "Good-bye, Mr. Onatu."

The outer airlock door unlatched and there was a terrible whoosh, and Simon Onatu flew backward. For just a moment, he saw the stars and the pale glow of Enceladus through his freezing tears, blurry like on those warm Texas nights, long ago.

10

"What do you mean, you saw us die?" said Phoebe.

Liam fought another wave of nausea as the memories flashed through his head. "When I twisted the watch, everything started to speed up—like, the whole world. JEFF gave you the pills and—"

"Ha, ha, ha," said JEFF. Liam and Phoebe both looked at him. He'd stopped spreading the white powder on the floor and had replaced his normal claw-style hand with a vacuum nozzle attachment. A hose snaked around to a canister strapped to his back.

JEFF's eyes flashed. "Your statement that I had somehow already given Phoebe the pills was so illogical

203

that I assumed it was another example of humor. . . . Was that not funny?"

Liam shook his head. "No, JEFF. I know it doesn't make sense, but just hear me out. You gave her the pills, and then we went to the cockpit and watched the rescue team land, and I think we started to take off, but then . . ." Liam closed his eyes, his head still spinning. The mushroom cloud flashed in his mind. "There was this huge explosion, and it swallowed us up. And then later there was ash and smoke and everything was destroyed."

"Did our parents get out?" Phoebe asked.

"No, that's what I'm saying." Liam's voice wavered. "Nobody did. Not our parents, not the rescue team, not even us. We all died in the explosion."

"And you're saying that's our future?"

"I don't know, exactly. But I think so." Liam glanced down at the watch. It was still blinking fast. "I think it really is warning us."

Phoebe hugged herself. "That we're about to die."

"I guess."

"But so, what do we do?"

"I don't know." Liam tried to ignore the pain in his head. "When the watch blinked on the mountain, we were in danger, but we survived. Maybe what I saw is what will happen if we wait here for the rescue team to show up. So . . . maybe we have to do something different. Like come up with a way to rescue everyone faster. JEFF, can you call Marco on the ship's link?"

"Acknowledged." Liam heard the hiss of an open channel over the ship's speakers.

"Liam, is that you?" said Marco. "Are you back on your ship?"

"We are, but we need to get our parents out faster."

"Well, we're doing our best," said Marco. "They're still stable, and the team will be here soon."

"I don't think we can wait for the team," said Liam. "The turbines are going to explode, or melt down, or whatever they'd do."

Marco was silent for a moment. "Look, I know you're worried, but that's pretty unlikely. The turbines have multiple safeguards built in."

"But—"

"Liam, listen, I know how you feel. You wish there was something you could do. But I need you to just sit tight." There were voices behind him now, Mara and Idris, calling to him. "I have to go. We're trying to fix the elevator now and I need to get back to it. If you could keep your eyes peeled for the rescue team and make sure they know where to find us, that would be a big help."

The signal ended. Liam slammed his fist on the armrest of the couch. "He's not going to listen."

Phoebe stared at his watch. "What if that thing is

right and he's wrong? We can't just sit here."

"I know," said Liam. He had to think! How could they get down into the underground lab quickly? He pictured the narrow canyon, then the lava shaft. . . . "Maybe the skim drone could fit through there." Liam tried standing. He wobbled and leaned against the wall for balance. His stomach churned, his throat still sour from throwing up, but he swallowed hard and stood straight. "Marco said there are canaries down at the turbines. JEFF, can you confirm that?"

"I will check the inventory," said JEFF. His eyes flashed. "Yes, there are four canaries stored with the emergency supplies in the underground lab. They should be charged and ready to go; however, because we've lost communication, I am unable to access their real-time status. They may have been damaged in the explosion."

"Okay, so . . ." Liam picked at the skin on his thumb. "I could fly down in the skim drone, get everyone on a canary, and then send them out."

"And if they're damaged?" Phoebe asked.

"I can take someone in the cockpit, maybe even stuff two people at a time. I mean, I could be down there in five minutes, and then ten minutes to get out and back. I could probably get everyone out before the colonial team even arrives." His heart raced. "I think it's our best chance."

"You'd know," said Phoebe. "You're the one who saw us get blown to bits." She glanced at the watch again. "If you think this will work, let's do it."

Liam nodded. "Okay."

"What should I do while you're gone? I can't just sit here. . . ."

"You be ready to help get our parents on board as fast as you can." Liam started zipping up his pressure suit. "JEFF, once I leave, get this ship airborne. And get ready to lock on the canaries and guide them to you."

"Acknowledged," said JEFF.

Liam checked the watch. It was blinking a bit slower. He held it up to Phoebe. "Maybe that means we're doing the right thing."

"Like the future's not written yet," said Phoebe.

"I hope not." Liam slipped on his helmet, breathing hard. Fingers tingling. Head swimming. "Okay, I'm gonna go. Um . . ."

"Good luck," said Phoebe. "Don't die."

"Right."

Liam zipped his helmet closed and climbed down through the hatch into the skim drone. He glanced at the watch again. It was nice to see it blinking slower, but it hadn't stopped blinking, either. Maybe he'd made one good decision, but needed to make more if they were really going to get out of this alive. Maybe he'd actually only delayed their deaths by a few minutes. He thought about spinning the watch again. Would what he saw be different now? But just thinking about it made his stomach lurch and a splitting pain shot through his head. He remembered, too, how he'd felt at the end, that sense that he was being torn apart, and stranger still, that sense of wanting to keep going, even farther. . . . What would have happened if he had? The thought made him shudder. But it didn't matter right now. They had a plan, and very little time.

He gripped the controls and powered up the drone. He checked the battery level, saw that it was nearly back to full, and detached from the cruiser.

"Hey," said Phoebe over the link. "I'm right here if you need me."

"Thanks."

Liam edged out from beneath the cruiser, fired the thruster, and rose up over the research station buildings. As he flew toward the canyon mouth, he glanced up at the giant orange sun. It was hard to believe that just this morning he'd been sad about leaving a place that now seemed so determined to kill him.

The drone passed into the cliff shadow. Liam fought crosswinds and lined up the canyon entrance. The craft was still flying with a slight pull to the left due to the damaged stabilizer. He could keep it straight, but the faster he went, the more it pulled and vibrated.

The cliff face loomed overhead, and he slid into the canyon. Darkness and smoke closed in. Liam turned on the ring of white lights around the drone, but they barely penetrated the smoke. One of the proximity sensors blared and the edge of the drone dashed off an outcropping of rock. The compartment shuddered.

"Liam, are you okay?" Phoebe asked.

"Yeah," he said, but he slowed down and switched on the sensor scopes, which outlined the twists and turns of the canyon in bright blue lines on the canopy.

Ahead, he saw flickering white lights. Marco, Mara, and Idris, working on the elevator. Their headlamps swept up toward him.

The skim drone's communicator blinked to life.

"Liam, is that you?" Marco asked. "What are you doing in here?"

"I'm going to get our parents."

"Liam, no. It's way too dangerous down there. The rescue team is on the way and they have the proper gear. If we just wait—"

"We can't wait," said Liam. "You guys need to get out of here. Get in one of the cruisers and pull back to a safe distance before the reactors melt down."

"Liam," said Marco, "I told you, there's no way—"

"There is. You have to trust me."

"But how can you know that?"

Liam nearly laughed to himself. What could he say? *Because this watch I pulled off a dead alien told me?* "Just please get out. I'm going down."

He flew over the wide lava shaft and activated the vertical thrusters. Small jets fired upward, and the ship began to lower, straight down into the smoke and dark.

"Liam, we can't just—" Marco's voice cut out. "You don't—"

No Signal.

Liam switched channels. Tried the cruiser. "Phoebe?"

No Signal.

He looked at the watch. It was still blinking slowly. "You better be right," he muttered.

The craft's lights illuminated only smoke swirling on all sides. He'd descended fifty meters, then one hundred. Using the sensors, he moved the drone closer to the wall until its lights illuminated the elevator shaft. The shiny metal was kinked and twisted, and partially torn away from the rock. There was no way Marco and the team were going to be able to fix that.

Two hundred meters down. Then three. Liam flexed his fingers. His palms were slick with sweat. If he closed his eyes, he pictured the explosion, the mushroom cloud spreading, running them down.

After nearly four hundred meters of smoky black-ness, the proximity sensors on the bottom of the craft began to beep. Liam spied the outline of the lower platform, a square that stuck out into the shaft.

All at once he emerged from the smoke. The walls and platform came into view. He saw the elevator car, jammed cockeyed at the bottom of its mangled track, dented and covered with boulders. Across the plat-form from the elevator was the entrance to the access tunnel—except it was no longer there. A large slab of the wall had broken free and fallen onto the platform, completely blocking the tunnel except for a frown-shaped gap at the top. Much of the smoke was billow-ing out of this gap, while more poured from cracks in the wall above it.

Liam saw where a bright orange cable, the hard line, snaked over the slab and through the gap. Marco would have flown it down using a small robotic drone. It had no problem getting through, but the crack wasn't nearly big enough for the skim drone. Liam didn't even think he could crawl through it.

His heart pounded faster. There wasn't time for this! But the watch was still at a slow blink.

Okay . . . he needed to stay calm. The watch was telling him what was going to happen—well, not the exact details, but that his plan had a chance. He thought of what his mom said, how you could never really know what came next. Except now he could. Sort of. He at least knew that this boulder wasn't a problem, wasn't unexpected, or the watch would have started blinking faster . . . right?

If so, then in this future, he solved this problem. Now he just had to stay calm, and figure out how to actually do it. Deep breath. He looked over the skim drone controls. Maybe . . .

Liam turned on the underside camera. He tilted the craft upward while hovering in place, until he was nearly vertical, so that his view out the cockpit looked straight back up the lava shaft. Then he fired the topside thrusters, moving toward the slab that blocked the tunnel, until the bottom of the drone was only a meter from it. Liam activated a three-pronged claw on the drone's underside that could be used for moving cargo or attaching to things like asteroids or rock faces where the magnetic stabilizers wouldn't work. The craft shuddered as the claw unfolded. Liam inched toward the slab, then closed the claw. The fingers dug in with a splintering crunch.

He fired the main thruster. The ship shuddered but didn't move. He stopped, then fired again, a stronger thrust this time. . . . With a groaning crunch, the slab pulled free in a rain of dust and debris. It immediately fell, yanking the drone back to horizontal and dragging it into the abyss. Liam had already plunged twenty meters before he could hit the release button. The claw opened and the boulder fell into darkness. He slammed the thruster to halt his descent.

Liam exhaled hard and flew back up. The access tunnel was clear now, its wide entrance belching smoke. There were still big chunks of fallen rock here and there on the floor, but it looked like there was enough room for him to fit through, and there wasn't time to survey the tunnel on foot to be sure.

The watch was still blinking slow. Okay . . . Liam edged the ship slowly into the tunnel. Its sides glanced off the walls. The cockpit banged the ceiling twice. Ahead, he could see light through the smoke.

Ominous red light.

Liam increased thrust and flew into the underground lab. It was a massive cavern, two hundred meters tall and wide, its ceiling hung with a thousand stalactites. In the center of the cavern stood the two giant, cone-shaped terraforming turbines. Their metallic surfaces were streaked with burn marks. Thick clouds of black smoke spewed from their tops and sparks shot out of cracks in their sides. One of the turbines had split in two, and its upper half had collapsed and wedged itself against the cavern wall. The wide bases of the turbines, the fusion cores, glowed red like miniature suns about to go supernova.

The floor and walls of the cavern were covered with a jungle of green plants. Huge leaves, twisting vines. One area was plowed like a garden; another had a small pond. Beneath the vegetation was layer upon layer of wilted brown stalks and husks from the years of studies. Everything close to the turbines had been flattened and charred black. Where there wasn't smoke, a thin layer of gray clouds hung in the cavern, and the surviving plants were dappled with water.

Just beside the cavern entrance, a steep set of metal stairs led to the wide platform that held the control systems and equipment lockers. Some were still standing, but others had been knocked over. Smoke swirled around the computer consoles. Smoke swirled everywhere.

Someone was lying on the platform. Liam landed beside the stairs and hopped out. The sensors on his pressure suit began to blare. *WARNING: CRITICAL RADIATION LEVELS DETECTED. WARNING: TOXIC ATMOSPHERE DETECTED.*

Liam vaulted up to the platform. It was Dad, lying there on his side. Liam slid to his knees beside him. "Dad." Liam could see his chest moving through his pressure suit. A good sign, but a shrill alarm was blaring from his link, and a red message blinked: *OXYGEN LEVELS CRITICAL. RADIATION EXPOSURE CRITICAL.*

"I'm here, Dad. Hold on." Liam jumped up and ran to the lockers. He started throwing open their metal doors. Chemicals, electronic equipment, gardening supplies. The canaries were in one of the units that had toppled over. A large rock was lying on top of it. Liam pulled three of the meter-wide, disk-shaped machines out of the locker, but the fourth was pinned beneath where the rock had fallen, and spitting sparks.

But that was okay. Liam could take the fourth person out in the drone. What did the watch think? Still at a slow blink. Liam raced back to Dad and placed one of the canaries beside him. It worked on small turbo propellers and was programmed to find its way to the surface.

"You're gonna be okay, Dad. I'm sending you out."

An earsplitting hiss tore through the cavern. A white-hot bolt of electricity spidered around the partially collapsed turbine.

Liam switched on the canary. As its propellers whirred to life, he activated the injury setting. The canary rose, and four thick cables extended from beneath it. There was a roll of fabric between two of the cables. Liam unfurled it and attached clips to the other two cables, creating a stretcher. He rolled Dad onto the fabric, the disk hovering above him. Three sets of straps hung from the sides of the stretcher, and Liam buckled them around Dad, securing him in place. He stood and pressed a flashing green button and the canary lifted Dad off the ground, his body sagging in the stretcher, and then buzzed off toward the tunnel, yellow lights flashing on its sides.

Okay, one down. Liam gathered the other two canaries, one under each arm, and stood. More sparks shot from the turbines. He looked around the platform, checking behind the fallen lockers, but saw no sign of Mom or Phoebe's parents. He vaulted off the side of the platform, threw the canaries in the skim drone, and hopped back in. He lifted off into the smoky air and edged toward the turbines, peering down into the plants. Clouds of black smoke obscured his view. The canopy was beaded with condensation. The craft shuddered in waves of heat coming off the turbines. So many of the skim drone's sensors were screaming at this point that Liam didn't bother checking them.

But the watch. It was blinking faster again. What had changed? Was it that canary being damaged?

Wait, there they were: three black shapes among large ferns, on the slope that led down toward the turbines. Liam landed, crushing a patch of plants, and jumped out. There was less smoke down here, but his radiation sensor chirped furiously. Liam could hear the reactors buzzing like hives of angry bees.

Mom, Paolo, and Ariana were all lying on their

stomachs, facing away from the turbines, like they'd been on the run when the explosion had happened.

"Mom." Liam knelt beside her. Her oxygen and radiation warnings were also flashing. There was a stun rifle lying just beyond her hand. They kept those down here for security. . . .

"Liam," Mom said faintly. Her eyes fluttered open. She coughed hard. "Is that you?"

"Yeah, Mom. It's me."

"What are you doing down here?" she asked weakly.

"It's okay. I'm going to send you out on a canary. It will just be a second."

"Where's your dad?"

"I already sent him up. Just let me get you—"

Mom grabbed his wrist and pulled herself up, leaning on her elbow. Her eyes were red, and there was a thin line of blood down her temple. "Liam, listen to me. You have to get out of here now. It's not safe."

"Yeah, I know," said Liam. "But trust me, this will work. I—"

"No." She strained to look back at the turbines. "Something wasn't right. With the readings—*cough*— We tried to fix it, but . . ." She fell back, and gasped for breath. "It was sabotage, Liam. They . . . You need to go, right now."

Liam glanced at the rifle by Mom, and then wildly

around the thick plants. Sabotage? But by who? Who could possibly be down here when everyone was off-planet? And who would want to destroy the terraforming project? There had been that one group, the Planet Defenders, who protested colonizing Aaru because they thought humans would just ruin any new planet like they'd apparently ruined Earth. But they hadn't been violent. And that was years ago. Besides, without the terraforming, the entire human race might die out in deep space somewhere. . . .

Mom grabbed his arm again. "Take this with you," she said, tapping her hip pocket.

"Mom, just give me your hands," he said, taking hold of her wrists.

"No!" Mom wrenched her arms away and slapped at her hip again. "You have to listen—*cough*—In my pocket, there's a data key. It's the final Phase Two trial—*cough*—it worked! You have to take it to your father, or Wesley or the secretary general, and don't—*cough*—don't tell anyone that you have it. Do you understand? You—" A fit of coughing overwhelmed her.

"Mom, this is crazy, I—"

"I'm serious, Liam!" She winced. "Now go! I love you so much—" She tried to grab his hand and pull it to her, but just then her suit emitted an earsplitting shriek and she fell back, her eyes fluttering closed.

SUIT SYSTEMS FAILING. SURVIVAL CRITICAL.

Liam searched for a tear in her suit somewhere, or maybe the radiation had fried her batteries, or the smoke had overwhelmed her oxygen filter.

The watch. Blinking faster still. That symbol in its right side had started to glow. Was it because of these saboteurs? Were they closing in on him right now? He looked around again but saw nothing. And what did Mom mean he couldn't tell anyone? He looked at the rectangular outline of the data key in her pocket. . . .

But no. There was no way he was leaving her here. He pressed the power switch on the canary—

No response.

He pressed it again, jabbed it, slammed it with his fist. "Come on!" He flipped the disk over. There was no other way to turn it on, and no way to access its inner workings without unscrewing the casing.

The ground rumbled, and a huge blast erupted from the turbines. Stalactites broke free and plunged to the cavern floor. One landed ten meters from them, shaking the ground.

Liam hurled the broken canary into the plants. He grabbed the other one and it powered up, lights glowing, systems humming. He looked from Mom to Paolo to Ariana. One canary, one seat in the skim drone. Three people to get out.

Unless . . .

Liam glanced at the stun rifle by Mom's hand. Back to Phoebe's parents. Around the cavern again. *Sabotage.* There was no one else down here. . . .

But Phoebe's parents couldn't have done this. Liam had known them for years, and even though they were stern and maybe not the friendliest adults to be around, they'd dedicated their lives to saving humanity, and kept their family on Mars until the bitter end, just like Mom and Dad.

Another shriek of metal. More lightning shot from the turbines. A stalactite crashed way too close. The watch blinked even faster.

Liam nearly screamed. He had to think! Okay, he could send Mom on the canary and put Phoebe's parents in the skim drone. Could it fly with two extra adults? Fast enough to escape the meltdown? Maybe a canary could hold two people. . . .

A blast of hot air knocked Liam sideways.

The watch. The watch knew what was going to happen. It was blinking faster because things were getting worse and none of his ideas were slowing it down. . . . Liam had to use it. He couldn't afford to make any mistakes now.

But the pain, the nausea; how would he even fly afterward? What if the effects were worse the second time?

Then they'd all be dead either way.

Liam took a deep breath. It was worth the risk. He clenched his midsection and clicked the dial forward.

The world began to blur, and pain immediately sliced through Liam's mind. He saw himself attaching Mom to the canary and then activating it. Once again, his future self was moving at a blur but then he was also still right here, kneeling right beside Mom, two versions of him, one inside and one outside of his life. He saw the canary shoot off, but it only just reached the exit tunnel when the cavern wall collapsed, crushing his mom.

The turbines began to explode, jets of flame shooting in all directions—

"Hello there," said a man's voice from behind him.

Liam whirled around, his head splitting with pain, his gut quaking, to find someone standing just a few meters away from him. A figure in a nearly black metallic space suit, not part of the blurring future, but right here, with Liam, in the space in between.

11

Liam lurched to his feet and staggered back. "Who are you?"

"Who exactly are *you*?" the man asked. His suit was much thicker than a pressure suit, and even bulkier than the suits used for space walks. It almost looked like one of those old deep-sea diver outfits that ancient explorers wore on Earth, except that its dark metallic surface was crisscrossed by wires that glowed gold, and the helmet was sleek and rectangular, with a headlamp and a shiny lavender-tinted visor. Liam couldn't see the man's face.

Around them in the blur of the future, rocks were crashing down. A spear of light from somewhere above . . . now flames everywhere. Liam wanted to pay attention to what was happening, and yet somehow, impossibly, here was this man, with him, seemingly outside of time.

"Did you do this?" said Liam. "Did you sabotage the turbines?"

"The what now?" The figure stepped closer. "I'm afraid I have no idea what you're talking about. Then again, you're about the last thing I expected to find when these time anomalies started popping up."

Liam took another step back.

"You certainly don't look like one of those time-keeper beings. So how are you— Ahh." The man pointed with his thick-gloved hand. "You took its watch. But it doesn't quite work for you, does it? That figures: three-dimensional being with four-dimensional technology. . . . I shouldn't have left that behind in the observatory, but I was short on time, which I'm aware is a funny thing to say at the moment, isn't it? Well, no matter, I'll take it now."

The metal-suited man held out his palm.

Liam's head thrummed, his vision swimming. Around them, everything was dark now. The future streaming by. The meltdown and the explosion already over. He wanted to run, but where? And how? His arms and legs felt like breezes.

"Just give me the watch, boy," said the figure.

"You're not meant to have that kind of power. You're only human, after all."

Liam kept retreating through the pitch-dark blur around them, he and the metal-suited man lighting each other with their headlamps.

"I need it," said Liam. "To save my family and friends. To get to the starliner."

"Aw," said the man. "That's sweet. Listen, if you really want to save your family, come with me. My people and I can take you away from all of this."

"What do you mean, your people?"

"It's not who we are," said the man, "it's who we'll become that matters, though certain nearsighted beings around the universe have taken to calling us the Drove. I think they mean it like we're an oncoming storm. Maybe *swarm* was taken, who knows? Though I have seen the word *drove* defined as a 'broad chisel,' which, if you think of the universe as a big stone, then I maybe see where they're coming from. Personally, I would've gone with something suggesting a little more precision, but anyway." The man stepped closer, reaching. "The watch, please. Then you can come with us to the Dark Star. Your family, too. You don't have to die here."

The words were slipping into and through Liam. He could barely make sense of them and he still didn't get how there could be someone here with him in the time stream, someone offering to save him. But there was something else he'd just said . . . about taking the watch. . . .

"You killed her," said Liam.

The man shrugged. "I did do that. But it's not as bad as you might think." He kept advancing. "Just come with me and I'll explain. After all, there's so much to know. So much more than we could ever possibly imagine."

Liam looked at the watch, which was still blinking fast. This man, the Drove . . . *the oncoming storm* . . . He turned and tried to run, but everything hurt, and he felt that slipping sensation again, like soon he would dissolve into dust, scattered throughout the space and dark. Stumbling instead of running. Falling to the ground, which wasn't even ground anymore. . . .

The spaceman loomed over him. "It's okay," he said. "It will be over in just a moment."

Liam dragged his distant-feeling arm toward his other hand. The watch. That symbol blinking in the right semicircle. Last time when he'd pressed it . . . stretching, another centimeter . . .

He jabbed it with his finger.

"Oh no, don't do that," said the man.

But there was the lurch and the feeling of being pulled, being stretched to his limits and then rubber-banding back, through the dark, then the fire, all the way to the cavern, the ground, his mom right in front of him.

"See you later," the figure called from somewhere far, far away.

Liam toppled over onto his side, clutching his stomach and wincing. Pain everywhere, his insides like jelly, spots in his vision . . . but he forced himself to his knees and looked wildly in all directions.

Could the metal-suited man follow him here? Or could he only appear in that strange out-of-time state? *Time anomalies*, he had called them. An effect of the watch. Whoever he was, there was no sign of him in the cavern now.

A shrieking wail from the turbines. Their sides had started glowing molten red.

The watch still blinked fast. What had he seen in the timestream? His mother being crushed, but what else? He needed another look, but if he turned the dial, would that man be there? Also he felt like if he time traveled again, his brain would tear in two.

The turbines screamed and hummed and shook.

Liam looked from Mom to Paolo and Ariana to the skim drone. Everyone at once: that was the only way, wasn't it?

The watch slowed down. But only a little.

More rumbling from the turbines, more chunks of the ceiling and now the walls starting to crash to the cavern floor. No more time to think it through. Liam grabbed his mom by the shoulders and hoisted her up. He dragged her to the skim drone, dumped her in the cockpit and ran to Ariana and dragged her too. His muscles burned and his shoulder screamed in pain. His head was a den of hissing snakes. He laid Ariana on the front left side of the drone. Ran back and dragged Paolo. Out of breath, legs threatening to collapse beneath him . . . He hoisted Paolo up onto the other side of the drone, then lunged into the cockpit and grabbed his safety line. He yanked the cable out of the winch, unspooling it all the way and making a tangled pile on the ground, and clipped the hook to one of the towing rings. He ran around and threaded it through a ring on the other side of the ship. After cinching it tight, he doubled back and threaded it again, and then a third time, strapping both of Phoebe's parents firmly in place.

Flames were spreading from the turbines now. Metal whined and gave way. The turbine that was still standing wobbled and crashed into the other.

Liam jumped into the cockpit and closed the canopy. He fired up the main thruster and the drone rose, laboring under the extra weight. He turned toward the tunnel—but it had already collapsed, like he'd seen in the time stream.

Suddenly everything exploded. Jets of fire burst from the sides of the turbines, and the skim drone was tossed across the cavern. Liam barely avoided slamming into the wall. He banked the ship in a near vertical turn, then arced around. Fire in every direction. The ground shook, the walls shook, chunks coming down. A stalactite narrowly missed the ship. Dust and rocks clouding the air. And the fire, growing. This was it.

Liam spun around. All the sensors were blaring. They had seconds at best—

And then bright light speared down from above. Liam remembered this moment from the time stream. He looked up and saw that a great section of the ceiling had collapsed, revealing a wide hole that shot diagonally all the way to the surface.

It might work! Liam pushed the thruster to maximum and aimed for daylight, swerving back and forth to avoid falling rocks. Behind and below, fire bloomed, consuming the turbines completely. Any second now, the reactors themselves would blow.

Dust, smoke, falling rock. Liam shot up into the hole, a section of lava tube, a circle of daylight hundreds of meters above.

There was a sucking sound. . . .

And then the full blast.

A fireball grew in the rear camera. Surging. Racing after them.

The concussion of the blast tossed the drone forward, rattling every joint. The cockpit clipped the wall.

Liam jammed his thumb on the thruster even though it was already at maximum. The battery was draining so fast he could watch the bars going down. Sensors screamed from every possible spot on the dashboard, the craft wobbling with the bad stabilizer, nicking the wall again, and again, sparks flying.

Flames licked at the back of the craft. Out the rear-view camera, all he could see was fire. Engines redlined. Liam's heart slammed, his lungs pumping, his hands pressing so hard against the controls they hurt. The flames danced up on either side now, like fingers about to close around them. The glow on the cockpit window brightened, the little cabin getting hot.

But they were almost there.

Fire wrapping in front of them now . . .

The skim drone shot free of the lava tube and into a half-collapsed section of the canyon. Liam leveled off and darted back and forth between the craggy canyon walls, the fire right behind them.

"Liam, we see you on our sensors!" Phoebe called. "We have your dad, but—"

"I've got everybody else!" Liam shouted. "Back the ship up! Here comes the blast!"

He caught a glimpse below of the metal walkway and punched at the communicator. "Marco! Do you read me?"

No Signal.

The drone banged against the wall. Liam struggled to keep it straight. More smoke, more fire . . . And then they were out. Shooting into the daylight. Liam saw the Cosmic Cruiser glinting in the distance. He aimed straight for it.

Fire shot from the canyon behind him. The earth collapsed and the field-station buildings began to tumble into a smoke-filled fissure.

"This is colonial extraction team on our approach—come in, project leader," a voice called over the long-range link. "Marco, this is Captain Reyes, do you copy? We're being told to steer clear by one of the children of your team members, and we're picking up abnormal heat readings. We're standing by up here. What's the situation?"

Liam craned his neck. There, directly above, a boxy colonial craft was hovering over the area. Liam punched at the radio. "Turn around! Get out of here! The reactors are melting down!"

"The what? Who is this?"

Liam saw the colonial ship beginning to veer.

And then it felt like the skim drone had been kicked from behind, the blast wave catching them. Everything turned upside down as they were thrown out over the landscape.

Liam found himself looking back at the volcano, inverted, as the entire side of the mountain exploded in a ball of light and heat and the mushroom cloud billowed skyward. Even in this future, the colonial transport never had a chance. It had just started to bank a sharp turn when it was consumed by the fireball.

Liam fired thrusters on all sides of the craft, trying to get it back upright, trying to stop the spinning. The force of the blast had thrown them far out over the wasteland.

"Liam!" Phoebe called. "We're going down!"

Liam righted the drone, got the spin under control, but the ground was rushing up to meet him too fast. He tried to pull up. . . . All the controls went dark, the battery dead.

They plunged toward rock and sand, still spinning. Liam's vision blurred, the world losing focus. . . .

Everything went dark.

12

Give me the watch, boy, the metal-suited man said through the darkness. Liam turned to run, but he tripped and fell onto his bed. His room in their apartment, the orange daylight through the window . . . and his alarm was going off, only the walls were also the cavern and they were collapsing, and the floor around his bed was falling away to black like a bottomless lava tube, the red sun somehow beneath it. *It's got a tummy ache,* said a voice from beside him. Liam turned and there was his mother, but she was dressed in the dead alien's robes, and her face blurred when she moved, becoming a skull, like the ghosts in *Roid Wraiths*, dead for centuries. *We tried our best,* said Mom, *but these*

232

things happen. Liam tried to run but his legs didn't work, and now his bed was gone, his room gone, no colony anymore. There was only dark and the sound of the alarm as he began to fall toward the sun, which was growing brighter, opening its molten jaws. . . .

Liam blinked, the dream dissolving, the world coming back to him. He slowly opened his eyes.

Copper sunlight streamed through half the cockpit canopy. The other half was covered in sand. Paolo and Ariana were still strapped to the front of the drone. Paolo was mostly buried in the same sand drift that covered half the ship. Liam saw his chest rising and falling. Ariana appeared to be alive too, but both their links blinked red. Inside the craft, Mom's was flashing too, but she was breathing. Somehow, they were all alive.

Something was still beeping, somewhere. The dream flashed through Liam's mind. Falling toward the sun again . . .

He sat up, blinking hard. The Cosmic Cruiser lay cockeyed in the sand about a hundred meters away. Its landing gear had failed to deploy, but otherwise it seemed to be intact. Its windows were dark; maybe it had lost power, too.

Craning his neck, Liam saw Olympus Mons a few kilometers behind. The mushroom cloud had died down, but smoke still poured skyward. The cliff had collapsed all around where the canyon had been, leaving a gaping hole. The colonial team, Marco and Idris and Mara . . . none of them had made it out.

The ground between here and there was littered with debris: chunks of rock and wreckage from the research station buildings and the other spacecraft. Some scraps still burning. The skim drone had carved a deep trench in the sand.

Liam glanced at the alien watch. It had stopped blinking. They were safe. He wondered how long it would last.

But that beeping . . . Liam shook his head. He looked at the console but it was dark: the skim drone's battery dead.

Then it clicked. He checked his link.

Four zeroes flashed on the screen, over and over.

Red Line.

A light caught his eye from above: high in the bronze sky, flickering like a nearby star, only now it was beginning to move, making a streak of brilliant fire.

Red Line . . . and the *Scorpius* was leaving.

"No!" Liam pressed the canopy button, but all it did was click uselessly. He pushed up on the flex-glass surface, then slammed it with his palms. After a few hits, his shoulder ached.

"Wait!" He wrenched open his suit and fumbled at his thermal shirt and pulled out Mina's radio beacon. He pressed the top, over and over.

"Don't go!" he shouted. But of course they were leaving. Colonial command would have registered the explosion of the research station. They would have known the rescue team was lost. If the Cosmic Cruiser's power was out, there was no way that the starliner would know anyone was alive down here. Satellites would only have shown two crashed ships. They could have sent someone to investigate . . . but why would they risk it? The *Scorpius* had a hundred million people to protect. And how could they know that Liam had the final data they needed? They'd assume it was gone along with everything else.

The flash of light kept moving across the sky, a shooting star arcing faster and faster.

All Liam could do was watch it go. "Come back." Tears slipped down his cheeks.

And then the beacon blinked. Liam's breath caught in his throat. He pressed it. It blinked back again. And again.

He laughed out loud. "Mina!" She knew they were alive! She could tell them, and they could . . .

But what could they do? Stop a trillion-ton star-ship that was accelerating at thousands of kilometers per second? Starliners didn't exactly have brakes. It would have to use fuel to slow down, fuel it needed for its journey.

The streak of light curved toward the horizon and began to disappear.

At least Mina knew: that was something. She could tell Shawn. She could tell Wesley and colonial command and maybe they could slow down, at least wait for them to catch up. . . .

Which meant Liam had to figure out how to get everyone off Mars.

The light of the *Scorpius* faded out on the far rim of the horizon. In its place, waves of blue and green light swept toward them. The solar storm. The one strong enough to force Red Line. Bringing another huge dose of radiation right at him and his mom and Phoebe's parents.

The wind gusted. Sand pelted the canopy.

Liam tapped his link and tried to call the Cosmic Cruiser.

No Signal.

He tried Phoebe and got the same message.

Had they been injured in the crash? The ship didn't look like it was too damaged, but . . .

Liam zipped his suit back up. He hugged his legs to his chest and slid down until his back was flat on the seat and his feet were above him. He kicked the canopy as hard as he could. Nothing. Kicked again. Had something cracked? He kicked a third time—still nothing.

Come on! He paused, breathing hard. Outside, the shimmering energy waves blew closer.

Liam's gaze fell, and he noticed a small red-and-white-striped handle in the shadow beneath the rim of the canopy. The emergency release! He'd been so busy worrying, he'd totally forgotten about it. He unlatched it, then leaned over Mom and pulled a second handle. There was a hiss as the canopy opened a sliver, just enough for the pressurized air to escape, but then it stopped. Liam shoved his fingers in the gap and pushed up. The canopy wouldn't budge any farther. The sand was too heavy.

He slid down on his back and kicked again. It opened another little bit, and a tiny waterfall of sand cascaded onto Mom. He kicked again. A few centimeters, if that. This was going to take too long—

"Liam!"

He sat up and saw Phoebe limping toward him, using a shovel for support. JEFF rolled behind her. He'd switched to a larger pair of wheels with thick treads.

"Hey!" Liam shouted back, waving.

Phoebe reached the drone and bent down between her parents. She touched their shoulders, and looked up at Liam with tears in her eyes. "You did it," she said through her speaker. "You got them out!"

Liam nodded. "I'm kinda trapped in here, though."

Phoebe started digging at the sand pile. "Just a sec."

"How's my dad?"

"JEFF says he's stable right now, but his lungs are in bad shape, and he has radiation burns. JEFF thinks the best thing to do is put our parents into stasis pods until we get help, so they don't get any worse."

As she scooped away sand, JEFF unstrapped Paolo and Ariana. "Excellent work, Liam," he said. He took hold of Phoebe's parents by the oxygen packs on the backs of their suits and started dragging them across the sand to the cruiser.

The wind whistled through the rocks. A gust nearly knocked Phoebe over. Fingers of blue-and-green energy reached overhead.

"Hurry," said Liam.

"Help me out and keep kicking," said Phoebe, tossing sand aside.

Liam leaned back and kicked the canopy, over and over. More sand poured in, Phoebe kept digging, and finally, one of Liam's thrusts moved the canopy up a whole half meter. He flipped around and pushed it the rest of the way open with his back.

As Liam stood, his link began to beep, radiation sensor flashing yellow. He staggered out and Phoebe threw her arms around him. Her balance was off, and their helmets clanged into each other, and they nearly both fell over.

"Thank you for saving them," said Phoebe. "And good job not dying."

"Thanks," said Liam, hugging her back. "I tried to call you before."

"My link was dead," said Phoebe. "A bunch of the Cruiser's systems shorted out when we crashed and my link was charging at the time. Had to replace the chip. JEFF's been working to get the power back on."

Liam knelt down and pulled Mom out of the cockpit. He held her by her armpits and dragged her toward the ship, the wind buffeting his back. Phoebe limped along beside him. Their radiation sensors flipped from yellow to red.

"The *Scorpius* left," said Liam, breathing hard.

"I know," said Phoebe. "I saw it go."

The air began to sizzle. Liam dug his heels in harder. His legs burned and his shoulder throbbed.

They reached the side of the ship, which was leaning at an angle in the sand. Liam climbed into the doorway and pulled Phoebe up. JEFF lifted each of their parents and Liam dragged them one at a time into the main cabin.

Wind blasted through the airlock. Once they were all in, Liam slammed the doors shut. He glanced out the window. The sky had turned green, the air dancing with shimmering curtains. Gusts rattled the ship.

"Are we shielded in here without power?" Liam asked.

"The hull of the ship and your pressure suits will be enough protection for one storm," said JEFF.

"How about for a few storms?" Phoebe asked.

"That would not be advisable," said JEFF.

"Can the ship fly?" Liam asked.

"It appears so," said JEFF. "I have a few more circuits to repair, but then I believe we can reboot all the systems. We need to attend to your parents first."

They carried their parents into one of the two back rooms, where JEFF had lowered four stasis pods from the wall. Dad was already in one. The pods were long black cylinders with oval windows in the top. Each had its own independent battery system, in case of a ship power failure. Dad's pod glowed a mellow amber inside. He was in his black thermals, his eyes closed. There were long red burns on his cheeks.

"When we take off their pressure suits, we will have to move quickly," said JEFF. "There is no oxygen or pressure in here, so we need to move them into the pods immediately."

"What about the fluid lines and the muscle stimulators?" Liam asked.

"I suggest we wait to administer those until we

have restarted the ship. For the moment, we can just put them safely into the pods. I can activate the initial stages of stasis without those features."

They gathered around Ariana first. Phoebe knelt by her legs.

"JEFF should probably help lift her," said Liam, "since your leg—"

"It's feeling better," said Phoebe. "And I want to do it."

"We will lift on three," said JEFF, standing by the control panel at the back of the pod. "One, two . . ."

They unzipped Ariana's pressure suit, tugged it off of her as fast as possible, and then hoisted her into the pod, Phoebe wincing as they did. The pod top closed with a hiss and the amber lights lit around the inside.

"Is she okay?" Phoebe asked, watching her mom's face.

"Yes," said JEFF, tapping the panel. "Pressure, temperature, and oxygen levels are normal."

They did the same for Paolo, and for Liam's mom, and then stood back, breathing hard.

JEFF gathered their pressure suits, hung them up, and plugged them in, and then returned to the cockpit, but Liam and Phoebe stayed, gazing at their still parents.

Liam realized he was trembling. He didn't know

241

if it was from exhaustion, the leftover effects of the time stream, or anxiety about their current predicament. Maybe all of the above. His throat started to feel tight, his eyes hot. Or maybe it was actually relief. He gazed at his parents' faces; he'd almost lost them. The thought made tears spring from his eyes.

"I don't know what I would have done if they died," said Phoebe. Liam saw tears on her cheeks too.

"Me neither," said Liam.

Phoebe breathed deep. "What happened down in the lab?"

"The canaries were broken and I ran out of time. My dad and your parents were unconscious. My mom was awake for a second though, and . . ." Liam paused.

"What?" said Phoebe.

Mom's words still echoed in his head: *Don't tell anyone.* And his suspicions down in the cavern . . . He glanced at Phoebe's parents.

"Liam . . ."

Liam shook his head. He looked at Phoebe's wide sad eyes. She was his friend and the only person he had right now. And besides, Mom had been injured and out of it down there. She'd been asking him to leave her behind. . . . Who knew how accurate anything was that she'd said?

"Mom thought that somebody sabotaged the turbines," said Liam.

"Sabotaged?" said Phoebe. "But why?"

"I don't know—she didn't say. But I guess the last trial they ran worked." Liam stepped to his mom's pressure suit, unzipped the front pocket, and held out the tiny silver data key. "She said we have to get this to the starliner, either to Wesley or to the secretary general. She wanted me to leave them all behind down there and just take this, but . . ."

"You did the right thing," said Phoebe.

Liam turned the key over in his fingers. "I don't understand who would want to destroy the terraforming data."

"People are crazy. There were those Planet Defenders."

"I thought about them. But that was a while ago."

"Yeah." Phoebe shrugged. She looked out the window, toward the distant smoke. "Well, if someone else was down there, we don't have to worry about them anymore."

Liam followed her gaze. "True." When he turned back, she was eyeing him. "What?"

"I was just thinking that right now, you have the terraforming data that will save the human race, and also the alien data that explains what happened to the sun."

Liam laughed. "Yeah." He slipped the data key

into his right pocket, then tapped the bump of the alien crystal in his left. "One in each pocket."

"That makes us kind of the most important people in the galaxy right now," said Phoebe.

"I guess," said Liam. "There's something else. . . ." Liam explained about using the watch, and the metal-suited man who had shown up.

"The Drove?" said Phoebe. "Who are they?"

"I don't know, but this guy was the one who killed that alien we found. Maybe the Drove are the ones blowing up the stars."

Phoebe shook her head and clenched her fists at her sides. "Bastards."

"They could also be behind the sabotage," said Liam. "Like they're trying to wipe out humans or something. Except I asked him that and he acted like he didn't know what I was talking about."

"We have to get out of here," said Phoebe. "Everyone needs to know about this." She started back toward the cockpit.

Before joining her, Liam stepped between his parents' pods. He put his hands on the oval windows. "I love you guys," he said, and a big wave of fear shuddered through him. Stranded on Mars, only hours until either the next solar storm or the frigid nighttime, with the *Scorpius* gone, sabotage, even the Drove . . .

How was he ever going to do this without them?

We'll take it one unknown at a time, his mother had said, only hours ago. That was what he had to do now. Focus.

"Okay . . ." He tapped their pods. "See you guys later."

Liam joined Phoebe and JEFF in the cockpit. The big panda was sitting in the pilot's seat. A thick electrical cord ran from his belly button to a port beneath the main control panel. "Is it working?" Liam asked.

"Yes," said JEFF. "We did not have a replacement for the main data processor, but I am using my own internal processors to run the system. Once we are fully rebooted, I should be able to run the ship and simultaneously rebuild the software architecture, but I will have to do it one packet at a time."

"How long will that take?" Liam asked.

"Many hours," said JEFF, "but I can do that in my backup memory."

"So once the ship is rebooted, then what?"

"Assuming it can fly, I believe our safest course of action is to depart at once. The *Scorpius* will use a low-level engine burn along with its solar sails to get to Saturn Station. When it arrives, it will slow briefly to receive its fuel supply of water and to pick up all remaining colonial personnel. After that, it will use a gravity slingshot around Saturn to increase speed, then make its primary burn to Delphi. The *Scorpius* should arrive at Saturn in approximately thirty-eight hours. Once we've left Mars, at our max speed, we can reach Saturn a little bit faster: in about thirty-five hours. They have a head start of about forty-five minutes— Ah, there we are."

All around them, lights began to illuminate. There was a rumble as the life-support systems clicked on, heaters buzzing, air blowing.

"So we have a little over two hours to spare," said Phoebe. "How fast can we get out of here?"

"I will know that momentarily," said JEFF.

"Can we call them?" asked Phoebe.

"We will also know that as soon as the system is back up."

They watched the main console display. Beneath the Cosmic Cruiser logo, a little progress bar steadily filled to green. As soon as the main menu appeared, JEFF brought up a holoscreen and accessed the ship's system reports.

Lights flashed to green on Liam's link, indicating that air pressure, oxygen, and temperature levels were normal. He and Phoebe pulled off their helmets and breathed deep. Phoebe coughed, then left the cabin. She returned with her atmo pack.

"It appears our long-range antenna was torn off in

the crash," said JEFF. "But if we can get close enough to the *Scorpius*, we might be able to hail them over the link."

"How close?" asked Liam.

"Within ten kilometers or so," said JEFF, "but we should show up on their radar before that."

"But if they're not looking for us, they might not even notice us," said Phoebe.

"They will," said Liam. "Mina knows we're alive. I told her with this." He showed them the beacon. "She'll get the *Scorpius* to keep an eye out for us, even wait for us."

"Acknowledged," said JEFF. "That would be ideal. I would caution, however, that the *Scorpius* has one hundred million lives to protect, and a limited amount of fuel."

"What if they won't wait?" said Phoebe. "Can we get to Delphi in this?"

"In theory it would be possible," said JEFF. "But while our top speed can beat the *Scorpius* to Saturn, it's less than twenty percent of what their maximum speed to Delphi will be. Plus, this engine was only designed with fuel stores for trips within the solar system. We would need to make frequent refueling stops."

"So how long would it take us to get to Delphi?" Liam asked.

JEFF's eyes flashed. "My rough calculation is twenty-five years."

"Is that a joke?" said Liam.

"I am not sure. Is math humorous?"

"Twenty-five . . ." Phoebe trailed off.

"They'll wait," said Liam. "I know it."

"The good news," said JEFF, "is that while many of our electrical systems shorted out, we sustained minimal structural damage. It looks like most systems on board are working, but I will need to run diagnostic tests to be sure. We can't risk trying to launch out of the atmosphere until we know the ship can take it."

"How long for those tests?" asked Liam.

"One hour."

"Anything can we do?" asked Phoebe.

JEFF flipped through holoscreens. "Please finish digging out the skim drone, and be sure that the Cruiser's starboard thruster and wing are clear of sand as well."

"Got it." Liam started toward the hatch. He heard Phoebe behind him and turned—

"Okay, before you say it, just listen," said Phoebe. "From now on, every time you think to ask me whether I'm up for something, or say that I should rest my injured leg, don't."

Liam smiled. "Understood."

They climbed outside, each with a shovel, and

trudged back to the skim drone. The sun hung low in the afternoon sky, fattened even more by the horizon. The solar storm still raged beyond Olympus Mons. Smoke still poured out of its injured side.

They sank their shovels into the heap of sand covering the right side of the skim drone. Dust whorls gusted by them as they worked. Neither of them spoke.

The temperature fell, the shadows growing long. Liam gazed around at the rock cliffs and mountains, the yawning washes of sand. He shivered. Mars felt lonely in a way it never had before. Not only were they the only living things here except for the cockroaches and a few microbes, they were the only living things for millions of kilometers.

"I think that's it," said Liam after twenty minutes of digging. The top of the drone was clear, and they'd dug sand out from beneath most of the craft's edge. He started back toward the cruiser but didn't hear Phoebe. He turned and saw her staring back at the volcano and smoke. "Hey," he called. She eased herself down onto one knee and started gathering small rocks. Liam walked over to her. "What are you doing?"

"Making memorials." She'd started piling rocks into three cairns. "Just because everyone will be gone doesn't mean we shouldn't remember the dead."

"Can I help?"

"You do the other three."

"Other—"

"Marco, Idris, Mara," Phoebe said, pointing at her piles. She counted three more on her fingers: "Wallace, Misha, and Ed."

"Oh man." Liam had totally forgotten about them. He knelt beside Phoebe. "I'll make theirs hamster-sized."

They stacked the piles a meter tall for the humans. They left the hamster ones tiny. When they were finished, they stepped back and surveyed their work. Six cairns, facing the smoking ruins. Phoebe sniffed from fresh tears.

"I wish we could have saved them all," said Liam, "but I think we did everything we could."

"Maybe," said Phoebe. "I don't mean you. Of course you did everything, but while you were down in the caves, I could have at least gotten the hamsters. Saved *someone*."

Liam patted her shoulder. "You saved my dad."

Phoebe nodded. "Yeah."

"The memorial looks really good."

"Thanks."

"We should go work on the wing."

They returned to the Cruiser, cleared the sand, and then climbed back inside.

Liam pulled off his suit and pressed the radio

beacon. He watched it for a few seconds but it didn't blink back.

"Okay," JEFF called from the cockpit. "All systems check out. I believe we are ready to take off. Our timing is fortunate, as another solar storm is rolling in."

Liam and Phoebe joined him in the cockpit and buckled in. The thrusters rumbled to life, and with a jolt, the cruiser lifted out of the sand.

"The only system that is offline is the landing gear," said JEFF. "Our landing in the *Scorpius* may be a bit rough."

The cruiser rotated and edged over the skim drone. JEFF lined them up and activated the magnet latch. There was a loud bang on the underside of the ship.

"Skim drone secure," said JEFF. "Please go and make sure the canopy is properly attached."

When Liam returned, they were passing by the blast area and rising steadily. Liam gazed down into the cavernous crater where the canyon and research station had once been. Smoke still poured up from the darkness. He thought of Marco and Idris and Mara. The little hamsters too. He hoped their last moments hadn't hurt too much. The blast had been so strong, maybe it had been over in an instant.

"Hey, look." Phoebe pointed up the mountainside. The silver sphere was lying far in the distance, about halfway down the slope. "We should have built a seventh cairn for that alien." She sighed. "That's seven victims that the Drove need to answer for."

Liam nodded. He glanced at the watch. Still not blinking.

Something flashed out the other side of the cockpit. Liam leaned over and spied the distant geometry of the colony dome, gleaming in burning sunset light. He could just make out the silhouettes of buildings. The gossamer lines of the space elevators flickered now and then, stretching up and out of sight. The place he'd spent his whole life, no longer anyone's home. Someday, it could be an ancient ruin for some other race of beings to find, except . . .

"It's weird enough leaving," said Liam, "but it's even weirder to think that soon, all of this will be gone forever."

"Yeah," Phoebe said quietly.

Liam clenched his jaw and looked back out the window, at the colony, at the red landscape. There was a lump in his throat. "Bye," he said so no one else could hear.

JEFF increased their angle and thrust. The red lands of Mars fell out of sight completely, and now there was only the copper sky, the last high wisps of flint-colored dust clouds, the last gusts of thin, frigid air bucking and rattling the ship. A moment of lavender . . .

And then black.

The engines went silent. The wind ceased.

Gravity fell away. Liam unbuckled, grabbed a handle on the wall, and floated away from his seat.

"Huh," said Phoebe, doing the same. She kicked her feet up, floated sideways, and smiled. "It's been years since I was off planet."

"The only other time for me was a field trip up and down the space elevators back in Year Eight," said Liam.

Phoebe spun onto her back, looking out the top of the cockpit. "It's awesome."

"Yeah," said Liam. Stars in all directions, brighter than he'd ever seen them . . .

"I'm going to orbit Mars to generate more velocity," said JEFF.

Liam watched the orange-and-red planet slide by below. They passed over abandoned colonies, like coins lying in the sand. Much closer: the hulking skeletons of the many space docks. They rounded the dark side . . . then there was the sun again, enormous and orange, but no longer looming above them.

Liam took a deep breath. His heart was pounding, his fingers tingling. "Which way to Saturn?" he asked. This was it, and now that they were going, he felt . . .

Actually he felt ready . . . so ready.

"I'm setting the autopilot now," said JEFF. "But . . ." He pointed to the right. "Roughly that way."

They passed by the space dock above Haishang. Red lights still blinked at its ends.

They passed over Olympus Mons, an anthill on the surface, the smoke not even visible.

"Okay, we are nearing alignment and will need to fire our primary burn. Who would like the honors?"

Liam looked at Phoebe. She raised her eyebrows. "Same time?"

"Definitely."

They placed their index fingers side by side on the console touchscreen, over a red button.

"Initiate burn in three . . . ," said JEFF. "Two . . . one . . . and go."

They pressed the button and held on tight. There was a low rumble within the cabin, and they floated back as the engine ignited and they shot into the dark.

"Come on," Liam said to Phoebe. He pushed himself out of the cockpit, flying hands first through the living quarters and back into the empty room opposite where their parents were. He arrived at a round window on the back of the ship, Phoebe beside him.

"Actually, I'll be right back," said Liam. When he

returned a minute later, he had pulled off his pressure suit. Over his black thermal shirt, he was wearing his official Dust Devils jersey.

Phoebe smiled. "Did I get the right size?"

"Perfect," said Liam, smiling back. "Thanks."

They gazed at Mars, just a little island now in a vast sea of night. It shrank to a marble, then to a dot. The sun went from an angry fireball to just another star.

Traveling at eight thousand kilometers per second, the last humans left the inner solar system forever.

Liam felt that lump in his throat again, because who knew? What came next, where they'd end up, and no matter what it was, it would never be the same. . . .

Phoebe elbowed his shoulder. "I'm starving."

Liam laughed, and his stomach growled. "Me too."

13

They slept tethered to the couch, and JEFF woke them when they were passing Jupiter.

"Is it morning?" said Liam, rubbing his eyes.

"By official *Scorpius* time, it is just after nine a.m."

They floated to the cockpit and gazed at the solar system's king. It was marble sized in the distance, its moons like fireflies. Liam could just make out its red spot. He took a picture with his link.

"I always wanted to go there," he said to Phoebe.

"Me too," she said. "Remember when they were going to build that ice hotel on Ganymede?"

"That sounded so cool," said Liam. "So did

methane ocean voyages on Titan, until the stupid solar storms sped up and everything got canceled. Mina at least went to the asteroid belt once." He watched Jupiter shrink. "Maybe at Aaru there will be cool trips to make. I heard it has a sister planet that's split in two or something."

"Three," said Phoebe. "They think it got hit by a comet."

"Sounds pretty neat," said Liam.

"Yeah." She spun around. "I'll be in back."

"How's it going, JEFF?" Liam asked.

JEFF's eyes were flashing on and off. A couple seconds passed before he answered. "The reprogramming is going well. I'm afraid I cannot disconnect until the process is complete. I suggest that you both eat some breakfast."

"Thanks," said Liam. "In a minute." He stayed in the cockpit, looking at Saturn straight ahead, still only a dot, but he could just make out its rings. He had the orange crystal sphere in his hand. He turned it over and over, picturing the man in the time stream. Liam had been thinking of using the watch again, to see if they'd be able to rendezvous with the *Scorpius*, but if he did, the metal-suited man might be there. He'd said something about time anomalies; maybe he could detect every time the watch was being used. Not that Liam was eager to feel like his body was being spun like a dust whorl again anyway.

He wondered why the Drove wanted to blow up stars. Where were they from? And if there were blue-skinned aliens, and the Drove . . . how many more aliens were there? Liam glanced around at the trillions of stars. So many possibilities.

Before they'd slept, he'd put the orange crystal in its square reader again and listened to its message. Then he'd plugged the coordinates it gave into the Cosmic Cruiser's computer. They pointed roughly toward the Helix Nebula, which was almost seven hundred light-years away. That made the trip to Aaru look like a walk to your neighbor's apartment. What chance did humans stand against such power, and such distances? And that didn't even count the fact that someone else was trying to destroy the Phase Two project, which they needed for the only planet they actually could reach.

Liam pressed the beacon again. He counted. One . . . two . . . It blinked back five seconds later. Before he'd slept, the gap had been eight. Radio waves traveled at the speed of light, and the delay was due to distance. Assuming Mina had been pressing her button the moment she saw it blink, they were catching up to the *Scorpius*.

He left the cockpit and floated back to their

parents' room. He found Phoebe between her parents' pods, talking quietly. She turned as he braced himself on the doorway to slow down.

"Didn't mean to barge in," said Liam.

"That's okay," said Phoebe. "I was just telling them about everything that's happened. I mean, I know they can't actually hear me, but . . ."

"I get it." Liam floated in and checked on his parents for probably the tenth time. They looked the same: still and peaceful. The only change was that JEFF had attached a fluid line to their right arms through a small flap in their thermal-wear sleeve, and wires to their wrist and ankle cuffs, which powered the thermal wear's muscle-stimulating fibers. "Hey guys," he said quietly. "We're doing good. We'll be with Mina soon and get you both fixed up." He tapped the windows on their pods and pushed back toward the doorway. "Want some food?"

"Yeah. Be right there," said Phoebe.

Liam returned to the living area. He looked through the food supplies, all pretty boring, and picked two "island"-flavored nutri-meals. He removed their foil wrappers and placed the clear, covered bowls in the oven. He heated them for a few seconds and pulled them out, steaming hot. A salty, tangy smell wafted from the bowls. Liam opened the drawer and got out two forks and buckled himself into the couch. Phoebe joined him. The bowls had a rubber flap in the side where you stuck your fork to grab the brown cubes of food floating around inside.

They ate and then played hours of *Roid Wraiths*, soaring through the asteroid belt in single-flyer suits and battling demons. At one point, after getting burned alive by some sort of sun mutant, Liam pressed the radio beacon. Mina's reply came in four seconds. Closer . . .

After the game, they started watching season four of *Raiders of the Lost Planet*.

Liam pressed the beacon. Three seconds.

At some point in the sixth episode, he dozed off.

"Hey." He opened his eyes to find Phoebe shaking him awake. "You can see it."

Liam followed her to the cockpit. His insides hummed with nervous energy. Saturn had grown to fill half the window, its stripes and wide rings of dust and ice even more stunning than he'd imagined. Closer, in a hazy ring far beyond the planet, was a brilliant white dot.

"That's Enceladus," said JEFF, pointing to the dot, "and there"—he pointed to a small blinking light between them and the icy moon—"is the *Scorpius*."

Liam's heart raced. He pressed the beacon again. The response was nearly instantaneous.

"Tracking indicates that they've begun their slowdown to intercept with Saturn Station," said JEFF. "We will be catching up to them faster every second."

"When are we going to start slowing down?" Liam asked.

"In just another moment," said JEFF.

"And how soon can we call them?"

"We should be in maximum link range in twenty minutes."

They sat and watched in silence. Enceladus became brighter, and you could begin to see the gridwork of metal surrounding it. Meanwhile, Saturn grew and grew, until it towered above and below their cockpit window, even though they were still a million kilometers away.

JEFF began firing the retrorockets in short bursts, once a minute.

"Look, there are the solar sails," said Phoebe. She traced her finger on the cockpit window along the golden corona around the *Scorpius*.

"Five more minutes," said JEFF.

Liam tried to calm his breathing.

Enceladus was as big as a dinner plate now. Liam could see the central space station and docking area facing them. Far in the distance, they'd spotted the gleaming gold casino among the rings.

And the *Scorpius*! They could see its six cylindrical cores, each nearly twenty kilometers long, the blue glow from its six egg-shaped engines, the shimmer of those massive solar sails, the bursts of its retrorockets as it slowed.

Liam pressed the beacon again and it blinked back right away. *Almost there, Mina. . . .*

He wondered if she was on the bridge. Was she with Shawn and Wesley? Were they already in the landing bay waiting for them?

"We're nearly in range," said JEFF. He motioned again to the cable running from his stomach to the console. "I am using my own internal transmitter to boost the signal."

Phoebe's link flashed on her arm. A white light.

"Are you getting a message?" asked Liam.

"I don't know what it is," said Phoebe. She hunched over her wrist, her hair falling around her face. "It's been acting weird since it got fried in the crash."

"But maybe it's from the *Scorpius*."

Phoebe nodded and tapped at it. "I guess it could be." She huffed and kept fiddling with it.

"Okay, I am going to attempt to hail them now," said JEFF. "*Starliner Scorpius*, this is Cosmic Cruiser Delta Four Five from the Phase Two Research Station, come in."

They sat frozen, staring at the console display where words blinked: *Message sending. . . .*

JEFF tapped the retrorockets again. "I'll resend." He repeated the message.

Liam looked at the *Scorpius*. It had slowed further, coming right up beside Enceladus. Lights blinked in a line, a procession of ships leaving the Saturn Station docks for the starliner. Large water tankers, supply ships, personnel transports. *Come on. . . .*

Liam checked his own link. He still wasn't connected to any network. He checked the console again. *Transmission sending. . . .*

They were so close! But if the *Scorpius* finished loading those ships before they made contact . . .

"And again," said JEFF, pressing the send button. "*Starliner Scorpius,* this is Cosmic—"

"Cosmic Cruiser Delta Four Five, this is *Scorpius* command, can you hear us, over?"

"Yes!" Liam shouted, thrusting his fist. He punched the seat, a wide grin on his face. He and Phoebe slapped hands.

JEFF motioned to Liam. "Go ahead." He pressed the send button.

"*Scorpius!*" said Liam, his voice shaking. "This is Liam Saunders-Chang! We're alive and so are our parents and JEFF. . . ." He couldn't stop laughing as he talked. "Our parents are injured from the explosion on Mars but we have them in stasis pods and—"

"Liam!" Her voice maxed out the speakers in the cabin.

"Mina!"

"You made it! We knew you were coming, we've been calculating your distance using the beacon signals."

"Yeah! We lost our long-range antenna. Mom and Dad are hurt; they're in stasis, but they're alive, and we're okay, and we have the final data from the station!" The words came out of his mouth in a rush. But whatever, they'd made it, and relief was flooding through him.

"Just get over here!" Mina said.

"We're coming!"

"Cosmic Cruiser," said the *Scorpius* officer, "please proceed to landing bay six. We are transmitting a course vector now for your autopilot."

"Acknowledged," said JEFF. "Please be advised our landing gear was damaged, so we may be coming in a little hard."

"That's all right, Cosmic Cruiser. We will have personnel standing by."

"Liam, it's Wesley. You guys are just in the nick of time. What happened down there? You say you have the final data?"

"It's a long story," said Liam. "I don't even know where to start—"

"Liam." Phoebe's face had gotten serious. She nodded to his wrist.

The alien watch had started blinking.

"Um . . . ," he said.

Now faster.

"That's okay, Liam. You can tell us all about it when you get here."

Liam looked out the cockpit, up and down in space around them. At the giant face of Saturn. "JEFF, go as fast as you can."

"Acknowledged, Liam, although we have to be cautious on our landing approach."

He turned to Phoebe. "Do you see anything?"

She shook her head.

Liam hit the link send. "*Starliner Scorpius*, is, um . . . is everything all right there?"

"Yes," said Wesley. "We're fine here. What do you mean?"

"I'm not sure." Liam gazed at the blinking watch, then out into space again. "We just, um, we were worried, because back at the research station, my mom said that the turbines had been sabotaged."

"Sabotaged?" Wesley repeated. "By whom?"

"She didn't say—"

A deafening whine howled out of the speakers.

Liam clapped his hands over his ears. "What's that?" he shouted.

JEFF tapped the console and the speakers muted. "Some kind of electromagnetic interference. Our communications have been jammed."

Light flashed outside the cockpit. A geyser of fire and debris burst from a hangar at Saturn Station. Then more and more explosions, and all at once, Saturn Station tore apart in fiery bursts, its wreckage flying in all directions.

"No!" said Liam.

One by one the ships flying toward the *Scorpius* were pulverized by the blast, exploding in quick gasps of flame, blown into a million pieces. The water tankers shattered into sprays of ice.

"Get out of there!" Liam shouted uselessly at the *Scorpius*.

A hundred thrusters fired on the near side of the *Scorpius* and it hurtled sideways, but not fast enough. The wave of debris from the explosion slammed into it, tearing the solar sails and sending the ship rolling through space.

"We need to go," said Phoebe quietly.

"No no no," said Liam. He hit the link send. "*Scorpius*! Are you all right? Mina! Wesley! Can anyone hear—"

There was a loud clang, like something hitting the hull of the ship.

A teeth-chattering buzz . . .

All the lights went out in the cabin. The holo-screen winked out. The console went dark. The ship's systems coughed down to silence.

"What happened?" said Liam.

"It appears we—" There was a bright flash from JEFF's eyes and he slumped over.

"JEFF!" Liam hit his shoulder. Nothing.

He looked back out the window. Saturn Station was just a floating field of wreckage, its last pockets of oxygen bursting into flame here and there. The *Scorpius* was apparently okay; it fired rockets on all sides, slowing the roll and stabilizing itself. But part of the front array was popping with bursts of fire.

"Wake up!" Liam hit JEFF again, then he slapped at the controls, at the power button. Nothing.

Except the watch, blinking madly. And his link. It still glowed. Liam tapped to the transmission screen—

A brilliant flash of blue from outside. The *Scorpius*'s fusion engines burning full-on. The ship leaped forward, hurtling away from them.

"Wait!" Liam shouted. He jabbed at his link, looking for the *Scorpius*, but it was already out of range. Phoebe still appeared in the local link.

As well as another name, below hers: *Simon Onatu*.

Small bits of shrapnel from the explosion reached them, peppering the cruiser.

"This is bad," said Phoebe. Her eyes tracked up toward the top of the cockpit just as a shadow fell over her face.

Liam looked up. Something was slipping above them, a dark silhouette blocking out Saturn.

A spaceship. Right on top of them.

14

Liam and Phoebe stood frozen in place, staring out the cockpit, as the sleek spacecraft fired retrorockets and aligned itself directly above them. Liam recognized the model: a Moon Racer IV.

"They must have overridden our systems," Phoebe whispered.

"Who are they?" said Liam. But he glanced at the wreckage of Saturn Station and remembered his mom's warning. "The people who destroyed the turbines."

"They—" Phoebe doubled over coughing.

Liam shivered. The air was getting colder and thinner by the second. "We need to get into our pressure suits," he said.

They hurried to the back of the ship, flinging themselves from room to room. Their suits were plugged in, charging, and as Liam pulled his off its hanger, he worried that it would be as dead as the rest of the ship. The charging docks were indeed dark, but when Liam unplugged the cable and inserted his link, the suit's systems activated. The suit made his Dust Devils jersey bunch up but he kept it on, and he slipped the alien watch over the outside of the cuff. He pulled the helmet on, but before he zipped the suit fully closed, he pressed the beacon.

No response. Liam pulled the beacon over his head and zipped it into a tiny pocket on the chest of his suit. He finished putting on his helmet and leaned against the back window. He could just see the *Scorpius*, already tiny and distant, its engines glowing. Of course they were running. They'd just been nearly destroyed and they had no idea by whom, and they had all those people to protect. "They're going around Saturn," said Liam through his speaker. "We've still got time before they leave."

Something banged against the side of the cruiser's hull, and a metallic grinding sound vibrated the whole ship.

"It's coming from the door," Phoebe whispered, her eyes wide.

Liam swallowed hard. "Let's go look."

They floated back to the living area and carefully pulled themselves toward the airlock, pausing just to the side of its small window.

"You go," said Phoebe.

Liam met her gaze. "Okay." The watch was still blinking rapidly. He held his breath, grabbed the door frame, and peered through.

The grinding sound ceased. The outer door popped open a few centimeters. Thick gloved hands grabbed it and wrenched it the rest of the way. A man floated into the airlock, wearing a blue, space-grade pressure suit with lights on both shoulders, and holding a large device that Liam thought was a magnet drill. He had dark eyes and a dark beard. He looked at Liam, held up his wrist, and motioned to his link.

Liam backed away from the window. "He wants to talk to me."

"Don't do it."

Liam shrugged and swallowed hard. "What are we supposed to do? We can't restart the ship. We've got nowhere to go." Liam tapped his settings and found the local link. He selected the second name there: Simon Onatu.

"Liam, don't—" said Phoebe.

Liam connected. "What do you want?" He glared out the window.

"Nice to meet you too," said the man. "Hey, open

up this door, okay? You'll save me a lot of time."

Liam felt frozen in place, his heart pounding up into his throat. "No," he said.

"Come on, be a sport. I'm just going to open it anyway." The man held up the drill. "Hey, where are all the adults? They were injured, weren't they, back on Mars? Or maybe they're all dead?"

"They're not dead," said Liam.

"But if they were okay they'd be at this door instead of you," said the man. "Which means it's just you and the girl. Where is she? Let me talk to her."

Liam looked over at Phoebe. She shook her head.

"Kid, look . . ." The man glanced back over his shoulder. "We don't have a ton of time here. We've got a starliner to deal with. All we really want from you is the final data for Phase Two."

Liam's mouth felt dry. These *were* the saboteurs. His pulse raced as he tried to think of something to say.

"Look, I know the data survived, and I can tell by your face that you know where it is. That actually makes things easier. Thought I might have to kill you and then search your parents for the data. I mean, kill them too. But if you have it, you could just give it to me, and then we'll be on our way."

"You're lying," Phoebe said. She'd joined the local link.

"Ah, there she is."

Phoebe pulled herself over so she could see through the window.

The man's eyes flashed at her and he smiled.

"Hello there—"

"Phoebe," she said. "But your name's not Simon, is it?"

"Obviously not," said the man. He eyed the two of them. "Over on the space station, while my associate and I were planting those explosives, I was Corporal Reynolds. My real name is Barro. But do you really want to go by *real* names?"

"Stop it; you're a liar," said Phoebe. "You'll kill him if he tries to give you the data. Just like you killed all those people at Saturn Station. But you don't have to."

"Come on, *Phoebe*," said Barro. "Of course we do. This is all part of our big plan. I'm not exactly sure what went wrong back on Mars, but here we are, and you have the data so all's well that ends well."

"And how does it end?" Phoebe asked.

"You know how it ends," said Barro. "Now let's stop playing games and—"

"We're not your enemy," said Phoebe. "We all need each other. There's a bigger threat. We've seen it."

Barro's eyes sparked with interest. "What threat is that?"

Phoebe glanced at Liam, and nodded toward Barro. "Tell him."

"About the Drove?"

"The who?"

Liam breathed deep. He checked the watch. Still blinking fast. This didn't seem to be helping, but at least Barro was listening instead of drilling open the door.

"They're the ones who blew up the sun," said Liam. "Or started it going nova. And they've done it to other stars, too. All over the galaxy, maybe even the universe. They can travel through time, I think."

"They're the real enemy," said Phoebe. "If it wasn't for them, we'd all still be living peacefully on Earth, and the colonies and the starliners, all of it, would never have happened."

"Wouldn't have happened *yet*, you mean," said Barro. He glanced away like he was in thought. "It does change some things, I suppose. I can see why you'd want to tell me." But when he looked back through the window, his gaze had grown cold. "But it cannot change what the humans have done." Barro looked directly at Liam. "It cannot undo Phase One."

"What are you talking about?" said Liam.

Barro shook his head. He closed his eyes for a moment and seemed to say something to himself.

"Who are you guys?" Liam asked. "Why are you

trying to kill your own people?"

Barro's eyes opened. "I'm here for the data." He looked from Liam to Phoebe. "They *will* be counted."

"What?" said Liam.

Phoebe yanked him away from the door.

A motor whined and the airlock door began to vibrate from Barro's drill.

Phoebe switched from the link to her speaker. "We have to get out of here."

Liam's head felt crowded, his gut doing backflips with nervous energy. "What was he talking about with Phase One and counting?"

"Who knows?" said Phoebe. "He's crazy, and we can't let him have the data. What are we going to do?"

Liam looked around the dark ship. His gaze fell on their parents' glowing stasis pods. If only they could wake them up. He glanced at the ceiling. "As long as they're attached to us," he said, "they're overriding all our systems. We have to get them off us to restart the ship."

"Okay, so how do we do that?"

The vibrating rattled Liam's teeth. He had to think! Somehow through the noise and his pounding heart and quick breaths . . .

"Maybe," he said, "we give them what they want."

"Liam, we can't!"

"No, I know, but . . . come with me."

Liam pushed himself to the back of the ship. He unlocked the hatch that led to the skim drone.

"Isn't the drone shut down too?" Phoebe asked.

Liam lowered himself through the hatch. "Yeah, but there's a manual release. If I got in the drone, you could release me. Our pressure suits worked once they were disconnected from the cruiser's systems. Same thing should happen with the drone. Then I could take the data and run, and they could follow me."

"But then what? They catch you and kill you?"

Liam looked up at her. "I don't know what they'd do." With a deep breath, he tapped the alien watch. "But this does."

Phoebe eyes grew wide. "What about the Drove? Won't they come after you again?"

A loud grinding whine joined the vibrating from the airlock door.

"I don't know," said Liam, "but they're not here now, and *he* is."

Phoebe bit her lip and nodded. "What do I do?"

"Restart the ship the minute they come after me. Then head for the *Scorpius* and get our parents to safety. I'll meet you there. Tell them to wait for me. And if I don't make it . . ." He reached into his pocket and handed Phoebe the orange crystal sphere. "Get this to someone who can figure it all out."

"But we can't let them have the data. Leave that with me, too."

Liam shrugged. "If he figures out that I'm bluffing, he won't take the bait. We can't risk it. The information about the Drove is more important, anyway."

"What if he doesn't follow you?"

"Then I'll head for the *Scorpius* and we'll come back for you."

Phoebe nodded. "And if they do come after you . . . what are you going to do?"

Liam took a deep breath. "Try not to die."

He climbed down the tunnel to the canopy, pulled the manual latches on its sides, and lowered himself into the drone. He locked the canopy and then motioned to Phoebe. She tapped her link.

"Good luck," she said in his ear.

"Thanks."

Phoebe closed the hatch. A moment later, there was a metallic click and a hiss. The skim drone popped free of the underside of the cruiser and floated beneath it.

Liam sat in the cold and dark and counted down from ten. It only now occurred to him that if the power didn't work, he was going to freeze to death in a matter of minutes. Maybe that was why the watch was blinking. There were so many possibilities when it came to how the future might go wrong.

The drone bounced against the underside of the ship. Liam pressed the power button. *Please work.* . . .

The skim drone hummed to life, lights flashing, vents and heaters blasting, thruster glowing.

Liam gazed around. The *Scorpius* was gone, on the far side of Saturn by now. The station wreckage around Enceladus was twisted and dark. Saturn was so massive, arcing above and below him. Its brilliant rings reaching out . . . Liam tapped the main control screen for a map. He spread his fingers, drawing a line on the screen, calculating the distance to the rings. How fast could this drone even go in the vacuum of space? And how did it maneuver? Another thing he'd have to learn while he did it.

He fired the lateral thrusters and slid out from beneath the cruiser. He saw the Moon Racer in profile: such an awesome ship. And so fast. He and Shawn had been to the showroom in the VirtCom, though this one had different-looking engines on the back than the standard design.

Liam almost just fired the main engine and shot off, but then he had another idea. He raised the drone alongside the cruiser and edged forward until he was right outside the airlock door. There was the man called Barro, standing at the door, drill at his side. Phoebe was on the other side of the airlock window. She must have been trying to stall him. Her helmet tilted up as she spotted the drone.

Liam checked the environmental controls. Air and heat were good. He pulled off his glove and fished the data key out of his pocket. Then he tapped his link and connected.

"Hey, jerk," he said.

Barro turned.

Liam held up the key so that it glinted in Barro's lights. "I've got the data right here. If you want it, come and get it."

"Kid," said Barro, "I really admire your nerve, but that is a terrible idea."

"Well, I'm not letting you hurt my family and friends. So . . . yeah."

Liam tucked the data key in his chest pocket, then fired the side thrusters and slid away from the door. He rotated and faced the distant plains of Saturn's rings, aiming at the stark black line where the planet's shadow plunged the rings into pitch black. Then he burned the main engine at full power. The ship leaped forward, shoving Liam back against his seat.

He watched the battery meter, and cut the burn when it reached 75 percent remaining. He set the ship's controls to maintain course, heading straight toward the rings and the shadow line. The damaged stabilizer still made the ship shudder, but less so in the vacuum of space.

Liam checked behind him. A few seconds later, a light flashed. The Moon Racer was in pursuit and gaining fast.

Now it was time to find out how he was going to die.

Liam locked the controls into position, put his gloved fingers on the alien watch dial, and clicked it one notch forward. His stomach lurched, his heart hammered, his mind stretched and ached, and the world blurred around him.

Saturn's rings raced toward him. Chunks of ice, from the size of apartment buildings down to single crystals. In the future, the skim drone would make it over the edge of the rings and glide across their surface. Lights would start flashing on the console. Proximity alerts. Liam looked back. Two silver projectiles closing fast. The Moon Racer would fire its debris pulses, small explosives for defending against asteroids or other objects along your flight path.

Liam would swerve, and again, and then—
Impact.

The skim drone would be thrown by the blast, pressure lost, engines erupting, the canopy cracking. A flash of fire . . . and then space. Its wreckage would slam into a giant ice boulder the size of a cruiser that was half in and half out of Saturn's pitch-black shadow. Liam would be thrown free, floating in the black, his body bouncing off the ice, pain and the deathly cold of space seeping in. . . .

The Moon Racer would lower over him. Barro would float down on a tether. He would reach Liam and, with a flash of steel, slice his pressure suit open.

Liam watched it all from the weird blur, there but not. His own future eyes clouding over with ice, his skin cracking, his cells freezing, bursting. . . . Saw Barro cut open his chest pocket and remove the data key, saw Mina's beacon flung free in the process. Floating away, blinking green. . . . Barro would return to his ship, leaving Liam's body adrift, bobbing among the shadows and ice.

Something whined in the cockpit, making Liam wince. A sound not from the future but happening here in the time stream. Liam fought to turn and look past the blur, and he saw a strange shimmer in space, happening in his now, not the future, and making his mind ache just to conceive of it. The blur was like liquid, but metallic too. It was another ship, sleek and black, an oily teardrop against the backdrop of Saturn. It raced toward him, rippling, humming. . . .

"Hello again, time traveler!" The voice crackled over Liam's link. That same voice from back in the underground lab.

The man in the metal suit. The Drove.

There was another flash in the future. An explosion

in the distance, and an arc of burning rockets. Had the Moon Racer just destroyed the Cosmic Cruiser?

"Here you are again!" said the metal-suited man. "This is becoming very intriguing. Ready to come with us now?"

Liam reached for the alien watch, steadying his finger.

The liquid-black ship hurtled closer.

His future corpse disappeared into the rings.

All of it tore at his mind. . . .

"Not now!" Liam said to the Drove, wincing. "Sorry."

He pressed the blinking button in the right semicircle of the watch, and his body screamed in a white-hot blur of pain. Everything stretched and then rubber-banded and he was back inside himself, alive, in the skim drone. He clenched his stomach, fighting nausea. His eyes watered. He checked out the side window. No black ship coming toward him. Ahead, he was just passing over the outer rim of the rings. And behind . . .

The Moon Racer was closing fast. Two flashes of light, and the debris pulses hurtled toward him.

Liam scanned the fields of ice and dust ahead. He tried to remember what he'd seen with the watch, how far he'd made it before he was blown up. There, that giant ice boulder, where his wreckage hit. He figured he had ten seconds, at best, before those pulses caught up with him.

He neared the edge of Saturn's shadow. On one side, millions of ice chunks glittering; on the other, a void.

A proximity alert flashed. The debris pulses were closing in.

The watch was blinking faster than ever. Seconds before impact. Liam tapped the control panel. Increased energy to the forward and topside thrusters. He scanned the sea of ice chunks below—there. A gap just big enough that it might work. He could only guess at the exact angle he'd need to take. A hundred meters from the giant boulder . . .

Now! He burned the topside thrusters at maximum. The skim drone arced steeply downward, slamming Liam against his restraints. He dropped straight into the rings, threading between two large boulders and crashing into a hundred smaller ones that crackled against the hull.

The debris pulses raced overhead and struck the giant boulder, detonating in a spray of ice and dust.

Liam's fingers danced between thrusters, the craft zigzagging through the rings. Left, then right, clipping a larger one, ice smashing against the canopy and threatening to crack it open. He banked, slowed, barely slid beneath a long flat ice chunk the size of the cruiser, and nicked a jagged spear that could have impaled him. He dived again, sliding just between two more boulders bigger than the skim drone—

And he was through! On the underside of the rings.

Liam brought the drone to a halt and edged into the inky darkness of Saturn's shadow. He spun around and shut down the entire craft. As it powered down, he turned off his headlamp and cupped his hand over the watch. It was still blinking, slower than before, but not exactly slow.

The skim drone drifted silent and invisible in the shadow. Liam sat still, trying to calm his breathing. The Moon Racer arrived above the rings and slowed. Its underside lights flicked on and scanned the debris from the blast, refracting off the millions of ice chunks and crystals. No doubt they'd use infrared too. Liam hoped the rings offered enough interference, that the ship's thrusters cooled off fast enough, and that his body was a small enough heat signature not to be detected.

A light in the corner of his eye. Liam twisted and gazed out across the underside of the rings. Far off, not much bigger than a star from here, but moving fast: the *Scorpius*, coming around the far side of

Saturn. Once it broke free of its orbit, it would do a full burn and there would be no way of catching it.

Liam tugged the beacon from his pocket and pressed it. It blinked right back.

Above, the Moon Racer skimmed past but then reversed. He couldn't just sit here. But if he bolted for the *Scorpius*, he'd never beat the Moon Racer. And he didn't have any weapons, or even debris pulses.

A chunk of ice from the bottom of the rings thunked on the top of the drone's canopy. Liam looked up at the field of ice. Maybe . . .

The Moon Racer tracked away from him again, lights still searching. As it passed around the far side of the giant ice boulder, Liam powered on the skim drone and it hummed back to life. With two short bursts, he moved until he was beneath the giant boulder. Lights flashed. The Moon Racer was turning around, coming back his way.

Liam flipped the skim drone over, moving the underside toward the boulder. He opened the claw and grabbed onto the underside of the huge piece of ice, angling himself little by little, trying not to move the boulder except to rotate it.

He glanced over his shoulder; the *Scorpius* was streaking free of Saturn. Was Phoebe on her way there yet? He hoped so.

The Moon Racer closed. Liam flexed his fingers

on the controls. It was right on the other side of the boulder now, the skim drone still in the shadow. Now! He slammed the topside thrusters. Detached the claw, reversed thrust . . . the great boulder sailed away from him.

The Moon Racer's lateral thruster fired, slowing, turning . . . not quite enough. The boulder raked against the underside of its hull and sent the ship careening for a moment, but then it righted and spun back around. Its lights speared through the rings, illuminating the skim drone.

"Sorry, kid," Barro said over his link. "It was a nice try."

"Just let us go!" Liam shouted.

"Can't do that. They must be counted."

Liam started to turn, but there was no time to run. . . .

Two streaks of light lit up the black of space. Debris pulses. They hit the Moon Racer right in the side. There was a flash of fire and a spray of shrapnel. The Moon Racer was thrown into a spin. It plowed into the rings, dust and debris scattering, its lights going out.

"Liam, are you there?"

"Phoebe!"

There was the Cosmic Cruiser, streaking in over the rings.

"Are you okay?" said Phoebe.

Liam breathed hard. "I am—" He glanced at the *Scorpius*, close enough now for him to see its long body and glowing engines. "You were supposed to go to the starliner!"

"Yeah, I know," said Phoebe. "But that was a dumb plan."

"Thanks," said Liam. But then added, "No, really, thank you."

"Well, don't just sit there," said Phoebe. "We have a starliner to catch!"

"On my way." Liam shot out of the rings. The cruiser turned toward the *Scorpius*. Liam guided the skim drone underneath and activated the automatic landing. The drone fired tiny thruster bursts until it was beneath the hatch, then latched on. Liam opened the canopy. Halfway up the ladder he was thrown against the wall as the cruiser burned its engines full-on. He popped out of the hatch and thrust himself toward the cockpit, pulling off his helmet as he went.

Phoebe turned and smiled as he arrived. Liam almost grabbed her in a hug, but instead they slapped hands.

"That was amazing," said Liam. "I can't believe they didn't see you coming on their radar."

Phoebe shrugged. "They were so preoccupied with you, they didn't notice until it was too late. We're getting pretty good at this escape thing."

"Burning engines on intercept course," JEFF reported.

"JEFF, you're back!" said Liam.

"Yes, when that Moon Racer detached, my auto-recovery systems activated and I was able to restart both myself and the ship."

"I think it's because I kicked you," said Phoebe.

"Impossible," said JEFF. "I am not equipped with touch activation, no matter how forceful— Oh wait, that was humor."

"I did actually kick him," said Phoebe.

The cruiser sped over the rings. Liam looked out the cockpit, craning to see behind them, but he couldn't find the Moon Racer. Ahead, the *Scorpius* glowed gold and blue. Liam watched their progress on a holoscreen map. The cruiser was traveling along a diagonal line that intersected with the starliner's course.

"Are we going to make it?" he asked.

"We will if they maintain their present speed," said JEFF. "According to their original flight plan, they will make their primary engine burn . . ." His finger traced along the starliner's projected flight path. "Here. But I cannot be sure they are still following that plan after the attack."

Liam put the beacon around his neck and pressed it. It blinked back. "They know we're coming," he said. "They have to. How soon can we talk to them?"

"We're closing in on maximum link range again," said JEFF.

Liam watched the lines intersecting on the holoscreen. The two blinking dots getting closer. Out the window, the glimmering *Scorpius*, its long segments, its burning engines, the damaged solar sail, and the black burn marks here and there on the cores.

"Link range in ten . . ."

Phoebe grabbed Liam's hand.

"Eight . . ."

Something popped, a wail of shrieking metal. Liam was thrown into the wall of the cockpit. Phoebe slammed into him.

"What was that?" Liam shouted.

A siren blared, red lights flashing on the controls.

JEFF swiped through various images on the holoscreen. "That rear thruster has malfunctioned again. It's throwing us off course."

"I thought you fixed that on Mars!" said Liam.

"I did, but with limited supplies. I'm shutting it down now, and then we'll course correct."

Phoebe pointed at the holoscreen. "We're going to miss them!"

Their intercept line had adjusted and now crossed the *Scorpius*'s route behind where they would be.

"Thruster disabled," said JEFF.

"Hurry," said Liam. He pressed the beacon again and it blinked back.

"I am restarting, and calculating the course correction—"

A burst of brilliant light lit their faces, making Liam and Phoebe cover their eyes. Liam squinted through his fingers and saw the *Scorpius*'s engines ballooning with light, like small blue suns.

"No!" Liam shouted.

The engines grew brighter and brighter and the great starliner hurtled away from them.

In moments, it was lost among the billions of stars and the dark.

15

"How could they just leave?" Liam held his face in his hands. His tears were drying up. He lifted his head and looked back out the cockpit. "We were right here. . . ."

"I cannot be certain," said JEFF, "but I would theorize that the *Scorpius* could not afford to lose the massive amount of fuel it would take to slow down for us, and they were also extremely worried about the possibility of another attack. When they saw that we were damaged and would not catch them, they made the choice to depart."

"But we'll never catch up," said Liam. He rubbed his hands over his face and through his hair. "What did you say, JEFF? It's going to take us twenty-five years to reach Delphi? At that rate, we won't get to Aaru for *forever*."

"Two hundred and fifty years, approximately," said JEFF.

"That's a hundred years later than the *Scorpius*. Our families will be dead, our friends . . . Mina, Shawn, my grandparents . . ." Fresh tears fell.

Phoebe rubbed Liam's shoulder. "There's got to be something we can do."

"Like what?" said Liam.

"I don't know."

"It's hopeless. We might as well just fly back to Mars, or straight into the sun."

"Stop it," said Phoebe.

"Why?" Liam pushed out of the cockpit.

He sailed to the back room and checked on his parents. Seeing them only made him cry harder. Would they really never see their daughter again? And could they even survive such a long trip in stasis with their injuries? "I'm sorry," he said to their still faces. "I tried, but it didn't work out. I . . ."

A hand patted his back. "It's really not your fault," said Phoebe.

"But it is," said Liam. "How did that Barro guy know to come after us? That was me. I said we had the data when we talked to the *Scorpius*. My mom told me to keep it secret but I got too excited. They must have been listening. They might not even have blown up Saturn Station otherwise. It's all my fault."

"I think they were going to blow up the station no matter what," said Phoebe. "And they showed up so fast; they must have already known that we had the data, and they were waiting for us. It wasn't you, Liam. And we never would have escaped, or even come close to catching the *Scorpius*, if it hadn't been for your plan in the rings. If there's anyone who could have done more, it was me." She turned and left the room.

Liam followed after her, floating into the main cabin. "That's not true. You were great. Coming after them like that, and before when you tried to convince them to leave us alone."

Phoebe sat on the couch and buckled herself down. "It didn't work, though."

Liam sat beside her. He tried to think of something else to say, but couldn't.

"Your necklace thing is blinking," Phoebe said.

Liam held up the beacon. It flashed green again. He pressed it back. It blinked another time, and now another.

"Mina's never going to see us again," said Liam. Had she realized that by now? Was that why she kept pressing it? Was she saying good-bye?

"It almost seems like it's blinking automatically," said Phoebe.

Liam held the beacon in his palm. The blinking did seem kind of regular. Actually, it was getting faster, as if she was pressing it over and over.

Liam squeezed his eyes shut. *I miss you too*, he thought. He pressed it back a couple times. Soon they would be hours apart, the signal delayed. Eventually it would be days, months, years. . . .

A sensor started beeping in the cockpit. "Liam, Phoebe," said JEFF. "Can you come up here, please?"

Liam dropped the beacon around his neck and unbuckled. It was still blinking, almost every second.

"We have something coming our way," said JEFF. He pointed to the holoscreen. A small dot was approaching the square that represented the cruiser.

"Another ship?" said Liam.

"It is too small to be a ship," said JEFF. "I would have first theorized that it was a small asteroid, or a piece of wreckage from Saturn Station, except it is traveling on a course to intercept with us exactly."

"And it's not a debris pulse or a bomb or something?" said Phoebe.

"It is not registering as an explosive device. However, it does have electronic components."

"How long until it gets here?"

"Two minutes," said JEFF.

"And it's heading exactly toward us?"

"To the meter."

Liam glanced down at the beacon. Then at the alien watch, which had stopped flashing. "Can we take a look?"

"If you can take the flight controls," said JEFF, "I can step outside and retrieve it."

"Okay," said Liam.

JEFF rolled out of the cockpit. The object traced closer. Liam turned on the ship's cameras and they watched JEFF step into the airlock. He had affixed a bright light to his chest and a multidirectional rocket pack to his back, which looked like a metal mixing bowl with small nozzles sticking out in different directions. There was a hiss from his joints as internal seals closed tight. He clipped a safety line to a hook on his back and opened the outer door.

Liam switched to an external camera as the big panda floated out into space. JEFF's light illuminated a white equipment box, about a meter across. He adjusted his position and the box thudded into him. He retracted the safety line. Liam and Phoebe met him in the main cabin.

"That was refreshing," said JEFF, as his internal seals opened. A thin layer of ice steamed off his metal surface.

He placed the box on the table. It was made of

space-grade plastic. Its top had a thick rubber seal and locking clips. A small transceiver had been taped to the side, a little antenna sticking out of it with a red light blinking. Across the top, scrawled in black ink, it read:

For Liam.

Liam grabbed at the latches.

"Careful, it's very cold," said JEFF.

Liam's fingers stung, but he twisted the latches open. The box top popped up and Liam threw it back. Inside was a lot of empty space—

And lying on the bottom: a link.

Liam picked it up and turned it on. When the home screen appeared, an icon flashed that had been marked urgent: a video file. Liam pressed it and Mina's face appeared.

"Hey, little brother," she said, smiling, holding the link in one hand and wiping at tears that were making a mess of her eyeliner. Behind Mina, Liam heard sirens and shouting. He saw high ceilings, the tail of a military ship, and a tall rack of skim drones: the hangar of the *Scorpius*. She held up her beacon. "We used this to home in on you. Thanks for ruining my present to Arlo, by the way. You're taking good care of it, right?"

Liam laughed and brushed at tears of his own.

Phoebe leaned against his shoulder to see.

"They say we can't slow down for you . . . I guess it's too dangerous. Even my concert's been postponed." Mina sniffed. "Colonial doesn't know what we're up against. Lots of people are injured and there's some damage, so we're going to run for it. Wesley says I only have a second to make this. . . ." She wiped her eyes again. "So I have to be quick and say I love you! I love you, you little dork, so much, and Mom and Dad, I love you guys too and I miss you and it kills me not knowing where you are or how you're doing or when I'll see you again, but I'm okay."

Liam heard a voice from offscreen. Mina nodded, sniffling, and handed the pad over.

"Hey, guys." Shawn's face appeared.

Phoebe made a little sobbing sound but also smiled.

"I'm so mad at you guys," he said. "Having all that adventure without me, but things are getting pretty serious around here, too. Nobody knows what's going on." He looked over the top of the screen and nodded. Liam heard Wesley calling from somewhere nearby. "Listen, you guys be safe, okay? Don't do anything I wouldn't."

"We already did," said Phoebe, laughing. "Like ten things."

Liam laughed too.

Shawn smiled, almost like he heard them. Then he winked. "Okay, gotta run, um . . ." His smile faded. He glanced at Mina, and then handed the link back over. As he did, there were more flashes of people running this way and that on the deck.

Mina appeared again, fresh tears in her eyes. "So, Wesley says you won't be able to catch us. . . ."

Liam's chest tightened.

"But I told him you'll find a way, and so will we, do you hear me? This is not good-bye forever, just for now." She paused and gave a quiet sob. "We're gonna find a way, even if I have to stay behind at Delphi and wait for you. I don't care. We're all going to be together again. You got that?"

Liam nodded. "Got it."

Mina was nodding too. "I gotta go, but there's one more thing. There's another file on this pad with a code on it. It's called tap code. It's even more retro than these beacons, but it will let us communicate with each other, no matter how far apart we are. In a really slow and boring way, but still. We'll stay in touch with each other, and we'll find a way, I promise. So once you're done watching this, send me a message. Okay, that's it. We'll see you soon." She nodded. "Really soon."

Shawn appeared beside her and did his best to

smile. "See you soon, guys."

Mina lowered the pad into the box. Her eyes overflowed again, and she blew a kiss to the screen, her face trembling.

The video clicked off.

Liam wiped at his eyes and nose. Phoebe rubbed his shoulder. "We'll find a way," he repeated. He returned to the main menu and opened the photo file there. It showed a square grid that organized the letters of the alphabet into numbered rows and columns. Text below said: *First tap the number of the column, then the row. Wait one second in between letters, and two seconds in between words.*

"Okay . . . ," said Liam. He held up the beacon and tapped three times, then two, for an "H," and four times, then two, for an "I."

A few seconds later, the light flashed in return, a series of quick blinks. "H-i," said Liam, glancing between the grid and the beacon, trying to keep up. "B-a—"

"I think she said *Hi back*," said Phoebe.

"Yeah," said Liam. A smile crept across his face. He took a deep breath. "Okay, we can communicate. Now we just need a way to catch a starliner. JEFF, is there any way to make our engine go faster?"

"I'm afraid there isn't," said JEFF. "It just doesn't have the power."

"What about the casino?" said Phoebe. "Maybe someone there could help us."

"From the data available," said JEFF, "Rings of Gold is not considered a safe place for anyone, let alone children."

"We could steal a ship or something," said Phoebe.

"I am afraid I am not authorized to take part in an illegal activity," said JEFF.

"We have to do something!" said Liam. "The longer we sit here, the farther away they get."

Liam imagined arriving at Delphi to find it abandoned and cold. He thought of Aaru, two hundred and fifty years from now, a grave plaque with his sister's name on it . . . but what if humans couldn't live on Aaru without this terraforming data? What if they had to fly on, and ran out of supplies? Someday he might be looking out the window of the Cosmic Cruiser at the *Scorpius*, a hulking corpse in space. Or what if, long before that, they ran into another star going supernova? He should have told them about the Drove, but everything had happened so fast. The starliner could detect a supernova, and he'd only seen the Drove when he was in the time stream anyway. . . .

He gazed out at the stars and the universe felt bigger, and more lonely, more impossible, than ever before.

"Um," said Phoebe. "Would it be stealing if we

were salvaging a ship? Like, one that tried to kill us?"

Liam's heart skipped a beat. "The Moon Racer!"

"I calculate that this could be justified," said JEFF.

"It was damaged by those pulses," said Liam, "but it didn't explode or anything. Maybe its engine is intact? If it is, it's way faster than this ship." He looked at JEFF.

"You are suggesting replacing our engine with theirs," said JEFF. His eyes flashed. "Yes, a standard Moon Racer engine is quite a bit faster, and both it and the Cosmic Cruiser are C-class ships, with similar engine attachment configurations. In theory, it would be possible to swap them, if there is no significant damage."

"Could you do it?" Liam asked.

"I calculate that I could," said JEFF.

"But what about those people?" said Liam. "Barro, and whoever was with him? What if they're still there?"

"If they survived the impact, they would most likely have ejected from the craft by now," said JEFF. "Moon Racers are equipped with a variety of safety features, depending on the model. If they are still on board the craft, it is probable that they are seriously injured or deceased."

"I wasn't trying to kill them," said Phoebe.

"I know," said Liam. "Either way, it's worth going

back and checking it out. If we could just get that engine . . ." He tapped the beacon. Three seconds later it blinked back. They were already so much farther away. . . .

JEFF moved to the pilot seat and fired the thrusters, reversing direction. They flew back toward Saturn's rings. "I am returning to the approximate location of our encounter. I have the scanners on, but it will be difficult to spot the ship among the debris of the rings, and if it is still there, its engines will likely be cold."

"Is there any chance they can still fly it?" Phoebe asked. "That they might be gone? Or still be after us?"

"There is a small chance, yes," said JEFF.

They hurtled through the dark, no one speaking. As they passed over the outer edge of the rings, JEFF fired the reverse thrusters. They slowed to a float, the dark edge of Saturn's shadow a few hundred meters away.

"We are in the vicinity of where we last saw the Moon Racer."

Liam's eyes flicked from the windshield to the console. He couldn't help glancing above them, too, even though he'd seen how damaged the ship had been. . . .

"There it is," said Phoebe quietly. She pointed out the windshield.

Liam scanned the rings, and then he saw it. The back of the Moon Racer down among the ice and dust.

"No significant heat readings," said JEFF, "or signs of electrical activity. But the rings could be interfering." He tapped the thrusters again, slowing the ship to a stop. "It would be very risky to take the Cosmic Cruiser any closer to those boulders. I suggest using the skim drone to retrieve the vessel."

"Can we send it by remote?"

"Those systems need the long-range antenna. I am afraid you'll have to fly manually."

"Great," said Liam. He started zipping up his pressure suit.

"Be careful," said Phoebe.

Liam climbed into the skim drone and detached from the cruiser. He pulsed the thrusters, dropping down close to the rings; then he edged forward toward the Moon Racer. Its engine didn't look damaged, but there were scraps and chunks of metal floating around it. Liam saw a chair spiraling amid the debris, a stasis tube, and a scattering of freeze-dried food packages.

Liam pictured Barro's face. *Are you here?* he wondered, scanning the rings. He also realized that he didn't really know how many others had been aboard the Moon Racer. At least one person had been piloting, but there might have been more.

He passed a gap in the rings, a sliver of space he might be able to fit through. "I'm going to get a look from underneath," Liam said quietly into his link. He pointed the nose down toward the gap and slipped through to the underside of the rings.

He reoriented the drone, breathing hard, his eyes darting around and above him. He couldn't shake the feeling that they were here, somewhere, waiting.

"See anything yet?" Phoebe asked, barely above a whisper.

"No," said Liam. He edged forward, looking for the racer, for any movement. The shadows were too thick; he was going to have to risk turning on the exterior lights. When he flicked them on, metal reflected just above him.

The Moon Racer: a wide, jagged hole in its side, surrounded by twisted and mangled metal. And its front was missing; the ship ended at a flat metal wall with an open doorway. "The cockpit is gone," said Liam. "Like, completely gone."

"They must have had an ejectable cockpit," said JEFF. "A high-end safety feature, but one that would likely be available on a Moon Racer."

Liam exhaled hard, but he still scanned the rocks around him. "Where is it, then?"

"The cabin would have a small rocket for traveling a short distance."

Liam rotated in a slow circle. Something gleamed in the far distance. "Could they make it to the Rings of Gold with that?"

"They would be traveling slowly, but yes, the casino is within range."

"How far could they have gone since we left them?"

"Why are you asking that?" said Phoebe.

Liam's fingers flexed on the controls. He checked the battery life: over three-quarters full. If he chased them down, they wouldn't have to worry about being attacked again. . . .

"Liam, don't," said Phoebe.

But Liam kept peering into the distance.

"I have some very fortunate news," said JEFF. "My diagnostic scans indicate that this Moon Racer is equipped with a peculiar engine. A standard Moon Racer has a class-V thermal cell engine with a three-cycle ceiling; this one appears to be able to achieve a six-cycle burn without overclocking."

Liam shook his head. "What does that even mean?"

"It means this engine is unusually powerful. I can't be sure until we get a closer look, but it's possible that we will be able to catch the starliner at Delphi, or come very close, but we need to get started with the swap immediately."

"Okay." Liam took a last look toward the casino.

How could they be sure Barro and his team wouldn't come after them again? If he saw one little flash of light . . . But there was nothing, and any time they spent looking for the saboteurs was time they weren't using to catch the *Scorpius*.

"Okay." Liam turned the skim drone and flew back to the Moon Racer. He deployed the claw, carefully grabbed the ship by its strange engine, and pulled it back to the cruiser.

While JEFF worked on swapping the engines, Liam painstakingly tapped a message to Mina using the code table, which he had transferred to his link: *We found a faster engine. We may be able to catch up. Stay tuned.*

She replied: *Yes! But we're going into stasis in 22 hours. Wesley asks: can you send us your velocity before then?*

Ok, Liam replied.

It took JEFF nearly ten hours to complete the change. At first, Liam and Phoebe kept watch for any signs of Barro and his people, but after a couple hours, they settled into a long game of *Roid Wraiths*, followed by more episodes of *Raiders* and, eventually, a nap.

When JEFF updated that he was nearing completion, they placed two packages of slow-fuel nutrient supplement in the rehydration oven and heated them up. They squeezed the foil packs of warm paste into covered bowls, and used spoons with covered scoopers on their ends to eat it. The paste had little green flecks in it and nearly no taste. It would sit in your digestive system during stasis, slowly releasing vitamins, minerals, and electrolytes over the years.

"Grossth," said Phoebe, frowning as she chewed.

Between bites, Liam called JEFF on his link: "Will our parents be okay without the slow fuel?"

"I increased the concentration of nutrients in their fluid lines to compensate," said JEFF. "They will feel a bit ill on wake-up, and it will take quite a bit longer for the effects of stasis to wear off, but with this new engine, they will survive."

"Wait," said Phoebe, "are you saying if we had to use our normal engine, our parents were going to die?"

JEFF was silent for a moment. "That amount of time in stasis without medical attention was going to be a problem, regardless of slow fuel."

"Were you going to tell us this?" said Liam.

"Yes," said JEFF.

"When?" said Phoebe.

"I was still trying to calculate the most optimal time. Fortunately, now it is no longer an issue."

Liam glanced at Phoebe, eyes wide. She shook her head and kept eating.

Soon after, JEFF returned to the cabin. "The new engine is secured."

They gathered in the cockpit and buckled in. JEFF brought up a schematic of the ship on the holo-screen. He tapped the old engine and slid the software graphic for the new one on top of it. It blinked red for a moment, then switched to green. "The new booster is online. Ready?"

"Definitely," said Liam.

"Beginning gradual primary burn." JEFF powered the engine to 20 percent.

"Whoa," said Liam, as the force of their acceleration pressed them back in their seats. "That thing is fast. Did you figure out what kind of engine it is?"

"The booster seems to be modified with some kind of nanotechnology, but I have never seen anything like it," said JEFF. "I do not have access to the VirtCom, but I doubt it would be listed there anyway."

"It's the magic engine," said Phoebe, watching Saturn shrink on the rear camera.

"If we do a fifty-percent fuel burn," said JEFF. "we should be able to reach approximately thirty-five thousand kilometers per second."

"Thirty-five!" said Liam. "That's definitely faster than the *Scorpius*! High five, JEFF!"

Liam held up his hand. JEFF just looked at him, his eyes flashing. "One moment—I am searching for the correct response to this gesture."

"Jeez, never mind. I gotta tell Mina. Do you think we'll catch them?"

"It will depend on how long our refueling stops take. Our first will be in three years, at which time we make the first directional adjustment to reach Delphi. The starliner has enough fuel reserves to make these moves without stopping. We, however, do not."

"But we can still catch them."

"I think the chances are favorable."

Liam tapped the beacon as fast as he could. *Thirty-five kms! We can catch you!*

A few minutes later, Mina replied: *Yay!*

"And you'll be watching while we're asleep," said Phoebe, "for comets, or supernova?"

"Or saboteurs?" said Liam. "Do you think there are more out there?"

Phoebe sighed. "I really doubt they're working alone."

"I will be monitoring the ship's sensors at all times," said JEFF, "though not by a hard line this time. Should anything happen, I will know immediately. Now, we should prep you for stasis. Do not forget to use the bathroom. You cannot exactly get up in the night."

Phoebe raised an eyebrow. "JEFF, did you just make a joke?"

"I merely referenced the stasis best practices," said JEFF. "Though . . . I am aware that it was perhaps humorous."

Liam slapped his plastic shoulder. "You're learning, JEFF. And we'll work on that high five."

On his way to the back cabin, Liam stopped by his parents' pods and gazed at their calm, sleeping faces. He gave the top of each pod a hug, his cheek against the clear panel. "I love you," he said. "We'll be back together soon." He stood and pressed the beacon. Three seconds later, it blinked back. "Mina says hello."

He tapped a message to her: *Sleep now. See you soon. Love you.*

Mina: *xoxo. Until Delphi. Whatever it takes.*

Bye.

Good night.

Liam used the bathroom and returned to the room opposite their parents', where JEFF had lowered two stasis pods and opened their top panels. Phoebe sat up on the edge of hers, her heels under the pod to hold herself in place. She wore her thermal wear and was brushing her hair.

"Where's JEFF?" Liam asked.

"He's checking our acceleration," said Phoebe.

Liam ran his hand along the inside of the pod. The lining was a spongy foam covered in a soft, cream-colored fabric. "Have you done this before?"

"Nope," said Phoebe. "Are you freaked out?"

Liam shrugged. "If you'd asked me that two days ago, I would have said yes for sure, but now I feel like we have bigger things to worry about."

Phoebe nodded. "You mean like aliens and saboteurs and time travelers?"

"That's a way scarier list than I was thinking about yesterday morning on Mars. That was just like, asteroids and black holes and stuff."

"Those are all still out there," said Phoebe quietly. "Not to mention exploding stars."

"And engine failures," said Liam.

"Stasis malfunctions . . ."

"Navigation errors . . ."

"Slow-fuel farts."

Liam looked at Phoebe and they both cracked up, laughing so hard that they lost their grips on the pods and floated into slow somersaults, so hard that Liam's sides ached.

He took a deep breath and pulled himself back to his pod. Phoebe sighed, pulling herself down too. They shared a glance and giggled one more time.

But as Liam calmed, the thought still crossed his mind: that long list of dangers was only the things they *knew* about. This universe was so big, and there was so much they couldn't even imagine. . . .

"We're going to be okay," said Phoebe, almost like she was reading his mind. "You realize what we've survived so far? I think we can handle just about anything space throws at us."

"I guess," Liam said, smiling. "Mars feels like a year ago already."

"Yeah," said Phoebe. Her face fell. "I still miss it."

Liam pictured his room, the view off his balcony. Those gleaming space elevators zipping into the unknown. "Me too."

JEFF returned to their room. "All right, who would like to be prepped first?"

"I'll do it," said Phoebe. "Bring on the needles."

Liam sat up on his pod to watch.

"First we will attach the muscle stimulators, which will also be doubling as conductors for the simulated gravity field that each pod can produce. This option would not be required on the *Scorpius*, with its ship-wide gravity field, but it's necessary here."

"Won't that use up more fuel?" Liam asked.

"It will, but if we do not use it, your muscles will completely atrophy by the time we get to Delphi, not to mention a host of other issues." JEFF unspooled four wires from the inside rim of the pod. He clipped a wire into the small port on each ankle and wrist cuff of Phoebe's thermal wear.

"And next, the fluid line. For this, please lift up

the access flap on your right arm."

Phoebe peeled up the little Velcro tab and lifted a small window of fabric.

"What's that?" said Liam.

"What?" said Phoebe, pushing the fabric closed.

Liam motioned toward her arm. "No, under there. Is that a tattoo or something?"

Phoebe blushed. "It's nothing."

JEFF rolled closer with a needle attached to a thin clear tube. "Please open the access flap."

"I can't believe you never told me you had a tattoo," said Liam. "Come on, let's see it. Who cares? I swear I won't tell anyone."

Phoebe looked at her arm, and then at him. She shook her head. "You swear?"

"Duh, yeah, but it's not even a big deal anyway."

Phoebe sighed, her gaze on the floor. "Okay." She pulled open the access flap. Liam noticed that her fingers were trembling.

There, drawn on the bare skin of the inside of her elbow:

Three small black rings, like hollow circles.

"What is it?" said Liam.

Phoebe's finger traced slowly over the circles. "Just something I drew with a marker," she said.

"Is it a symbol? Like for planets, or a grav-ball thing?"

"It, um . . ." Phoebe glanced from the ground to the window, avoiding his eyes. A shadow crossed her face.

"Sorry," said Liam, "I didn't mean to—"

"No, it's fine. . . . I just don't usually talk about it, but we're friends, right?"

Liam cocked his head. "Of course we're friends."

Phoebe looked at him seriously. "Best friends?"

Liam felt his heart stutter a beat. "Yeah, definitely."

"Okay . . ." Phoebe bit her lip. She tapped the circles. "One is for my brother, and the other two are for my grandparents. They died."

"Phoebe . . . ," said Liam. He didn't know what to follow that with. "I . . . didn't know you even had a brother."

Phoebe wiped her eyes. "He and my grandparents were killed in an accident."

"You mean like a crash?"

Phoebe nodded. "He was sleeping over at their house. They were on their way to meet us. They died instantly—they . . . never saw it coming." She sniffed. "We didn't know it was an accident at first, but I do now. It's still hard for everyone in my family. They're still angry, and sad."

"Was that before you moved to Haishang? It must have been."

"Yeah, it was a little while before that."

Liam pushed away from his pod and floated to Phoebe and hugged her.

She gripped him tightly. He felt her wet eyes against his shoulder. "I still miss them," she said quietly. "It's not fair."

Liam nodded. "No, it's not."

Phoebe sighed and pulled away, her face red. "You can do the needle now," she said to JEFF. She looked back at Liam. "You won't tell anyone? Especially not my parents. They really don't like to talk about it."

"I promise," said Liam. "I didn't mean to bring it up—"

"It's okay," said Phoebe. "There's no way you could have known."

JEFF held the slim needle to Phoebe's arm. "Just relax," he said. She turned away and he slid the needle into her skin, just below the circle tattoo. He placed a piece of tape over the tube to keep it in place. "And the last thing," he said, bending back to the control panel near the foot of the pod, "is to connect your link. It will monitor your vital signs." He plugged a last wire into Phoebe's link.

JEFF repeated the steps with Liam. He found his breath getting short, and he started feeling lightheaded.

"That's it?" he asked when JEFF was finished.

"Yes. Now if you just lie back, before you know it, we'll be waking up to fuel the ship."

Liam swung his legs over and scooted them into the pod. He sat down on the foam base and buckled the strap at his waist. He looked at Phoebe and tried to smile bravely. "See you soon."

She smiled back. "May Ana wake you from pleasant dreams."

"What's that?" Liam asked.

"Something we say in my family. Good night, Liam."

"Good night, Phoebe."

Liam lay back, resting his head on a small foam pillow. He was breathing fast, and the sound echoed in the little space, making it feel even smaller. He gazed up at the ceiling and told himself to relax.

JEFF's smiling panda face appeared over the edge of the pod. "Ready?"

Liam breathed deep. "Okay."

The oval-shaped cover lowered and clicked into place. There was a humming of machinery, and then a hiss from tiny vents that lined the inside of the pod. The temperature began to drop, his view of the ceiling fogging over. Liam flexed his fingers. Tried to breathe slow. He raised his head and took one last glimpse at the alien watch. Not blinking at all. *It will be okay,* he thought. They'd made it off Mars. They'd escaped their pursuers. . . .

But there were still millions and millions of kilometers to go. Liam felt the orange crystal in one pocket, the data key in the other. They barely understood who they were up against. Had no idea what they would face next. Would they even be asleep an hour before someone came after them again? Could they possibly make it all the way to Delphi, to the *Scorpius*? Would they ever see Aaru-5?

And if they really made it all the way there, so long from now, what would their new life be like? Liam tried to picture it: a far-off planet around a different sun. He imagined the sister planet Phoebe had described, broken into three pieces. And would there be clouds, or mountains? Would their new home be an apartment, like Mars? A farm like he'd seen in pictures of Earth? What if it was none of those things?

Maybe it didn't need to be. Whatever Aaru was, that would come later. For now, he was safe. He had his parents. He had Phoebe, his best friend, and he had his memories.

Light dimmed inside the pod. Liam's breath slowed, and he began to lose track of his arms and legs. He closed his eyes and pictured their balcony on Mars, the view of the black buildings and the copper sky, the shimmer of the dome, and, looming in the distance, the great volcano, hiding more secrets than he'd ever known. The warmth of their old sun on his back . . .

And his mom leaning on the railing beside him.

We'll take it one unknown at a time.

EPILOGUE

RINGS OF GOLD CASINO

^62°22'E — B-RING — QUADRANT 3

12,086 KM FROM HUYGENS GAP

"Here's forty credits and you can keep the change."

"But, ma'am," the security bot began, "I am not allowed to accept—"

"Then throw it out the airlock for all I care," said Francine Luna, not breaking stride. "Money's useless in this solar system now, anyway."

"You're terrible," said her boyfriend, Antonio, putting his arm around her.

Francine tapped his Plasticine nose with her gloved finger. "You don't know the half of it."

Her grav-tronic heels clacked on the floor as she strode down the docking corridor of the Rings of Gold casino, her azure gown swishing behind her, and when Antonio paused to check his high wave of green hair in a reflective metal wall panel, he fell behind.

"Keep up, Tony. We're getting out of here before any more space stations blow up."

"Of course, Ms. Luna. But that was three days ago."

"Obviously," said Francine, "but I wasn't through playing yet."

She stopped at airlock seven and tapped her link, which was encrusted with Dionian amethysts. The airlock clicked to green and its inner door slid open. As it did, she gathered her gown to step over the threshold.

"Is this your ship?"

Francine looked up to find two tall people standing in front of her.

She scowled. "What are you doing in my airlock?"

The man and the woman just stared at her.

Tony arrived beside Francine. "Hey, who are these two?"

Francine was about to call security to take care of these impertinent intruders, but as her gaze took them in, she found that her words escaped her.

The man and the woman wore blue space-grade pressure suits, scuffed with black streaks. The woman still wore her heavy helmet. The man's helmet was off, and his hair was quite ruffled. But that wasn't the problem.

He was smiling, kindly, but that wasn't the problem either.

The problem was that he seemed to be missing half of his face. Or rather, he seemed to have two different faces, mashed together. One half of his face seemed perfectly normal, but then his skin ended at a ragged torn edge just past the bridge of his nose, and the other half seemed to be made of some kind of rough lavender covering with black speckles. The eye on the human side was dark brown. The eye on the lavender side was blue where it should have been white, like the midday sky back on Earth—a color that Francine knew, but Tony did not. Its iris was black and the pupil a brilliant gold.

"We'll be needing your ship," said the two-faced man. The lips on the lavender side were black.

"Who are you?" asked Francine.

The woman lunged and hit Francine across the side of the head with a mangled length of carbon shrapnel. She spun and hit Tony the same way. The two fell into a heap on the floor.

"They always ask the wrong question." Tarra knelt and slipped the link off Francine's wrist. "Thank you."

Barro and Tarra dragged Francine and Tony through the airlock and onto Francine's Nebula Class Comet H-6. Barro pulled off his space suit and floated to the cockpit. Tarra stayed in the ship's airlock with

Francine and Tony until the Comet had fired away from the casino.

"May Ana wake you from pleasant dreams," said Tarra, and she stepped through the inner door and flushed the two humans out into the black.

"Will this ship be fast enough to make the rendezvous?" she asked as she joined Barro in the cockpit.

"Barely," said Barro. "How long were we out there?"

Tarra checked her link. "Seventy-four hours. We're lucky to be alive."

"It's not the first time." Barro burned the engine. He sighed. "I can't believe she lied to us."

Tarra nodded. "She's young. I wouldn't give up on her."

"I won't. She'll still have a chance to do right by her brother—by all of them."

Tarra closed her eyes. "They will be counted."

"Yes," said Barro. "Very soon."

One bloodred afternoon two years later, a strange light fell on the microbes that lined a chunk of rock lying in the sand not far from Olympus Mons. The rock, once part of a cave wall, had flown hundreds of meters from the research station blast site, and just happened to land facedown against some other rocks, such that the microbes were granted a pocket of space and shade. Here, they had managed to survive while the rest of their species had been incinerated.

They didn't notice when the gravity started to change. Didn't notice when the ground began to crack and split apart, the sky to boil. They didn't know what a planet was, or a solar system, or a universe, never knew that they were the very last Martians.

As the red planet buckled and broke apart, their piece of rock was thrown skyward. In the process, it flipped around, and though the microbes did not exactly have eyes, they did have primitive light sensing spots, and for just a moment, they perceived a glow unlike anything they had ever known, so bright, so warm, so complete. . . .

A year after that, the great red star, its waist now nearly to Jupiter, all at once collapsed in on itself and exploded into a supernova that vaporized every remaining planet, asteroid, and comet of the eighteenth planetary system of the third spiral arm of the Milky Way galaxy.

A beautiful magenta-and-yellow wash spread through space, like spilled watercolors.

Sensors aboard the hundreds of starliners recorded the event, but even just a short time later, when the

Second Fleet would awaken near Delphi, those brilliant clouds would already be gone, and only a small, cold neutron star would remain, a celestial gravestone to humanity's birthplace.

But here, in this final moment . . .

As arcs of plasma glowed . . .

As stardust glittered . . .

As rare elements formed in the atomic foam . . .

A fleet of silent black ships, flickering like droplets, moved swiftly into the storm they had secretly created, and got to work.

END OF BOOK ONE

YOU JUST SURVIVED
THE LAST DAY ON MARS.
YOU PROBABLY HAVE SOME QUESTIONS

Dear Intrepid Readers,

Kevin Emerson here. When I'm writing science fiction, my biggest story inspiration comes from real science. Whether I'm trying to answer a big question, like *what is humanity's place in the universe?*, or a small one, like *what would we eat for breakfast on Mars?*, I try to think like a scientist would, and to do justice to the wonders of our world. With that in mind, let's tackle some of the biggest questions in *Last Day on Mars*:

IS OUR SUN REALLY GOING TO EXPLODE?

In a word: nope.

Key facts about our home star:

- **Star Type:** yellow dwarf
- **Age:** 4.6 billion years
- **How much longer will it burn?** 5 billion years
- **Then what?** It will grow to a red giant, then shrink to a white dwarf

In *Last Day on Mars*, it's two hundred years in the future and our sun is going supernova—an event that occurs at the end of a large star's life, culminating in a massive cosmic explosion. But unless I've been possessed by an alien consciousness and everything about the Drove is actually true (unlikely, although I do feel sorta fuzzy sometimes, especially in the morning before I've had coffee), then this is NOT going to happen in real life. There are many different types of stars in the universe, with big differences in size, color, and composition. A yellow dwarf star like our sun is not one of the kinds that will go supernova. It will expand when it runs out of energy, but only into a red giant, not a red *super*giant. When this happens, it may swallow the inner planets of the solar system, including Earth, but that will be a long, long, long time from now.

COULD WE REALLY LIVE ON MARS?

In nine words: Yes! But it would take a lot of planning.

Key facts about our next-door neighbor:
- **Day Length:** 24 hours, 40 minutes
- **Year Length**: 687 days
- **Average Temp:** -81 degrees F
- **Oxygen:** nope
- **Water:** ice only
- **Gravity:** 38% of Earth
- **Air Pressure:** 0.6% of Earth
- **Moons:** 2

As you can see in the list above, Mars is similar to Earth in some ways, but very different in others. While the days are about the same length (forty extra minutes for homework!), the conditions are pretty harsh. It's extremely cold, and we would need to create our own water and oxygen. Also, even on the warmest day and even if we were holding our breath, we wouldn't be able to go outside without a suit on, because the Martian atmosphere has such low air pressure that the water in our bodies would immediately evaporate. This *might* make our eyes sort-of boil. (Yikes!) And if all that wasn't enough, Mars has such a thin atmosphere, and weak magnetic field, that solar and cosmic radiation would be a constant threat. The gravity is much lower on Mars, which might be fun when we first arrived, but we're not sure yet how our bodies would fare in low gravity over a long period of time, so even that might turn out to be a danger. On the plus side, when you live on Mars, you get a bonus moon in the night sky! Though both moons, Phobos and Deimos, are very small.

WOULD IT REALLY TAKE SUCH A LONG TIME TO TRAVEL TO A NEW PLANET?

In a word: yup.

Key facts about distances and speed in space:

- Distance to Alpha Centauri, our closest neighboring star: about 4 light-years
- 1 light-year = 9.46 trillion kilometers
- Speed of *Voyager 1*, our fastest deep space probe: 17.3 km/s
- Speed of a starliner in *Last Day on Mars*: 30,000 km/s

One thing I wanted to do in this story was convey the sense of how big space really is. Everything is FAR and takes a long time to travel to. Alpha Centauri is over 40 trillion kilometers away! It would take *Voyager 1*, the fastest deep space probe we've launched, about 80,000 years to get there. Alpha Centauri may have a potential planet or two, but scientists suspect we'd have to go much farther in order to find one that humans could actually live on.

Aaru-5 is a made-up planet that is fifteen light-years away. (If you want to know where I got the name Aaru, take a look at ancient Egyptian mythology.) We have seen some evidence of possible planets around stars that are at about the same distance.

In the book, I imagined that we have designed engines that can travel at about 10 percent of the speed of light. At that speed, you could get to Alpha Centauri in a little over forty years. That doesn't sound very fast when you compare it to light speed in *Star Wars* or warp speed in *Star Trek*, but it is SO MUCH faster than any ship we have now. Will we someday design engines that will be able to go this fast? I think so, but we have a lot of research left to do.

HOW DO THE STASIS PODS WORK?

I get more questions about the stasis pods than any other topic in the book. I think we all want to know we'll be safe when we are sleeping on spaceships! Stasis, or suspended animation, is a classic science fiction idea. The pod slows down your body to the point where you stop aging. In *Last Day on Mars*, stasis is like very cold hibernation, using chemicals added to the body, and of course, near-freezing temperatures. We don't know how to create stasis in real life yet, and we would need to learn a great deal more about cryogenics (the study of how the human body operates at very low temperatures). You can't just freeze a person like an ice cube, because water expands as it turns to ice and this would cause our cells to burst. But there are some insects that have special chemicals in their blood that act like antifreeze. They can be frozen all winter, and when the snow melts, they can come back to life. If we can figure out how to do the same thing with our own bodies, as fictional scientists have in this book, maybe stasis will someday become a reality.

WHAT OTHER THINGS DID YOU RESEARCH?

Everything I could! Many little details in the book are based on real ideas, like how scientists are studying ways to make plasma force fields (which inspired the dome around the Mars colony), or how we might be able to mine asteroids for their water and use it for fuel, or how 3D printers could be used for building spaceships in orbit (it would be very hard to build a single ship as big as a starliner with today's technology, never mind a hundred of them!), or even how mealworms and crickets are a great source of protein that are far easier to grow than cows or chickens. (Did I mention what Nutri-Bars are made of?) I researched the landscape of Mars too, and put Liam and Phoebe's colony on the Amazonis Planitia (a real place) so they would be close to Olympus Mons (a real volcano).

As you can tell from what we've talked about so far, part of the fun of writing science fiction is making your own creative choices once you have the science in mind. Here are a few of the little things in the story that I had fun inventing:

VirtCom: This stands for Virtual Community. I imagine it like a vast virtual reality mall that you walk around using an avatar. So, to hang out with friends, or go shopping for just about anything, or even exercise, hike an Earth mountain, etc., you'd link into the VirtCom and do it there.

Grav-Ball: I imagine Grav-Ball to be something like soccer and basketball, only in a zero-gravity environment, so players have to move by thrusting themselves off the walls. The game is played inside a huge clear oval-shaped container. You can use your hands, feet, and head, but you can't grab the ball, you have to dribble it.

Starliner Engines: The starliners have nuclear fusion engines that run on hydrogen, which they get from water. They also use solar sails, which are giant mirrors that gather radiation from sunlight.

Link: A link is like a really advanced smartphone. It networks to whatever you need it to, like a spacesuit or a ship. Of all the technology in *Last Day on Mars*, the links are the most like what we currently have. It's hard to predict how phones and the internet will advance in two hundred years. Links will probably be very different than today's smartphones, but since there is already so much that's unfamiliar in the story, I thought it might be good if our main tool for getting information was something you could easily imagine yourself using.

I had a lot of fun writing this book. Now, want to try your hand at making your own science fiction story? Here are two ways to do it. For either one, you could create a story by writing, drawing, or filming:

OPTION 1: ARRIVING IN A NEW WORLD

Imagine a character arriving in a new place for the first time. This can be another planet or moon in our solar system, a planet around a different star, a space station (what is it orbiting, or is it in deep space?), or any other object.

To find a place, you can look in books or online to get inspiration from pictures. If it's a real place, you can read a little bit to get ideas about what the place will be like. If it's an imaginary place, like a far-off planet, you can read about what scientists think other planets might be like.

Start your story by showing the moment when your character is seeing this place for the first time. What's it like? Use vivid details. What is your character thinking and feeling? Also, who are they traveling with, and why are they there? What kind of gear and precautions will they need to take? Show the character making their way into this new world. Where do they go first? What difficulties or trouble do they encounter?

OPTION 2: FAN FICTION

When I was a kid, fan fiction was my favorite thing to write. I loved taking the characters, settings, and storylines of my favorite books and movies and writing my own versions. It was like playing with a Lego set of story ideas. This can be a great way to practice writing science fiction, because sometimes it can be hard to think up all the ideas, characters, and settings that you need to get started.

You can write fan fiction about any story. If you were writing about *Last Day on Mars*, I might suggest imagining a character we don't meet in the book who's already traveling on a starliner, maybe even as things go wrong back on Mars during this story. Or imagine another character having a different adventure on Mars, or Saturn, or on the way to Aaru-5. You could even write a story about an adventure that Liam, Phoebe, and Shawn had out at the field station, maybe exploring the volcano tubes, before *Last Day* took place. Or at a grav-ball game, or at school. Anything you want!

THE ADVENTURE CONTINUES IN THE SECOND INSTALLMENT IN

THE CHRONICLE OF THE DARK STAR

DON'T MISS THESE BOOKS BY
KEVIN EMERSON!

"This is perfect science fiction: a terrifying yet very cool vision of the future, lots of technological awesomeness, mind-bending alien mysteries, a mission to save the human race—and two funny, resourceful, very real kid heroes who I'd follow to the edges of the universe."

—TUI T. SUTHERLAND, *New York Times* bestselling author of the Wings of Fire series